A HARD WAY TO DIE

A HARD WAY TO DIE
Copyright © 2022 Lance McMillian

All rights reserved.
No part of this book may be reproduced
without permission of the author.

ISBN 979-8-9866332-2-0
Published by Bond Publishing

This book is a work of fiction. Any similarities to any person living or deceased to a character in the novel are purely coincidental.

Typesetting and Cover Design by FormattingExperts.com

A HARD WAY TO DIE

LANCE MCMILLIAN

To My Daughter Emily—For Always Making Me Smile

"Anger and contempt are the twin scourges of the earth. Mingled with greed and sexual lust, these bitter emotions form the poisonous brew in which human existence stands suspended. Few people ever get free of them in this life, and for most of us even old age doesn't bring relief."

—Dallas Willard, *The Divine Conspiracy*

1

The Smith & Wesson is heavy in my hand. I take aim and squeeze the trigger in rapid bursts—unleashing six shots, all straight at the heart. The ear protectors mask most of the noise, and only a slight pop reaches my ears at each discharge from the revolver. I squint at the results ten yards away but don't like the look of things. Pulling the slide in for a closer inspection of my work, I lament that the imaginary perpetrator before me still has plenty of life left in him.

One shot grazed the target's side, well away from the heart. A couple landed on the arm. Another nicked a finger. Two avoided the black outline entirely. All the misses are to the left. I frown and stare at the gun as if it might deserve the lion's share of the blame.

The Atlanta Police Department's shooting range is crowded, but then again, it's always crowded. Cops love to shoot their guns. Although a lawyer by trade, I'm no different. Usually these times are a therapeutic outlet for me to relieve the accumulation of stress that piles up like a landfill at my door. The medicine is a cure unlike any other. Something about unleashing a deadly volley of kill shots into a target satisfies a man's most primal desires.

Except lately I can't hit the broad side of a barn, which leaves me less than fulfilled. Compounding matters, my day job now requires that I tote around a gun on my hip. Inaccuracy is liable to get someone killed—most likely, me.

Scott Moore, my best friend and one of the best detectives around, wanders over. I don't even bother to glance at his results. The only uncertainty is how he decided to group his shots. A smiley face is the usual choice. Ten, fifteen, twenty-five yards, it doesn't matter. His shots always land in the exact spot where intended. He stares at my target in disgust. I offer a weak defense.

"Maybe the sight's off."

He sticks his hand out, and I hand the revolver over to him. Scott hates revolvers because reloading the chambers one by one is too time-consuming in a firefight. Switching out a pistol magazine cartridge, on the other hand, takes mere seconds. But I remain unpersuaded. Revolvers are simple and sturdy, which is about all the fun that I can handle. If I'm ever in a shootout, I will just have to make do with my six shots and hope for the best.

A dubious Scott closes one eye to scrutinize the sight. He reloads the gun with fresh shells and moves my target back down to its place in the line and then some—doubling the distance at which I was shooting. Revolver at his side, he jerks it up with sudden swiftness and empties the contents into the dark outline a couple of first downs away. I squint again but have trouble making out the small holes. The press of a button returns the slide back to us, and it doesn't take long to determine that the sight on the Smith & Wesson works just fine. Six little circles dot the target's fictional heart. Scott delivers his verdict.

"You might be better off just carrying around a baseball bat."

"Hey, I killed a man when it counted. Two holes in his stomach, just like I wanted."

"A shotgun blast from close range. My mother could make that shot, and she's practically blind."

Having met his mother, I don't disagree. But she's tougher and meaner than your typical octogenarian. No matter. I stood toe-to-toe with a man intent on killing me and did what needed doing. That counts for something. And regardless of how accurate Scott is on the gun range, he's never had the bad luck of having to deploy his talents against a living, breathing human on the other side. The real thing is a different game with eternal stakes.

But ever since that night when I faced death and managed to survive, my gun skills have gone on hiatus. I never was a marksman, but I could hit the target well enough once upon a time. Now, not so much. Is the problem psychological—a byproduct of residual guilt at taking a human life? Doubtful. The person on the other side earned his killing, and not even a faint hint of remorse has troubled my heart in the aftermath. Indeed, the flipside may be of greater concern. My hidden fear could be that I enjoyed the killing a little too much.

Scott asks, "Ready for your vacation?"

These days I head an elite investigative unit with wide-ranging authority to investigate and prosecute crime all over the state of Georgia—an untouchable group of lawyers and investigators dedicated to combatting violence and corruption at its source. Or something like that. Our team has an official name, but no one uses it. The local press quickly dubbed us the "Atlanta Murder Squad," and that label stuck. The unit is roughly half a year old now, and getting it operational has been a labor of love. But a different kind of love is a more pressing matter.

I owe Cate—my new wife—a honeymoon.

"If Italy is as nice as the brochures make it out to be, we might just stay there forever."

Scott grunts, which may be his way of saying that he would miss me. He reloads my revolver and hands it back to me. A serious expression clouds his face, and he studies me for a few seconds with great meaning. The shift in mood is unexpected, and I decide to wait him out.

"Can I say something?"

The question is rhetorical. Scott says what he damn well pleases and has for as long as I've known him.

"Cate's good for you. You're getting back to your old self. Warms my heart to see."

The sympathetic earnestness in his eyes is a departure from his usual no-nonsense demeanor. A warm heart is not one of his prominent traits. But more than anyone, he has had a ringside seat for my journey to the gates of Hell and back. Nearly five years ago now, an unknown assailant murdered my wife and four-year-old son. Scott was one of the first officers on the scene and saw Amber and Cale dead in their own blood—the unsolved case remaining a pain in his side to this day. In the aftermath, I buried my grief as far as I could manage, running from God and everyone else as part of the process.

Except one day the seams of that emotional straitjacket gave way to something much worse. Scott was there for that, too.

But that was then, and Cate is now. We married about six months ago, two tumultuous weeks after we first met. Each of us was broken in our own way—a cheating ex-husband on her side, the murder of my family on mine. But joined together, past hurts don't sting as much, and the prospects for the future appear hopeful. And Scott is right. My new wife continues to restore parts of myself that I figured to be lost for good.

"She's great, isn't she?"

"Besides marrying you in a fever, you mean?"

Fair enough. The speed of our nuptials took everyone by surprise, Cate and me most of all. But all love stories have their own unique DNA, and the circumstances that must conspire over generations for any two people to end up together defy all mathematical probability. Married the Friday before a weekend snow-apocalypse, we celebrated the impulsive wedding by riding out the storm at the Four Seasons in Midtown Atlanta.

Now, we're on our way to Italy—after a quick stop on Jekyll Island for a gathering of lawyers at the state bar conference. Cate is a justice on the Georgia Supreme Court and has meetings to attend. That leaves me free to get an early start on our honeymoon with some golf and beach time.

"Send me a postcard," Scott says as we part.

2

George the Alligator eyes me with disinterest from his customary perch adjacent to a dark pond on the fourth hole. Alligators can live as long as humans, and the mammoth George—all thirteen feet of him—seems intent on hanging around for as long as possible. I haven't visited Jekyll Island in over five years and wondered whether he would still be here. But there he is. His dependable presence satisfies something hard to describe within my soul, a timeless continuity that just feels right.

The positive energy doesn't extend to my golf game. My tee shot slices off to the right a little too close to George for comfort, and I yell at him that he can go ahead and keep the ball for himself. After taking a generous drop in the fairway, I line up to take another swing.

The phone rings.

I stand down and head to my golf bag to answer the call. The incomparable sound of Johnny Cash singing "I Walk the Line" alerts me that the caller is my wife. The interruption is a surprise as she has meetings all morning. She barely gives me a chance to say "hello" before rapidly speaking in my ear.

"You're not going to believe what happened! Donovan Kessler was murdered last night!"

A bell from somewhere in the past rings, but I can't quite catch the meaning. I scan the pond to ensure that no alligators are prepping a sneak attack and respond.

"The name sounds familiar. A lawyer maybe?"

"Not just a lawyer—the president of the state bar."

An image of an elderly man with perfect teeth and perfect gray hair comes to mind. Donovan Kessler. The epitome of lawyerly deportment. I think he even served in the state legislature with my father decades ago—around the time that I was a kid playing hide-and-seek in the nooks and crannies of the State Capitol. Kessler's hair was dark back then, more black than brown if I'm thinking about the right man. Now he's dead—more violence in a world already chock full of it.

"Who killed him?"

"No idea. They just found his body less than an hour ago on the beach, just down from our hotel. He lives on the island. Somebody smashed his skull. Everyone at the conference is freaking out."

Murder has that effect on people. And it won't just be the attendees at the conference disturbed by this news. Jekyll Island is a small, sleepy, idyllic kind of place. Killings are rarer than a white alligator. Crime is low, too. The island is owned by the state and requires a park fee to even get on the thing. The six hundred or so residents that live here are accustomed to their own quiet sliver of paradise. A smashed skull on the sand figures to provide them with an uncomfortable jolt into the darkness that stains the heart of man. Welcome to my world, I think.

I crane my head back toward the tee box to see if I'm holding any other golfers up. But I have the whole course to myself from the looks of it. That solitude is more alluring than the golf—just a peaceful morning surrounded by green grass and trees, the pleasing smell of salt in the air. I start itching to get back to my round.

"Shouldn't you do something?"

Cate's question puts a halt to my itching. I crunch up my face in confusion at the phone in my hand, a pointless expression since no living soul is around to see it. For his part, George—cursed with an alligator's limited eyesight—is much too far away to get a good view. But I allow my face to emote anyway and consider my next words.

"Not much I could do down here. All of my team and resources are five hours away in Atlanta. Besides, you and I are going to Italy in a few days."

The other end of the line sits silent for a few seconds before Cate half-heartedly agrees with my assessment. She sighs, "The world is messed up, Chance. I know you can't investigate every murder in the state. This one just hits a little too close to home for my liking. I've known Donovan for over a decade. Anyway, my meeting is about to start back up, even though I don't expect much work to get done. Love you."

"Love you, too."

Poor Donovan Kessler. But not my circus, not my monkeys.

One of my chief responsibilities as head of the murder squad is knowing when to exert my vast power. We cannot be everything to everybody, and throwing my weight around uninvited is a sure way to create enemies with long memories. My father, the one-time lieutenant governor back when I was in high school, taught me that. He also taught me that south Georgians trust folks from Atlanta about as far as they can throw them. And it's much too early in my tenure to kick up that hornet's nest of geographic Georgia politics for what figures to be a purely local crime. I go back to my golf game.

Right in my backswing, the phone rings again. I finish the follow-through and watch my ball slice straight into George's pond with a resounding splash. I slam the club into the ground. The sound of "The Emperor's Theme" from *Star Wars* keeps braying from my cell, a little joke of mine to unmistakably identify the caller.

The Governor.

I stare at Minton McReynolds' name for a full second before pushing the green button on my iPhone. It's too early in the morning for coincidences. One moment's thought is all I need to realize that he's calling me about Donovan Kessler. Sometimes you just know.

"Chance, how are you doing?"

"Enjoying my vacation, trying to get some golf in. But something tells me the universe has other plans."

"Golf! Never got into it. Couldn't see the point. Wasting hours of the day hacking away at some small ball. Life's too short."

His words fall into a silent void. Truth is, the game doesn't do much for me, either. Mark Twain once quipped, "Golf is a good walk spoiled." I kinda know what he means. The walking is more enjoyable than the playing—the feel of green grass under my feet rejuvenates me, especially in the secluded and laidback confines of Jekyll Island, where wearing jeans and tennis shoes qualify as proper golf attire. The Governor doesn't let the silence linger.

"You know, I hate to bother you when you're down there trying to get in some relaxation, but I just received some disturbing news from that neck of the woods. Donovan Kessler was murdered last night on Jekyll Island—"

"How on earth could you know that so quickly?"

"Son, I got my fingers in more pies than the world's busiest baker. Not that it's any of your business, but the state trooper supervisor for Jekyll used to work on my protective detail up here until his wife decided that she wanted to live by the beach. He gave me a call. Anyway, your being there strikes me as mighty good fortune. Donovan served with your Daddy and me in the state legislature back in the day. He was a good man. I want to know who killed him and why."

The Governor was my father's best friend, which is the reason I'm one of the few people alive allowed to call him Minton. Two years short of political retirement, he formed the murder squad some months back and appointed me—a former prosecutor of Atlanta's worst criminals—to lead it as his lasting legacy to the state of Georgia. "Restoring the public trust," he called it at the time. Sounds nice on a bumper sticker.

And now I'm standing on a golf course itching to find a reason not to do my job. After my last trial, I walked away from chasing criminals forever—quitting being the only way to preserve my dwindling supply of sanity. But the Governor had other plans and called me in from the cold to do his bidding. I answered the call but resolved to stay a better-balanced man this time around. My marriage to Cate only solidified that determination. She deserves the best of me, not the leftovers.

"Minton, you know I'm going to Italy in a few days. That's non-negotiable. Cate wants her honeymoon, and she's going to get it. Besides, I have no people in this part of the state. No resources. No anything. The folks down here are plenty capable. Let them do their jobs."

"Hogwash. Jekyll Island barely has a police force. Some state troopers, and that's it. Those boys don't know how to investigate a murder. The Major in charge down there—Jack Fitzgerald, that's his name—told me that himself. They want help. And I ain't trying to mess up your trip to Italy, either. I don't want that on my conscience. You have a team. Use it. That's an order."

He hangs up before I have the chance to tell him that he lacks authority under state law to order me to do anything. No matter. That legal nicety would be dead on arrival. Minton gets what he wants and always has. Call it the magnetism of his personality or something.

I check my watch to get my bearings. Today is Friday. The state bar conference ends Sunday. Cate and I are flying out of Atlanta to Rome on Monday evening come hell or high water, which doesn't leave a ton of time to arrange things before leaving the country. Maybe I won't come back from Italy, putting me forever beyond the reach of Minton's jurisdiction. That'll show him. I shake my head and drop another golf ball onto the fairway.

Clearing my mind of all distractions, I slowly unfurl the smoothest swing in my arsenal. The ball is unimpressed and makes like a heat-seeking missile to a watery grave. Seems about right.

A good walk spoiled, indeed.

3

The sand of Jekyll Island is never soft and fluffy. The tide runs so high at times that most of the beach disappears when the water reaches its apex—the barrier of the high dunes being the only thing keeping the ocean off the pricey residences that dot the edge of the sea. The result is a firm, wet compactness after the water recedes enough for the sand to be visible, which is good for walking around in tennis shoes at least.

I flash my badge to get through the initial perimeter of cops guarding the scene and spy an older guy wearing a finely-pressed blue state patrol uniform. The man's manner reminds me of a general supervising the work of his troops, and I figure him to be Major Jack Fitzgerald, Minton's former security man. I make my way over to introduce myself, but he beats me to the punch.

"You're Chance Meridian, ain't you?"

"Guilty as charged."

He studies me up and down. The disapproval of my sweatshirt, jeans, and sneakers is obvious. We shake hands anyway. His strong, macho grip is typical of police everywhere. I manage not to grimace. After confirming my hunch that he is Fitzgerald, he calls out for one of his deputies to join us.

Fitzgerald says, "Captain, this is Chance Meridian. Meridian, meet Captain Dave Ketchum. The Captain will be your point person with the state patrol station on the island. I'll leave the two of you to it. Holler if you need anything. I'll be in my office."

Without giving me much of any opening for a follow-up, he marches off with brisk precision. I know the type well—someone eager to avoid the threat of any responsibility. No wonder he called the Governor so fast, begging for help. The hot potato he was holding was probably scalding his hands raw. Dave watches his boss hurry away before returning a pair of sad eyes back to me. He extends a begrudging hand. I take him up on his offer. His grip is a reasonable one, at least. But the forced politeness seems to strain him, and I decide pretty quick that I'd rather be playing golf.

He complains, "I told the Major we didn't need any help from you Atlanta folks to solve this case."

"And I told the Governor the same thing, but here we are—two lowly public servants following orders."

The joke doesn't go over. Based on early returns, Dave is a frowner—the creases in his face matching the crispness of his clothes. I reflect that I've never met a state patrol officer with a wrinkled uniform. Most are ex-military—their whole lives an exercise in standing straight at attention with faithful hearts. I've always been more of a sloucher myself, positioning my body in whatever odd angle brought me the most comfort in the moment. My father once raised the possibility of my attending West Point. Minton was in Congress at the time, and my appointment would've been a cinch. I laughed, knowing myself well enough that I wouldn't have lasted a day. Too proud. Too independent. Too stubborn. The same qualities that made me a great trial lawyer.

I try to make Dave feel more comfortable about living under my authority.

"Why don't you show me what you've learned far?"

"Sure."

He takes the lead, and I follow him down the beach. It doesn't take me long to spot Donovan Kessler—or what's left of him. His skull is smashed all right, both temples crushed with nasty indentions at the points of impact. The position of the body rests awkwardly at the bottom of wooden stairs leading up to a walkway over the dunes. All of Kessler is wet, soaked to the bone and then some. He had to be submerged in water at some point. High tide, probably. If the blow to the head didn't kill him, he might've froze to death in the unseasonably cold morning chill. Or maybe he just drowned. I'll wait for the coroner to tell me.

Blood still sticks to Kessler's head. A lot of it. The water diluted some of the red to a more pinkish hue, leaving a sticky paste that clings to the dead man's wrinkled, white skin. On the staircase, above the waterline where the tide comes in, the blood retains its traditional color and reveals a fairly meaningful field of splatter. Good chance some of that splatter landed on the murderer, too. I take a bunch of pictures with my phone.

One curious thing. Kessler is wearing a vintage football letterman's jacket from the University of Georgia—with a big "G" on the front, the number "62" on one sleeve, and a white bulldog on the other sleeve. It doesn't take Sherlock Holmes to deduce that Kessler once played football for UGA, probably for the great Vince Dooley himself. Still, I've never known a grown man to wear his letterman's jacket, especially someone north of age seventy.

I glance around, notice who's not here, and ask, "Any crime scene techs coming?"

Captain Dave reacts with wounded pride. He explains, "The state patrol doesn't have our own folks who do that, you know. But a GBI team from Brunswick is on the way. Should be here in fifteen minutes. They're going to have to work fast, though. High tide's coming again in a few hours and where we're standing now figures to be underwater when that happens."

"Murder weapon?"

"Let me show you."

We head along the shore about ten yards and stop to peer down at a brick that appears heavy enough to have done the requisite damage to Kessler's forehead. One end of the brick is round, and the other side is concave, which would allow it to slot close to similar bricks to create a border. The rounded edge of this particular brick has traces of a substance that might well be blood. Like Kessler, it is saturated with ocean water. I can even see specks of salt dotting the red exterior. Dave fills in some details.

"The victim lives on the other side of that wooden bridge. Bricks like this one line the victim's backyard around flower beds and such.

Except one's missing from the other side. I don't figure it flew over this way by magic. Has to be the murder weapon."

"I reckon you figured right."

He takes the compliment with stoic resolve. I ask, "Anybody touch it?"

"No, sir."

"Good. Let's keep it that way, and don't call me 'sir.'"

"What should I call you then?"

The words are devoid of even a hint of sarcasm, but I tilt my head to study him to make sure. His whole being projects earnestness—a dour earnestness but earnestness all the same. Jack Fitzgerald referred to Dave as "Captain," and Dave returned the favor by addressing his boss as "Major." Maybe that's just how they do things in the state patrol. Chain of command and all that. I decide that Dave is being straight with me, and an honest question deserves an honest answer.

"'Chance' works just fine."

He nods with a pained expression—as if informality is as uncomfortable as a wrinkled uniform. But my investigation, my rules. I switch my attention back to the stiff corpse at the bottom of the stairs.

"Who found the body?"

"Early morning joggers—a married couple—attending some lawyer convention on the island. We're keeping them down the way on the beach right now. Want to talk to them?"

I shake my head and respond, "Maybe later. Have one of your men take their statements and then let them go."

Dave frowns again. No matter. Kessler's been dead so long that the people who discovered him won't have much in the way of useful information. My limited time is better spent elsewhere.

"Anyone staying in the house with the deceased?"

"Yes—a bunch of folks. His girlfriend lives with him all the time. She was there. Also, a son and daughter, along with their spouses, stayed the night. The whole family is full of lawyers, here for that convention."

He doesn't quite sneer at the mention of lawyers but comes close enough for government work. I doubt he knows that I'm part of that contemptible breed and decide not to ruin his morning even further by mentioning that fact to him. That Dave gets edgy at the mention of lawyers is no surprise. They teach cops not to trust lawyers as part of the standard training in police academy. I ask, "Any of those folks been down here to see the body?"

"Absolutely not. I was first on the scene. Once backup arrived to guard the body, I went to the house to notify the family of what happened and to make sure they all stayed put. One of my best men is up there keeping an eye on them with instructions that no one is to go outside."

I check my watch and then the tide. The sooner the GBI gets here, the better. The whole situation bugs me. The place should be crawling with technicians and photographers by this point. With every passing second, the physical evidence degrades further. Some of it may have even washed away already. And while Dave did good work in keeping the family off the beach, the house itself is close enough to count as part of the crime scene.

Could be that the murderer is up there right now destroying evidence.

4

Questioning the girlfriend and the family is the obvious next step, but I decide on a detour first—telling Dave that I changed my mind about talking to the people who discovered the body. He responds with an approving nod. With a spring in his step, he hurries me down the beach. In the distance sits the hotel where Cate and I are staying. The convention center hosting the conference is right next door.

Captain Dave stops short of another state trooper. A restless couple—a man and a woman—hover in the vicinity. They look like lawyers. Seeing me, the woman speaks first.

"You're Justice Slattery's husband."

No doubt. I wonder if I should know her, but no memories stir in the part of my brain in charge of facial recognition. Their matching running suits—red all over with white trim—tell much of the story. I pity their bad luck of having a morning jog on the beach turn into something horrible. But life's random like that. I ask the pair of them, "Who all have you told about Donovan Kessler?"

The man actually huffs, "No one."

That won't do. I unpack my blank face, which is my usual tool to express profound incredulity. The woman shows more emotion and flashes a disgusted look at her companion. Despite the reaction, she still holds her tongue. I decide to start again and give the guy a do-over.

"What's your name?"

"Burt Pressley."

"You a lawyer?"

"Yes, sir. For twenty years, Lois here and I have practiced down in Bainbridge. Do a bit of everything."

He turns to Lois for confirmation, and she offers a little nod without much feeling. I study the pair before me again.

Burt and Lois from Bainbridge.

Bainbridge is close to Tallahassee, and movie star Burt Reynolds played college football at Florida State in Tallahassee. Except Burt Reynolds would never be caught dead wearing a matching running suit with whatever woman he was seducing at the moment. Much too cool for that.

A gust of wind kicks up. I rub a hand through my hair and steal a quick glance at the sea. Part of me wants to march off into the ocean and keep on going until I sink. The thought of Cate and Italy brings me back to reality.

"You discovered Kessler's body, recognized him, and called the cops?"

"That's right."

"So you told the police?"

"Of course them."

"You also alerted someone at the state bar conference down the beach."

The words are a statement, not a question. Burt glances down at the sand and kicks at it with his bright white running shoes. People don't like to be questioned by authority, and Burt is no different. He's probably an important man back there in Bainbridge—the kind of person that tends to do the questioning. But everybody has to answer to someone. I wait him out.

"Understand, I personally find gossip to be unseemly. But Donovan was state bar president. I'm a former state bar president myself. People in charge needed to know what happened to him."

"No one said otherwise. I just need to know everything you said and everyone you talked to."

"Only Meredith Bixby—incoming state bar president. Told her Donovan was dead on the beach. She needed to know. That's all."

That's not all. Cate knew enough to accurately tell me that Kessler's head was bashed in. She didn't get that information from Captain Dave. Burt stands his ground. Maybe he honestly doesn't remember. Stress turns a lot of minds to jelly, but Lois knows the score. She gives her husband a dose of side-eye with a slight frown. Because she seems a better bet at this point, I turn my attention to her.

"You want to take a try?"

Lois exhales. The sense is that she's had to expend a lot of breath on Burt's behalf over the years. I reckon the matching running suits was also his idea. But while he is as prickly as a porcupine, she's as calm as a dove. After taking my measure for a couple of seconds, she answers the question.

"I'm a former prosecutor and can tell what you're getting at. You want to figure out who all knows about the details of how Donovan died—the location of the body, the cause of death, what he was wearing, all that stuff. Am I right?"

"You're getting warm."

"Thought so. Well, it's like Burt said, the two of us called Meredith Bixby, putting his phone on speaker so everybody could hear the other. We told her that Donovan had been murdered, that someone had smashed him in the head good and hard. But that was all we said. The conversation was a short one."

"How did you know it was murder? Maybe he fell down the stairs to the beach."

Burt stiffens a little, but Lois and I pay him little heed. She offers a grim smile and appreciative nod at me before responding.

"This isn't my first rodeo. I've seen plenty of corpses on the autopsy table. Donovan's head had contusions of all shapes and sizes, consistent with repeated blows with a heavy object. A fall down the stairs wouldn't cause so many diverse types of wounds. Someone hit him hard and often. And I'd have to be blind to miss the nearby brick. That's your murder weapon."

Lois is growing on me. Competence these days is in short supply. Any time I come across a person who knows their business, I mentally offer up a "Hail Mary" to thank God for small miracles. And I'm not even Catholic.

"No mention of the brick to Meredith?"

"Do I look like I fell off the turnip truck or something?"

She kinda does, actually. But appearances can be deceiving. Anyway, I credit the response as a denial of any mentioning of the brick to Meredith.

"You stayed with the body while waiting for the police to arrive?"

"Yes."

"Anyone else come upon the scene?"

"Not until this state trooper here showed up after the 911 call. We started out at the crack of dawn. Place was dead. Had the beach all to ourselves."

Burt chimes in, "We've always been early risers."

He says the words as if I should pat him on the head or something. Even the prim and proper Dave, otherwise stoic in my questioning to this point, breaks character to look askance at Burt's interjection of that little bit of useless trivia. But I'll let Lois deal with Burt later—the forbearance she must display on a daily basis a testament to suffering wives everywhere. Meanwhile, I have a couple more questions for her.

"Did you know that Kessler lived in a house on the other side of the dune?"

"Sure, we attended a party there last night for past state bar presidents and their dates. Big shindig. About forty people in all."

Burt nods importantly, in case I forgot that he used to be a state bar president. But I'm past paying much attention to him. Rather, the thought of now having to interview forty partygoers makes me weep a little on the inside. I don't have the horses to perform this investigation and certainly not before I leave the country for over two weeks. The whole thing feels like a heavy weight that I'm bound to drop on my foot.

Lois adds, "The party broke off around eleven. That's when we left. Donovan was still alive."

I ask her, "Any suspects?"

"Not really. Donovan was pretty vanilla. About the most boring guy imaginable, if I'm being honest. There's other state bar presidents that I would've expected to be murdered before him."

She may or may not be talking about her husband. I pivot to him to see if he took any offense and spy a lot of bother on his face. But not because of his wife's words. The frown he points at me suggests another source, and I call him on it.

"What's eating you now?"

"You asked about suspects. I have one. Donovan's girlfriend—Sadie Foxx. I don't like her. The woman barely wears any clothes. She might as well be in a nudist colony. And her sleeping in his bed while Judy's still alive. Barely old enough to drink, too. It's indecent. Makes me angry."

Much of that makes no sense to me, and I swivel to Lois with a look that invites her to fill in the gaps. She accepts the offer.

"Judy is Donovan's wife. Was, I guess, since he's dead. A couple of years ago, an eighteen-wheeler hit Judy, and she lost most of her brain activity as a result. She's now in a care facility in Brunswick. Sadie has moved in and sticks out like the sorest thumb you've ever seen—to the point that it was awkward at the party last night. But I don't know why she would kill Donovan. She's living on easy street. More likely that the rest of the family would want to kill *her*."

While I could spend an hour talking to both of them about that party and probably will at some point, getting in front of Sadie Foxx and everyone else in the victim's house is a higher priority. I stare into the eyes of both Burt and Lois—mainly him—to emphasize the importance of my next words.

"The two of you stumbled into something horrible through no fault of your own. It's traumatic. And you're going to have a burning urge to relieve that trauma by talking about what you saw. Except you can't. Nothing to no one. Everything about that crime scene needs to stay secret. If anyone asks you, just say that 'the authorities have instructed you not to talk about it.' Can you do that for me?"

They both nod, Burt vigorously, and I take them at their word, telling them that they are free to go. As I start to wheel around to make my way to the house, Lois asks, "Why are you even handling this case way down here?"

I stop in mid-turn and contemplate her for a couple of seconds before answering.

"That's a helluva good question."

***

Captain Dave and I shuffle back over the sand to the vicinity of the dead body, which is now swarmed by the arrival of the Georgia Bureau of Investigation's crime scene techs. Despite the rising threat of high tide, the leader of the group, Debbie Fincher, assures me that they'll get the job done. She looks the part, with the navy blue GBI pullover she wears fitting like a second skin. Her manner is brisk and efficient—the undercurrent being that the work will begin in earnest once everyone gets out of the way. I take the hint.

That leaves the girlfriend and the family. I make my way across the wooden bridge toward the weathered, white house over the dune. In the backyard, an array of perfectly arranged flowers decorate the landscape in a display of bountiful colors.

Only one false note is apparent. Dave points out the missing imprint of a brick in an otherwise neat border around one flower bed filled with yellow daffodils—beauty giving birth to something grotesque.

5

One peek at Sadie Foxx confirms the accuracy of Burt's words from just a few minutes ago. She barely wears any clothes. Sitting on the couch in a halter top that reveals plenty of shoulder and stomach—but no tan lines—Sadie glances up from a magazine with a bored expression. A pair of long, shapely legs stretch out in front of her. I think she might be wearing short shorts but wouldn't swear to it under oath. Everything about her oozes sex.

An embarrassed Captain Dave averts his gaze from the sight of it. He's probably a deacon in a Baptist church.

I introduce myself and ask if I can sit down.

"Sure."

Sadie closes the magazine—one of the celebrity gossip rags that my mother likes to read—and tosses it onto a glass coffee table. She tilts her head my way and slowly gives me a full going over, from the top of my brown hair all the way down to my dirty tennis shoes. I give her time to complete the inspection. When she returns to my eyes, I offer condolences for her loss.

"Thanks."

"Can I ask you some questions?"

She shrugs. The words aren't exactly flowing out of her. Granted, her boyfriend did just die. But any grief on her part appears to be in short supply.

"Your name's Sadie Foxx?"

"Uh-huh."

"Is that your real name?"

A staccato-sharp laugh accompanies a toss of her head. When she turns back to me, some type of unholy glee infects her bearing—a sultry smirk combined with taunting eyes.

"Why do you ask? Think that's my stripper name or something?"

"The thought did occur to me."

"You're not the first to think that. But alas, Sadie Foxx is my real name. Right there on the birth certificate. Blame my parents. I do have a stripper pole upstairs in my bedroom closet if you would like a private show. Maybe you want to start with a lap dance. Your friend over there can watch."

I turn toward Dave to make sure I heard her right. The rising red blush that fills his cheeks confirms that his ears are as good as mine. He stands apart from us uncomfortable in a corner, as far away as he can manage while still being polite. His stare back to me conveys its own message: "She's your problem, not mine."

True enough. I return my attention back to the witness—who may or may not have a stripper pole in her bedroom closet.

"Sadie, whatever the hell you're doing, knock it off. Your boyfriend was murdered maybe forty yards from here. Crime scene technicians are inspecting his dead body while we speak. A little later today, the coroner's going to cut him open and lay his insides out neatly on a cold steel table. Ugly stuff—all because somebody decided that Donovan Kessler didn't deserve to keep on living. My job is to find that person, and the search begins in this house."

The theatrics leak right out of her. She bends her head down to inspect her fingernails, which are adorned in some shade of pink. I let the moment breathe to give her plenty of opportunity to take inventory of the situation. After tucking her legs underneath the rest of her on the couch, she turns back to me and gives a little nod.

"Good. Let's start over. Tell me about your relationship with Kessler."

She sighs and says, "Donny was all right. I met him in his law office. His brother, Raymond, was handling a car wreck case for me where I got rear-ended and got some whiplash. Later I bumped into Donny at the grocery store. We went to dinner, and six months ago I moved in."

"The age gap didn't bother you?"

"Obviously not. We each had something the other wanted. I wanted his financial assets. He wanted my physical assets. The deal was unspoken, but both Donny and I knew what was up. And we were fine with it. Everyone else, not so much. Bothered the hell out of them. What about you? You're not one of those judgmental types that looks down on people from your moral high horse, are you?"

"The older I get, the more I lose the taste for judging other people. That's God's business. But let's be real. Something tells me that you get a pretty big thrill out of being provocative for the sake of being provocative. Kessler was still married when you moved in, wasn't he?"

"Nah. Judy's gone. Has been ever since that accident. Her body may still be barely alive but not her. Donny waited a respectful time. Life goes on."

"Did his kids see things the same way?"

Sadie makes a scoffing noise and utters a word still illegal in some parts of the South. She proceeds to give me her unfiltered opinion on the rest of the Kessler family. Sammy and Lucy Kessler—the deceased's son and daughter-in-law. Both lawyers, usually up in Savannah. Stuck up as hell and mean as rattlesnakes to boot. Katherine and Maxwell Matheny—daughter and son-in-law. She's a stay at home wife who takes too many pills—probably because her husband is a leering drunk. Maxwell works in the same Savannah law firm as Sammy and Lucy, although there's no love lost among the three of them. Next up is Raymond Kessler—the dead man's brother and next-door neighbor. Sadie says that Raymond is all right, apart from throwing her damning looks of judgment every chance he gets. But at least he has the decency to keep his mouth shut about it.

"Tell me about the party last night."

"Have you ever hung around lawyers?"

"A little bit."

"Most boring group of people on the planet. Only thing that makes them tolerable is their drinking. Last night I wanted to stab my eyeballs out with a knife. Donny was loving it, especially the reactions of his startled friends as he showed me off to them. I apparently was a shock to their conservative sensibilities, and he enjoyed the spectacle. The whole thing gave me a headache, but that's the price of being a kept woman. The second the last of them left, I went up to bed and crashed."

I'm guessing that Sadie hasn't hung around many accountants. Lawyers are a blast compared to them. But I can see where she's coming from. Being paraded around for the sole purpose of having a bunch of drunk lawyers gawk at you sounds about as much fun as slamming a hammer on one's hand. Even for an exhibitionist like Sadie. Too much like being on display in a zoo.

"Remember who left the party last?"

"Do you really believe I made any effort to learn a single one of those people's names?"

Fair point. I scan around the room to try and inspect it with an investigator's insight only to realize that I've neglected something important. Silent curses follow—including a few toward the Governor for dropping this mess into my lap. I excuse myself from Sadie and head over to Dave, who is still standing straight as a stripper pole in the corner. I motion for him to join me outside.

***

"We need a search warrant for the house. Can you spare one of your people to go find a magistrate judge and get one?"

Captain Dave accepts the assignment like a man happy to have something to do. Anything to get away from Sadie. He strides off with purpose, maybe even with a little trot to his step. I kick myself again for neglecting the search warrant until now and wonder how many other balls I'm going to drop through bad juggling before sundown.

I check my watch. On the way over from the golf course, I summoned Scott and J.D. Hendrix—the junior member of my investigative team—to get down here as soon as possible. But I don't expect them for a few more hours, leaving me feeling very much alone. Standing outside the front door to the house, I take a deep breath before heading back in.

She sits there as before, the long legs still curled up under her. The celebrity magazine has returned to her exposed lap. She flips a page just as I enter but flings the magazine back on the coffee table upon seeing me. It lands with a dull splat. Jennifer Aniston and Brad Pitt are smiling on the cover. Apparently, they are back together. Love conquers all.

When I return to my seat, Sadie turns toward me in a sensual manner that conveys the impression that handling her is going to be a chore. Reaching into what must be a deep bag of tricks, she licks the top of now-pouty lips and opens her mouth to speak.

"Wanted to get me alone, huh?"

And Jesus wept.

6

Sadie smiles at me with the self-assurance that only comes from not having lived long enough to know better. Proving the point, she proceeds to unfurl her long, brown legs in divergent directions—one along the length of the couch, the other at a right angle stretching out on the floor. Combined with the skimpy shorts she's barely wearing, the spread-eagle view on display figures to show off much of her womanhood. But I work to keep my gaze above sea level.

Maintaining eye contact, I remove my phone from my pocket, start the app that records conversations, and show it to her. She juts out her lips in a playful pout. Hoping that the knowledge she's being recorded will put a stop to the stupid games, I restart the interview.

"You decided to start misbehaving when I left the room. Why?"

"Hard-working man like yourself deserves an extra treat. Go ahead, get you an eyeful."

"Is this how you hooked Donovan? Putting it out there on a billboard that you were open for business?"

"You don't like it? What's the problem? You're straight, aren't you?"

"As an arrow."

"We'll see about that. But to answer your question, I like to push boundaries to see how men react, realizing that men like you have never been alone with a woman as beautiful as me."

"But I have."

"Don't be silly. Name one."

"Lara Landrum."

The answer lands. Hearing the name of the famous actress causes Sadie to do a double-take. And while my response is not completely accurate, it is close enough for purposes of her challenge. But I still wince a little on the inside.

Lara Landrum—the jagged memory is so seared into my brain that even absent my slavish devotion to Cate, Sadie's sexual hijinks are wasted on me as an audience. I've seen that movie before and have no appetite for a sequel, which would be akin to swimming in a bathtub with a hungry crocodile. Once is enough.

Sadie shoots a glance toward the celebrity mag on the table before circling back to give me a fresh going over with her eyes. A question forms on her lips.

"Are you famous or something? You're starting to look familiar."

"I have that kind of face."

She doesn't appear convinced but at least repositions her legs to a posture approximating the vicinity of normal. From a sociological perspective, she might make an interesting study, and I try to map out her future. The prognosis isn't promising. Looks fade away, but vanity and shallowness endure forever. A job seems out of the question, so the search for Kessler's replacement will probably start soon after his funeral, followed by a tour of duty as someone's trophy wife—assuming Sadie's not in jail for killing Donny.

"Any idea who murdered your boyfriend?"

"Of course not. How could I? Are you sure it's him? The state troopers wouldn't let me go look at the body."

"People from the party last night made a positive identification."

"Maybe they killed him."

That's an interesting thought. Kessler has been dead much too long for Burt and Lois to have murdered him on their morning run. But maybe they killed him late last night—motive to be determined—and went out early on a pretend jog to see if anyone had discovered the body yet. The hypothesis doesn't really move me, but it has a certain symmetry. I answer her.

"The timing doesn't work. When did you see Kessler last?"

"When the final guest left, I headed straight to bed. He wanted to stay up for a bit and go for a walk on the beach. He liked doing that. Every night. Always by himself. The only time I'm on the beach is when the sun is out. I told him not to wake me and that I would see him in the morning."

"What time?"

"Around eleven."

On the way in, I observed a Ring camera mounted to the front door. I ask Sadie if I could check the Ring app's history on her cell. She shrugs, pulls an iPhone out of the back of her shorts, and hands the device over. I pull up the saved recordings. The first one I open is time-stamped 10:56 p.m. from last night. Kessler steps out of the doorway with another woman. The two of them stop on the front step for a conversation. I turn the volume up.

He says, "Damn it, Meredith, these allegations are serious. I should serve as president for another year to allow an investigation and put this thing to bed. You can take over next year, without a dark cloud hounding your presidency."

The woman responds, "You don't get to make up lies about me just because you want to serve another year as president. That's not how it works."

Back to Kessler: "Don't fight me on this. No need for the situation to get ugly."

The woman again: "It's already ugly because of you."

She turns around and storms off. Based on what Burt and Lois told me earlier, the woman reckons to be Meredith Bixby, incoming state bar president. I worried before whether the Pressleys had shared too many details about the crime scene with her. Now, the scent is much more particularized in Meredith's direction. I text the video to myself and ask Sadie, "Any idea what that was about?"

"Take a wild guess. You think I give a single damn about anything in that conversation?"

"Your boyfriend ever say anything about wanting to stay on as state bar president for another year?"

"If he did, I wasn't listening."

Figures. The next video in the Ring's history has a timestamp of 12:39 a.m., which is close enough to the probable time of Kessler's death to scratch me where I itch. I push play and watch a middle-aged man with disheveled hair stumble up the walkway. He grabs the handle to the front door and jerks it up-and-down with increasing agitation. A hard kick follows, but the door wins. After much cursing about his now-injured foot, he staggers off to the side of the house, heading toward the backyard. After texting that video to myself, I play the clip again for Sadie and ask, "Who's this?"

She rolls her eyes and responds, "That's Maxwell—Donny's son-in-law. I told you he was a drunk."

"Any reason he would have to kill Kessler?"

"Sexual frustration. He'd do about anything to get into my pants."

"Does he have a chance now that Kessler's dead?"

The salute of her middle finger lets me know what she thinks of the question.

* * *

"Anyone else in the house besides Maxwell have a motive to murder your boyfriend?"

"The whole family is whacked out. Safe bet is that they all wanted to kill each other. But I think I would've probably been at the top of their list before Donny. I'm the outsider now sleeping in their mother's bed. Things were tense."

"Have you had the thought that the person who murdered Kessler might have a similar urge toward you?"

Her eyebrows frown and give birth to a concern that strikes me as awfully authentic. I keep silent and allow her fears to marinate for a spell. After giving the matter a good think, she speaks.

"You really believe that?"

Before I can answer, heavy footsteps from another room announce the arrival of another man in an archway that leads to the kitchen. The man's height is medium, his scowl possibly permanent. I recognize him at once. Maxwell Matheny—the drunk on the Ring video, who has combed his thick, black hair since the late-night altercation with the front door.

He barks at me, "Who the hell are you?"

"Chance Meridian. I'm investigating the murder of your father-in-law."

"You don't look like a cop."

"Because I'm not a cop. I'm a lawyer."

"You don't look like a lawyer, either."

I glance down at my jeans, sweatshirt, and sneakers. He's not wrong. I shrug my shoulders in sympathy and respond, "Well, I'm down here on vacation and didn't plan to do any investigating at all. But the Governor had other plans."

"Governor McReynolds?"

"Is there another one I don't know about?"

The scowl escalates into a sneer. But his puffy eyes—still reeling in the aftermath of the previous evening's alcoholic excess—drain most of the fierceness away. Hangovers can have that kind of deflating effect. He mutters, "Come to think of it, I've heard about you."

"All the way down here? I'll take that as a compliment."

"Don't."

After shooting me a mean look—and one to Sadie for good measure—Maxwell departs for another part of the house. I can still hear his receding footsteps when Sadie says, "He's mad because you were alone with me. He's always jealous like that even though he has no claim to. I told you how bad he wants to get in my pants. Bastard probably killed Donny."

A beautiful woman can make a man dumb in a hurry. Maxwell and I figure to have a lot to talk about. Sadie starts to speak again.

"So you're a lawyer, huh? Can I ask you a legal question?"

"You can ask."

"How long do I have to let Donny's family stay in this house?"

The words don't compute, and I stare at her confused for a few seconds. When I finally catch on, I begin to wonder just how good a deal Sadie negotiated for herself.

"Donny didn't leave everything to you, did he?"

"Not yet. Something about still being married to Judy. But he was divorcing her, and we were going to get married. Then everything could be mine. In the meantime, he made me a joint tenant with him on this house with the right of survivorship. He told me that if he died the house would be mine. Well, he's dead. So how long do I have to wait before kicking those people out of my house?"

A house this size on Jekyll Island, right on the beach, might fetch $5 million. Multitudes have been murdered for much less—although by her telling, Sadie had an even greater payday coming her way. Maybe she got impatient. But her information also points a giant finger at everyone else under this roof last night. Killing Donovan Kessler before he could change his will figures to keep a whole lot of money in the family. While I mull over these thoughts, she presses me again, "Well?"

"I'm not that type of lawyer. Real estate and probate aren't my thing."

"What kind of lawyer are you?"

"The type that puts murderers away."

"Not a lot of money in that, is there?"

"Nope."

"Too bad."

7

After asking Sadie for directions, I knock on an upstairs door to a room that supposedly contains Sammy and Lucy Kessler—the deceased's son and daughter-in-law, alleged to be as mean as rattlesnakes. I considered first finding Maxwell to continue our abbreviated chat but decided to gather more information elsewhere before tackling the person who stands as the best suspect at this early stage.

My knock is answered by a skinny man with an angular face. Thinning hair, more gray than brown at this point, decorates the top of his head. He blinks twice upon seeing me.

"Sammy?"

The man nods. I introduce myself and explain the purpose of my visit. He hesitates, peers back scared-like over his shoulder, and answers, "As you can imagine, my wife and I are still in shock. Can't we do this later?"

"Unfortunately, no. Speed is of the essence with a killer on the loose."

Sammy chews on that a bit. Eventually he nods without much enthusiasm and widens the door to allow me entry to a large bedroom. Lucy Kessler sits on a cushioned green chair. Unlike her husband who is dressed in a polo and khakis, Lucy's attire is all business—a dark pantsuit paired with a white blouse. Except for her oversized bare feet, she is ready for the courtroom. A tight grimace creates unattractive lines around the outside of her mouth.

She snaps at me, "I don't appreciate being kept like a prisoner in my own home."

"Is this your home?"

"Close enough."

With his arms crossed in a posture of strained tolerance, Sammy nods—this time with plenty of enthusiasm—in agreement with his wife's declaration. Figuring that a talk with the two of them will take a while, I sit down without being invited on a couch perpendicular to Lucy's chair. Sammy stares down at me like he wants to say something but ends up taking the chair opposite his wife with a silent pout.

I say to her, "Apologies for your detention. The morning has been hard on everyone involved, especially your father-in-law. Any idea who killed him?"

"Really? I think not."

"You must have thought about it while sitting up here."

"Some transient probably. They're all over now, clustered at that campground on the north end of the island, acting like the whole place belongs to them. I barely feel safe walking around after dark these days."

Her face is full of concerned earnestness, which is a remarkable window into her worldview. Jekyll Island is one of the safest places on earth. The fear that roving transients are somehow wreaking havoc around here is so divorced from reality so as to be comical. Except Lucy isn't laughing. I'm left to wonder if she is lying.

But could Donovan Kessler have been killed by a random stranger? Wrong place, wrong time—that kind of thing. Not likely. The big problem with Lucy's theory is the murder weapon. Captain Dave's earlier conclusion remains sound. The missing brick didn't fly from its spot around the flower bed and land by magic on the sandy shore. Someone took a brick from the backyard and across the wooden bridge. Someone who knew that Donovan Kessler was on the other side of the walkway and wanted to kill him with that brick.

Or as I used to call it when arguing my case to the jury—premeditation.

I turn to Sammy and ask, "What about you? Any suspects?"

"You should start with Sadie. She moved in six months ago, and now my father is dead. That can't be a coincidence. Have you met her yet? Make sure you keep your guard up. She's a seductress! Men lose all their senses around her."

"Like your brother-in-law?"

He opens his mouth to say something but thinks better of it. Lucy holds onto to her tongue, too, but does allow herself to purse her lips. She's plumper than her skinny husband—not fat, just the normal body type for middle age. She also spends a lot of money on her brown hair, which is short with long bangs—professionally trimmed, professionally colored. I make these observations while the three of us sit in silence. Wanting to hear whatever they might say about Maxwell, I decide to wait them out. Sammy breaks first.

"What would possibly move you to utter such a horrid thing?"

"You said yourself that Sadie has a certain effect on men. Maxwell is a man. Could be that he wanted what your father had. Jealousy is a green-eyed monster, you know. Straight from Shakespeare. Ever seen Maxwell get violent? Maybe when he was drunk?"

Lucy hisses, "Don't answer that, Sammy."

Sammy doesn't answer. When satisfied that her order will be obeyed, she scoots up to the edge of her chair, leans forward, and sticks a thick finger in my direction.

"Look here, Maxwell is family. He's also our law partner. You don't get to come into this house and make us turn against each other. We don't have to talk to you at all. If you want this conversation to continue, ask about something else."

"What did you and your husband do last night?"

"Had dinner with old friends at their place on St. Simon's. Got home about eleven-fifteen."

St. Simon's is a neighboring island about thirty minutes from Jekyll by of way of Brunswick, an important port city on the Georgia mainland. Lucy gives me the names of their old friends, and that part of the story will certainly check out. I ask, "How did you get in the house?"

"Through the door to the kitchen in the garage."

No Ring camera for that point of entry. No cameras are at back of the house, either. Just the front door.

"Then what?"

"We went straight to our bedroom and took turns showering."

"Who went first?"

Lucy scowls, probably in disgust at the impertinence of asking about her bathing habits. But she's the one that brought it up. Sammy butts in, "I did."

"How long did it take you?"

"Fifteen minutes."

I turn to Lucy and ask, "Did you leave the bedroom during that time?" Through clenched teeth, she spits out, "No."

"And how long was your shower after your husband had finished?"

"Twenty minutes."

At least that's what I think she says. The gravel in her mouth from digesting more of my impertinence makes it hard to hear her words clearly. I return to Sammy and say, "Did you leave the—"

He squawks, "Stop harassing us, damnit! You might not realize it, but we're important lawyers in Savannah! I know damn near everyone in this state and have a mind to call them about you! So watch your step!"

That's cute. Sammy is full of sound and fury, signifying nothing. He blusters loudly to project a strength that just isn't there. The smile on my face is wide in response to him. He is not the first person to try to pull rank on me and won't be the last. But the Governor set me up with so much independence that I'm free to ruffle as many feathers as I want—especially folks like Sammy who think they are untouchable. It's all right there in the Georgia Code.

"You're going to report me to your friends? Really? Who are you going to call? I answer only to God and the Governor, and I'm on a first name basis with both."

I raise my voice a little for effect. Sammy slouches down a little—his bony elbows jutting out over the arms of the chair. Maybe now he'll be in a mood to answer my question. I try again.

"Someone murdered your father maybe forty yards from where we are now. That means I need to know the whereabouts of everyone in the vicinity around the time that killing occurred, including you. I'll ask again. Did you leave the bedroom while your wife was in the shower?"

"No, I did not."

"And when your wife finished her shower, neither of you left after that?"

"Correct."

Their story is on the record, at least. Not that either of them has much of an alibi. Both were occupied in the shower long enough to allow the other to slip out, smash Donovan Kessler over the head with a brick, and make it back inside.

A new thought hits me. I stand up and stroll to the bedroom's window, which faces the ocean. The view of the ocean in the distance may be worth millions, but my interest lies in what's visible closer to home. The entirety of the backyard sits in plain sight. If either Sammy or Lucy were gazing out the window at the right time, they would've seen Kessler heading to the beach over the wooden staircase. Maybe one of them seized the golden opportunity. I also check for signs of the GBI technicians working over the body on the sand, but the dune hides the murder scene from the house, which is about how I figured it.

Lucy asks, "What are you doing?"

"Seeing if it might rain. Do either of you know anything about your father's dealings with Meredith Bixby?"

The sudden change in topics throws them. They sit there perplexed for a couple of seconds before Lucy asks, "What does she have to do with anything?"

"You tell me."

"She's going to be the next state bar president. The swearing-in is tomorrow night."

"The two of them get along?"

"Meredith gets along with everyone. She's the nicest person on the planet."

Sammy nods for effect. Their confusion seems genuine enough. For whatever reason, Kessler didn't share his squabble with Bixby with them. As I start to plan my exit, Lucy addresses me with a hard edge.

"I know you're a lawyer—a former prosecutor—but now you're also a cop of sorts, right?"

"Something like that. I have a gun and a badge."

"That will work for my purposes. I want you to escort Sadie out of our house as soon as you leave this room. She's not welcome anymore.

Throw her out on the street for all I care. She'll fit right in with all the other stray cats on the island. But get her out of here!"

Seems like the trouble with Meredith Bixby wasn't the only thing that Donovan Kessler kept from his family. I make a big production of exhaling most of the breath I can muster. Sammy and Lucy are not going to like what I'm about to say.

"Here's the thing—Sadie says the house is now hers. Your father-in-law left it to her. Joint tenancy with the right of survivorship. Truth be told, she beat you to it. She wants me to throw you out."

"What!"

Sammy's bellow doesn't fit with his slight mouth. His eyes bug out in a way that makes it uncomfortable to keep looking at him. Slack-jawed and drowning, he faces Lucy for any kind of life preserver. But his wife is more focused on her own anger. She seethes, "Where is that slut?"

"Down in the living room."

They both bolt for the door.

8

Lucy is quicker than appearances would suggest. Probably her big feet. She descends the stairs with the speed of a frightened jackrabbit. The carpet that covers the stairs does a poor job of masking her descent, and the boom of each step rattles throughout the house. Sammy nips at his wife's heels—his own steps creating a modest echo in her wake. I follow them down at a more moderate pace.

A panting Lucy stops short of Sadie, who remains anchored to her perch on the living room couch. Sadie glances up at the new arrival and unleashes a bemused grin twice as powerful as any yell. The tactic works. Lucy exclaims, "You bitch!"

"Good morning, Lucy."

"You bitch!"

"Yes, you already said that."

"If you think you're stealing this house—"

The front door opens. Captain Dave strides in and stands beside me—no doubt brought like a moth to the flame by the rising sound of disorderly conduct, the catch-all charge that police officers everywhere deploy to make arrests when nothing else can stick. His arrival pauses the action in mid-breath. After a short interlude of everyone just looking at each other in silence, Sammy moves to a spot next to his wife and whines in Sadie's direction, "I grew up in this house. It's my home. And you think it belongs to you? Over my dead body."

"A small price to pay."

Sammy takes a step forward, his hands balled up into little fists. Dave moves to intervene, but I arrest his progress with my arm and whisper to him, "I want to see how things shake out." He stares at me with his mouth slightly open in shock at my methods. I return my attention to the unfolding family drama.

Out of the corner of my eye, I spot a woman coming from the staircase into the periphery of the living room area, right behind Sammy and Lucy, who fail to notice her. Almost simultaneously, Maxwell emerges from somewhere and places his hands on the woman's shoulders. The woman flinches but relents. In a loud voice, Maxwell says, "What the hell is going on?"

Without turning around, Lucy answers, "This bitch claims that Donovan gave the house to her."

The woman in Maxwell's grip—who I presume to be Katherine Matheny, Maxwell's wife and Donovan Kessler's daughter—blanches at Lucy's announcement. She wiggles out from her husband's grasp and moves around to face both Sadie and Lucy.

Katherine asks, "Is this true?"

She turns her head from Lucy to Sadie and back again a number of times, awaiting an answer. Sadie says, "Afraid so, Kat. But if you're nice to me, I might let you visit for old times' sake."

That missile hits its target. Katherine starts to shake. I inch forward a little in case she makes a frantic grab for Sadie's neck. But instead she rushes back up the stairs, forcefully pushing Maxwell out of the way when he tries to stop her. A door slam puts an exclamation point on her departure.

The energy deflates out of the room. Sammy unclenches his fists and huffs, "Even if you're telling the truth about what Father did, this fight isn't over. We will see you in court. And don't even think about showing your face at the funeral!"

Lucy takes hold of his arm and directs him out of the living room. They make their way back up the stairs a lot slower than the hurry in which they came down. Maxwell remains in place and leers at Sadie with stalker-like, smoldering intensity. She returns the glare with a thin parting of her lips—part taunt, part smirk. Lois Pressley told me that the family would be more likely to kill Sadie than Donovan. I am coming around to that view and wonder if another murder may be in the works. But in no event can all of these people sleep under this roof tonight.

Maxwell blinks and loses the staredown. He whirls to head back to the kitchen. I anoint him as the next person I should interview, if for no other reason than to give Katherine time to stop shaking.

Sadie Foxx picks up her magazine.

* * *

"Where are we on the search warrant?"

Dave and I stand off to the side by ourselves in the dining room. He gazes back in the direction of the living room, disturbed. A complaint forms on his lips.

"The situation could've gotten out of control in there. What if someone had gotten hurt? That would've been on your head."

I pat him on the arm in sympathy. My methods often disappoint me, too. But doing a hard job requires making hard choices. I try to explain the facts of life to him.

"Sometimes it's best to see how animals behave while out in the wild."

"What does that even mean?"

"Investigations are hard because witnesses lie—all of them. Even when honest, they still tell a false story because they always want to put their best foot forward. To make themselves look better than they are. Kinda like the happy couple on social media who suddenly gets divorced. Smiling pictures never present the full picture. In contrast, what we just witnessed was a glimpse at a group of people momentarily unconcerned with how they would be perceived. That's valuable reconnaissance."

He doesn't believe me, which is not a surprise. Rule followers such as Dave often have trouble seeing gray. He shakes his head and counters, "And what did you just learn?"

"Plenty. Katherine can barely stand her husband. Did you see her flinch at his touch? Sammy came close to punching Sadie right in front of all of us. How violent would he get absent the watchful eyes of other people? How about Lucy's racing down the stairs all hot and bothered? She might have hit Sadie herself. But why? Lucy didn't grow up in this house. She's only the daughter-in-law. Also, Maxwell's simmering obsession with Sadie was on full display just from being in the same room with her. And what about the fact that the only visible emotion in this house is anger? No grief. No red eyes from crying. Don't you find that strange?"

Seemingly oblivious to our presence, Sadie turns another page in her magazine in the next room. Dave focuses on her—the beginning of a thought bubbling to the surface of his face. He points his head toward her and says, "What about Miss Foxx? You said witnesses, even when they're telling the truth, put their best foot forward. But she sure didn't care about appearances when you questioned her before. She was trying to push your buttons."

"Who says she's telling the truth?"

9

Maxwell sits at the kitchen table in an angry mood. A large hand, disproportionate to the medium-sized rest of him, holds a beer bottle. A European import if I read the label right—medicine for his hangover. My arrival doesn't improve the feeling in the room. He takes too much of a sip upon seeing me and has to jolt upright when the beer goes down wrong. After a wipe of his mouth with the sleeves of a button-down shirt, he glares at me with full vigor. I plop down into a chair and initiate a conversation.

"Making the rounds. You're next on the list."

"I've got nothing to say to you."

"That's fine. I'll just take the opportunity to get away from Sadie for a while. Does she ever wear clothes? Bet your father-in-law went through a lot of Viagra. Even for a happily married man like myself, that woman is damn tempting."

The confessional tone accompanying my words slackens some of the coiled tension in his posture. I slouch down in my chair to further the subliminal message that I pose no threat to him. As he takes another drink from the bottle—slower this time—I ask, "Where does a woman like that come from anyway?"

"Hicksville. Some driver rear-ended her. She saw Raymond's face on a billboard. He took the case, and that's how she met Donovan. In no time at all, he was the one rear-ending her. Lucky bastard."

He emits a twisted chuckle, and a feeling of being unclean from play-acting with him in this way disturbs my insides, even if the ruse is for the greater good. But the information checks out with Sadie's story. Raymond Kessler—the deceased's brother and law partner—represented Sadie in a car wreck case. The rest is history. I joke, "Guess his luck ran out."

Another laugh from him, followed by an offer to fetch me a beer.

"No thanks. On duty. Think she killed him?"

"Why would she? She has it made here, living high on the hog. Even if Sadie wanted to screw some dude on the side, no problem. Donovan worked all day. Sneaky bitch like her could have everything she wanted and then some."

"That's a thought. Is there another guy in the picture? Someone who might've wanted Sadie all to himself?"

Maxwell shakes his head and works on the beer. I watch him with a disinterested manner—somewhat surprised that he has opened up to me at all. But men have a near-unlimited capacity to commiserate with each other about the poisonous fruit that is a beautiful woman. And this particular man has a lot of pent-up angst about the particular woman sitting in the living room reading a gossip magazine. He licks his lips and gives me an answer.

"You understand that I live in Savannah, and she's still fairly new on the scene. I can't say for sure, but yeah. Sadie's the type to spread it around."

And so are you—although I keep that editorial to myself. Instead, I ask, "Who killed him then?"

"Hell if I know."

"Sammy got a bit heated in there."

He scoffs out a loud grunt and replies, "Him? The man's a mouse. Does bond work because that's all the conflict he can handle. He once got assigned a pro bono criminal case, and the experience nearly broke him. He shrinks from confrontation. Trust me, I've been his law partner long enough to know. His ballbuster wife, though, that's the one you need to keep an eye on. She's capable of anything."

"Why would Lucy kill Donovan?"

"She was in love with him."

***

Maxwell regrets the words the instant they escape out of him. I pretend not to notice. With exaggerated surprise on my face, I say, "Really?"

"Forget I said that. Lucy couldn't kill anyone, either. How did Donovan die anyway?"

"We're keeping that to ourselves right now. I'll let you know when I can. But what you just said about Lucy—her own father-in-law? Did Donovan reciprocate her interest?"

"No—I told you to forget about it. Drinking beer this early in the day makes me say stupid stuff sometimes."

Some revelations are too hard to forget. If Lucy truly had a thing for Sammy's father, that would give both wife and husband powerful motives for murder—a toxic brew of reverse Oedipal, in-law emotions or something. I set aside the thought for safe-keeping and change the subject.

"How's your wife holding up?"

"Kat's okay. Donovan was her dad and all, but she was much closer to Judy, her mom."

"Judy is in a care facility somewhere?"

"Yeah, over the bridge in Brunswick. A car accident damaged her brain for good. Kat still struggles with it and is pretty depressed."

He finishes off the beer in contemplative silence, and I reflect that being in this house makes me a little depressed, too. A sickness—some condition of rot—permeates the pores of this place. Like a mold that infests the innards of the walls. You can't see it, but the fungus is there, working its damage, attacking the lives of everyone who breathes its contaminated air. Me included.

Wanting to be done with him, I say, "Might as well give me your alibi while we're here. What were you doing last night?"

The spirit of fellowship evaporates out of the room. Maxwell spins a bottle top around in quick little circles, frowning hard as he tries not to look at me. He stops the spinning top with a jab of his index finger and slowly maneuvers his head to meet my stare. The frown gives way to a crooked grin.

"Why do you have to go and ask something like that? We were having such a nice little talk."

"A standard question in a murder investigation. You shouldn't take offense."

"Who says I'm offended?"

But his tone and body language betray him. I wonder why. That he would be asked such a question is a given. Any fool knows that. While I could confront him head on with the Ring video, I'm more interested in whether he'll tell the truth without compulsion. I say, "Don't make this more difficult than it needs to be. Where were you?"

"I'm done talking with you."

"At least tell me what time you returned to the house."

"No doing."

"How did you get in? I know you were too drunk to open the front door."

His eyes go wide then retreat into narrow slits of hostility. The soft touch with him has outlived its usefulness. Time to push hard.

"You were seen heading toward the backyard well after midnight. Come across anything interesting out there? Donovan maybe? Did you think that with him out of the way you might get to first base with Sadie?"

He slams his fist on the table with violent force. The bottle cap jumps a full inch into the air.

"Talk like that is liable to get a man hurt. Just because you carry a gun on your side doesn't mean you're tough. You're a lawyer playing dress-up as some type of fancy cop. My money says you don't even know how to handle that gun."

Anger flushes his face a deep red. I've seen men on tilt before, and I adjust my body for quick action if the situation turns physical. He taunts, "Have you ever killed anyone, Mr. Pretend Cop?"

"Have you?"

The response gets his goat, and I can almost visibly see the last drops of reason seep out of him. I stand up—wishing like hell that Scott or even Captain Dave were here as a counterweight to the rising volatility across the table. Looking up at me now, he asks again, "You gonna answer or what? Ever kill anyone?"

"Yes."

"Shoot some unarmed punk in the back so you could call yourself a hero?"

"Not quite. He was a Navy SEAL, with a gun in his hand, trying to ambush and murder me. You can Google it."

10

I ponder the state of the world at the bottom of the staircase. According to Dave, the search warrant should arrive shortly, giving me time to talk with Katherine Matheny before kicking everyone out of the house. But first—an experiment.

Supposing someone descended the staircase to commit a murder, how much noise would that person make? Lucy's earlier sprint down the stairs—made with the grace of a rhinoceros—created enough commotion to wake Lazarus. But what if someone had a mind to be stealthy? Old homes are known for having all kinds of creaks in their joints, especially when amplified in the stilted silence of the night. I take a step.

The carpet deadens most of the sound as I tiptoe up like a burglar on the prowl for jewels. And while the ambient background noise of daytime helps to mask my ascent—cars traveling along the main road, birds chirping, a child's squeal, music playing in the distance—I conclude that it wouldn't take a ninja to slip away without being noticed, which is bad news for the people upstairs at the time of the murder, a group that likely includes Katherine. I knock on her door.

No response. I put my ear close to the door to listen for signs of life but come up empty. I knock again, louder this time, and detect faint stirrings from the other side, followed by the shuffling of heavy feet. Katherine opens the door.

"Oh," she says.

"Mrs. Matheny, we need to talk."

"Who are you?"

I answer the question, explaining slowly because the grogginess in her eyes suggests that she just woke up. Or maybe she is on something. Sadie did tell me that Katherine had a problem with prescription pills.

We sit down—me in an uncomfortable wooden chair with a straight back, her on the edge of the rumpled bed. The room is more compact than Sammy and Lucy's quarters. A queen bed, small desk, and a dresser occupy most of the space. Generic depictions of beach living, the kind found everywhere in homes near shore and sand, decorate the walls. The overall feel is of an outdated beach motel. Katherine rubs her face, and I wonder whether she might fall asleep on the spot. The signs are there to confirm Sadie's information. Drugs.

"I'm sorry about your father. I know this must be difficult. Any idea who killed him?"

The question gets her attention, and a new alertness starts to creep into her manner. I wait for her to answer.

"I … I really can't fathom why anyone would do such an awful thing. It's … monstrous."

"Did your father have enemies?"

"Father? Enemies? That's absurd. He was a corporate lawyer who represented the shipping companies that use Brunswick as a port. Why would he have enemies?"

Everybody has enemies, whether they realize it or not. The human heart is a cesspool full of rage, envy, fear, hatred, and lust—powerful forces always in search of a landing spot. And not even the most innocent and pure of us can avoid becoming a target of those pathologies. The world killed Jesus, after all.

"You say he didn't have any enemies, but my impression is that moving Sadie into this house caused a lot of hurt feelings."

She doesn't take the bait, choosing to stare distractedly out of the window to the backyard instead of answering. I follow her line of sight and see nothing but gathering dark clouds on the ocean's distant horizon. It's that kind of day.

"Your dad was still married to your mom, right?"

Katherine jerks her head back toward me. She sizes me up, and I return the favor. Unlike Lucy, her hair is its natural color, fading black with gray aggressively on the march. Like the room, her attire is out of step with the times. She's too dowdy, making her appear older than her true age. Mid to late forties, she could pass for sixty. She's also thin—not a healthy thin, but an unhealthy thin, one of the known side effects of drug abuse. Could she physically pick up a brick, carry it across the wooden bridge, and swing it with enough force to spray her father's blood all across the beach? Difficult, but not impossible, especially if she was amped up, chemically or otherwise.

"Yes, Father was still married to Mother."

"How did you feel when Sadie moved in?"

"What do you think? Angry, of course. Mother isn't dead yet."

"Is it true he was going to divorce her?"

The affirmative recognition in her eyes is unmistakable. She stands up off the bed. A nervous twitch starts to plague her left arm, and she wraps herself in a bear hug—almost like what people do when they are freezing—to stop the movement. I remember the earlier shaking downstairs and catch her making furtive glances to a pill bottle on the nightstand. Katherine is obviously a sick woman, the kind for whom rehab could do wonders. Part of my heart aches for her in compassionate sympathy but only a part. I resume the questioning.

"How did you spend last night? Did you and Maxwell go out?"

A strange expression overtakes her, as if I inquired whether she had dinner with extraterrestrials as opposed to a meal with her husband. Even so, the change in topics away from her mother calms her down a little—the sense of relief palpable. She responds, "Oh, no. Max went over to a cocktail mixer early in the evening at the hotel hosting the state bar conference. I stayed here and read a book."

"What time did you go to bed last night?"

"Ten or so. I need a lot of sleep. Can never seem to get enough. No matter what, I always feel fatigued."

She allows herself a nervous laugh, a likely coping mechanism to make light of her obvious struggle with depression. Married to Maxwell, her father murdered, her mother mentally gone, the family home given away to a woman half her age in the form of Sadie Foxx—the immediate prospects for Katherine's life don't suggest a lot in the way of good cheer. And that's assuming she didn't kill Donovan Kessler herself.

"Did you wake up at any point during the night?"

"Oh, never. My sleeping pills knock me right out."

"Not even when Maxwell got into bed?"

"Oh, no. He usually sleeps on the couch in the living room. Says I have nightmares and thrash about too much. Sometimes I even sleepwalk, too. But I never remember."

"You sleepwalk?"

"Crazy isn't it?"

"How can you tell?"

"People have seen me do it. And sometimes I wake up in bed wearing a coat or shoes that weren't there when I fell asleep."

The explanation is completely matter-of-fact on her end, but my imagination runs wild with the information. Could she actually have murdered her father in some kind of unconscious state and not even know it? The possibility is not a fun one from a legal perspective. Not guilty by reason of insane automatism, the defense is called. And Katherine would make a sympathetic defendant.

To make conversation while standing to leave, I ask, "What book were you reading last night?"

"Oh, *The Brothers Karamazov*."

A tingling runs through my body. I know that book, one of my favorites. All of Dostoevsky's books are among my favorites—his expert handling of the themes of sin and redemption sparking the deepest longings of my soul. But that's not the cause of the subterranean prickling I now feel all over.

"*The Brothers Karamazov*, huh? That's the one where a child kills his father, isn't it?"

Sitting perfectly still, she answers, "That's right."

11

Standing in the front yard, I savor what little sunshine can break through the convoy of clouds enveloping the coastline. Today was supposed to be one spent almost entirely outdoors, a chance for me to recharge after a frantic couple of months. But spending too much of my morning in that house has had the opposite effect. I feel worn down to a nub.

Taking a deep breath helps me to recalibrate. One of the spiritual exercises I've recently incorporated into my life is the practice of gratitude. I visualize Donovan Kessler's smashed skull on the beach and realize that things could be worse. I feel better already.

The tires of a speeding Lexus screech to a sudden halt in the driveway of the house next door. A man emerges from the vehicle. He wears a striped seersucker suit, white shirt, red bowtie. Scanning around, he directs his focus to Captain Dave and heads straight for him.

"Where's my brother?"

The man makes a move to walk the path between the two houses, but Dave blocks his progress.

"Easy does it."

"Where's my brother? My nephew called me and said that Donovan had been murdered. What's going on?"

"*Had been murdered.*" Passive voice. My English teacher in high school, Mrs. Boren, always admonished me whenever I slipped into passive voice and left out of my sentences the subject who was actively doing something. Example: "*Donovan had been murdered.*" The phrasing suggests that the dead man went off and got himself killed for no good reason. "Bad writing," Mrs. Boren would say. Rather: "A cold-blooded murderer smashed Donovan's head to a pulp on the beach." Much better. Violence is given, not received. But I was never a great writer and preferred arguing in court instead. I walk over to Dave and the man.

"Raymond Kessler?"

No mystery exists as to his identity. Beyond the open acknowledgment that Donovan was his brother, I recognize him from the billboards featuring his smiling picture that are plastered all around the state. Cate and I must've passed at least ten of them on the drive down from Atlanta. The rugged face, distinguished crown of white hair, and trademark bowtie give him a distinctive look that is hard to miss.

But I knew of him even before that. With multiple, record-breaking, nine-figure jury verdicts in his favor, Raymond may be the most successful trial lawyer in Georgia. As a baby lawyer, I attended a lecture he gave on the principles of cross-examination to a packed-out audience. The advice was so good that I started applying his tips immediately and kept on applying them all the way through my last trial, prosecuting Richard Barton for the murder of his wife, Sara Barton.

The man turns his attention to me, and I see recognition dawn in his hazel eyes. Raymond puts out his hand, and we shake. He says, "Yes, I am. And you're Chance Meridian. I knew your father way back when. Good man. I was sorry to hear that he passed. Also made a point of watching you work during the Barton trial. I'd record the trial during the day and spend my evenings catching up. Even learned some new tricks from you, which is something that I rarely say. But why are you standing in my yard and what happened to my brother?"

I long ago stopped being surprised about the number of people who knew my father. A politician, especially one slated to be governor until he walked away from the chance, makes it his job to meet all the folks he can. But ever since he died a few years back, I experience a small injection of joy every time a stranger remembers him to me. The recognition affirms that Daddy existed, that he mattered. Now is no different. The warmth of his memory fills me while I figure out how to respond to Raymond's questions.

"Your nephew was right, sadly. I'm sorry to say that your brother is dead. Murdered. The Governor heard about it, knew I was down here, and thought it would be a good idea for my team to handle the investigation, given your brother's stature. The two of them served together in the legislature, I understand."

Raymond nods. He lifts his eyes to the sky and fights back a tide of rising emotion. A tear runs down his cheek, and he swipes it away with an angry hand—almost embarrassed at the perceived show of weakness.

He asks, "Who did it?"

"Don't know. I'd like to ask you some questions about that."

"Where is he? May I see him?"

"Not right now. Can we talk?"

"Come on."

* * *

I follow him into his backyard and onto a large patio behind his house. The dune blocks any sight of the ocean, but the view impresses all the same. Flawlessly choreographed flowers adorn the area in a canopy of color, almost matching the same type of floral display in his brother's adjacent yard. Raymond catches me admiring the scenery and notes, "You like it? Judy—that's Donovan's wife—was a bit of a horticulturalist. What you see is her vision. I'm just the gardener."

He bends down to one of the flower beds to pluck a tiny weed from the ground and deposits it into a trash can.

The patio area is covered and bears the same sense of order as the nearby rows of plants. An immaculate backyard kitchen—stainless steel grill, ivory sink, mini-refrigerator, television, all the trimmings—dominates the space. A hand-carved wooden table that must've cost a fortune provides seating for outdoor dining. Raymond picks up a bourbon glass from the table, the melted ice leaving a ring of water in its wake. He wipes clean the spot with a dish towel, washes and dries the glass in the outdoor sink, and returns it to a location on a shelf in exact symmetry with the other glasses in a cabinet on the patio. The dish towel, too, returns to its place on a hook, folded in half at the same length of its neighboring twin.

The onslaught of neatness before me is jarring. My bias is toward comfort. Life is messy, and so am I.

Inside the house is more of the same. Everything orderly, sparse, efficient, clean. I consider whether I should remove my well-worn sneakers but decide to keep them on unless otherwise asked. Raymond leads me to his living room. Unlike the vibrant colors on display out back, the reigning palette here is all white. The smell of eucalyptus—just a hint—hangs in the air. I reluctantly sit down in a love seat, self-conscious about dirtying the cushions. Raymond takes the couch. He gets down to business.

"What do you want to know?"

"Can you think of anybody who would want your brother dead?"

He takes a deep, tired breath. The confident face on all those billboards seems haggard now, old. Even the seersucker suit suggests the vestiges of another era—a vanishing symbol of a dying generation, the Southern gentleman on the road to extinction. After taking a fair amount of time to gather his thoughts, Raymond asks, "How much do you know about what happened to Judy?"

"That she was in some type of car accident a couple of years back and lost most of her brain functioning. Now lives in a care facility in Brunswick."

"Sad, isn't it? Judy is one of the finest women I've ever known. She went all the way through grade school with Donovan and me over in Brunswick. Thought I might even marry her myself at one point. Before I realized I wasn't the marrying kind. My draft number came up, and I did a couple tours of duty in Vietnam while my brother played football at UGA. When I returned, Donovan and Judy were engaged. I was the best man at their wedding. That was over fifty years ago, and I watched from next door as they raised a family together. The point of this history is that Judy's accident wrecked a lot of people—Donovan most of all."

The tone is friendly and folksy. Raymond's renown as a storyteller is the stuff of legends. Juries warm to him not because he wows them with Aristotelian logic. Far from it. Philosophers get massacred in the courtroom. Just ask Socrates. Rather, Raymond possesses the gift common to all the great lawyers: capturing the audience's heart through the power of drama. The technique is not exactly new. Jesus taught in parables for a reason.

Raymond returns to his narrative.

"Ever heard of Rickie Savage?"

I shake my head.

"You should get to know him because he's the answer to your question about who wanted Donovan dead. Savage was a truck driver for a national hauler based in Savannah. Always drove his rig like his hair was on fire. But the deliveries were made with plenty of time to spare, and that improved the company's bottom line. During a squall one early spring, Savage didn't bother to alter his driving to account for the unsafe conditions. Lost control of his truck and slammed right into Judy out there on I-95. She was delivering a meal to a friend with leukemia. Now she can't even recognize her own face in the mirror."

He pauses. I sit there in rapt attention. A pin drop would sound like a cannon blast in the deep quiet. That's another trait of the great trial lawyers—pacing. Give time for your words to marinate in the bone marrow of each juror, making each of them partners in your thirst for justice. I lean back and wait for the rest of the story.

"The criminal justice system let Savage off with a slight slap on the wrist. Not surprising. I handled the civil case, of course. Judy is family, and you better believe I brought more Hell with me than at any other point in my career. Savage's company wanted no part of facing a jury on my home turf. They paid to make it all go away. More than enough to provide as much comfort as you can for someone in Judy's condition. Savage had already lost his job shortly after the accident. But the worst for him was yet to come."

Another pause. I realize that I'm holding my breath. The silence lingers. I haven't spoken in ten minutes but feel compelled to ask, "What happened?"

"Someone murdered Savage's daughter."

12

Raymond heads over to a mini-bar tucked away in a corner of the living room. He takes out a bourbon glass and pours himself four fingers of Johnnie Walker whiskey. I settle for a bottle of Coke—the chilled glass refreshing my dry lips when I take a sip.

The lunch hour is at hand, and my stomach informs me that it would be nice to get something to eat. My golf round would be about finished right now, and I had planned to head to the marina on the marsh side of the island for some oysters. While I think about food, Raymond downs his drink in short order. After washing and drying the glass and returning it to its proper place, he sits back down on the couch, ready to resume our conversation.

"Sorry about that. I'm not much of a day drinker, but this particular moment seems to call for it. Back to Rickie Savage. About a year ago, Savage's twenty-something daughter—I think her name was Becky—died of a pointblank gunshot wound to the head while leaving the restaurant where she worked in Brunswick. Late at night. No witnesses. Case remains unsolved. The police chalked it up to a robbery gone bad, but Rickie Savage didn't buy that. Told everybody who would listen that Donovan was the killer. Even swore to get even."

"And Savage lives around here?"

"Brunswick. Inland a little ways. At least he did when I took his deposition in the civil lawsuit. I hired a private investigator to unearth as many facts about Savage as possible—from when he stopped believing in Santa Claus to his favorite brand of underwear. Family, friends, everything. You can review the file, if you want. Except the settlement agreement. That's confidential. But I will tell you that it was a mighty big number. Mighty big. And you know the neighborhood where I typically hang out when it comes to settlements and jury verdicts. Anyway, consider everything else I have as yours."

"I'll start with an address."

"No problem. I'll send it to you. But one of the things we learned about Savage is that he spends most of his time on Jekyll. You know the fishing pier on the north end of the island, across from the campground?"

"Sure."

"He fishes there most days and nights. Or used to. Tries to sell what he catches to local fresh seafood markets. You might start over at the pier."

Lucy's theory that a drifter hanging around that part of the island killed her father-in-law may be closer to the truth than previously suspected. I say, "A picture would be helpful."

"Google him. His mug shot from the arrest for the accident should be one of the first results."

A few seconds later, the mean face of Rickie Savage—forever stuck on the wrong side of fifty—stares at me from my phone. The hair is unkempt, the teeth crooked, the hangdog look of defeat permanent. Irregular patches of gray stubble run from his ear to his chin. The whole aura about him screams a hard life. But then again, most mug shots tell the same story.

"You said he swore to get even with Donovan?"

"Multiple times—three months ago is the most recent I'm aware of. Donovan saw him at a gas station and told me that Savage made a throat-slashing gesture at him."

He goes on to demonstrate for my benefit, even though I got the gist from his description the first time around. The hunger in my belly lets me know that it's growing impatient. I compose my next words carefully.

"At the risk of being offensive, is Rickie Savage right? Did your brother kill Savage's daughter?"

"No offense taken. The question had to be asked. And while I have no way of knowing for sure, I fear the answer may be yes."

***

The pained expression on Raymond's face shows that the admission is not an easy one for him. He avoids making eye contact with me. In a firm voice, I say, "Explain." To his credit, he doesn't beat around the bush.

"Nothing concrete. Only that my brother changed a lot in the past year—around the same time when Savage's daughter was murdered. Judy's accident staggered him, of course. But he was still the same person underneath. The last year, though… Have you met Sadie Foxx?"

"Indeed."

"Then you know what I mean. Taking up with her was so far out of character from the man I knew for over seventy years. I suspect he had slept around on Judy during their marriage, certainly when he was gone for months at a time serving in the legislature. But his thing with Sadie was different. And so public, too. He always cared about his image in the community. Except now he was throwing away his reputation, everything he had built his entire life. That got me thinking—perhaps he snapped and killed Becky Savage. Wouldn't be the first old man to lose his marbles in response to tragedy. And he never really denied doing it. Just laughed the idea off, which made me suspicious. But I can't say for sure."

I despair that my murder investigation might necessarily grow into two with this Becky Savage killing, like a deadly cancer that metastasizes to everything around it. Hell, someone is liable to kill Sadie to complete the Triple Crown. I decide to raise this topic with Raymond.

"A lot of people in the house next door are angry about the living arrangements over there."

"How could they not be? The situation is absurd."

"Sadie says that Donovan left the house to her—joint tenancy with the right of survivorship. Know anything about that?"

He blinks twice, staring at me as if I am blurry. With surprising quickness for a man his age, he springs up and heads back over to the bar for another round of Johnnie Walker—completing the same ritual of drinking from the glass, washing the glass, and returning the glass to its home. Even in distress, he follows his method with precise attention to detail. No doubt he uses that same hyper-focus to never miss anything happening in the courtroom.

Back on the couch, Raymond buries his face in his hand and heaves a sigh. When he brings his head back up, what I see is a grim grin of pained exasperation.

"The house? Are you serious? Donovan bought that house right before he and Judy got married. Prices were dirt cheap back then. No one knew Jekyll Island from Gilligan's Island. I got this place right after, and the two of us formed a fearsome law firm. Sammy and Katherine were both born and bred in that house. I had the idea that both of our homes would stay in the family—one for Sammy, one for Katherine, didn't matter which. But I can't say that I'm totally surprised. Surprised that he changed the deed already, yes, but not that these types of thoughts were swirling around in his head. He told me yesterday that he intended to divorce Judy to marry Sadie. We had words over it."

"What did you say?"

"Told him that if he had any wild oats left to sow at his age to have at it, but he didn't need to divorce Judy and marry Sadie to have his fun. I'm not that type of man myself so I find it hard to understand. Never married. Women always struck me as a type of nuisance. The law is my mistress, and she's quite demanding. But Judy's still alive—seemed cruel to me for him to abandon her in that condition. He would've had to sue her to get a divorce, and she can't even defend herself. Court would have to appoint some type of guardian. Makes me glad I stayed single all these years."

His voice trails off, almost as if talking to himself. The reaction is a normal one. Death has a way of pushing people to a more contemplative frame of mind—reflections on a relationship forever gone on this side of eternity. And reflections that we ourselves are one day closer to that same eternity.

"I don't guess you persuaded him to your point of view about the divorce."

"Hell no. He got huffy and moaned that Judy was already gone. All of them over there think that, at least that's their rationalization for never visiting her. Not even Katherine, who was tight with Judy, will go to see her mother. So that leaves me to do all the visiting myself. But I can't even blame them. They just aren't equipped for it. That group has lived in a bubble all their lives. Being close to real suffering in the flesh is too jarring to their senses. I don't have that malady. My bubble burst in Vietnam. I witnessed enough horrors for a lifetime serving my country. Seeing Judy in her condition is just more of the same."

Looking at him now, the battle scars from that time seem almost fresh. I've known many men who fought in Vietnam, and not a one has ever wanted to talk about it. Tim O'Brien in *The Things They Carried*—the definitive account of serving in Vietnam—wrote that "you can tell a true war story by its absolute and uncompromising allegiance to obscenity and evil."

Obscenity and evil. Forget all the John Wayne movies I consumed growing up. No glory exists in men pointing guns at each other in order to kill the person in front of them.

I never wore the uniform, in combat or otherwise. My battlefield was the courtroom, where I dressed in suit and tie. But law and war share a symbiotic relationship. Law is the price the victors of history impose on the defeated, and a prosecutor's job is to wage war against those who think the terms of peace do not apply to them. Trials may lack the bloody violence of the jungles of Vietnam, but they are a species of battle all the same. The trial lawyer who doesn't go into court with the mindset of a warrior starts from a position of weakness. Raymond's transition from soldier to litigator was a change of degree, not of kind.

"You say you '*had words*' with your brother. Were you angry enough to kill him?"

Raymond casts a wary eye toward me. He says, "I suppose you have to ask me that."

"Comes with the job, yes."

"Well, the answer is no. I didn't kill my brother. For one thing, I couldn't afford to lose him as a law partner. Donovan managed the firm since we opened nearly fifty years ago. That allowed me to focus only on my cases. Without him in charge, things figure to be a mess. I don't even know where we keep the paper clips. Anyway, I was more disappointed than angry with him. But at the end of the day, his marriage is not any of my business."

"What about the rest of the family? How do you think your nephew and niece would react if their father told them he was divorcing their mother to marry Sadie?"

He smiles a crafty smile and shakes his head a slow, deliberate arc.

"Chance—can I call you Chance?"

"Please do."

"Chance, you're going to have to dig up your own dirt on that front. I am not biting. Sammy and Katherine are family, and I love them. Even if I witnessed one of them murder Donovan with my own two eyes, I wouldn't tell you. The family has suffered too much already."

"Did you see one of them? Is that why you put me so heavy on to Rickie Savage's scent?"

"For the record—no to both of those questions. And I put you on to Savage's scent because he stinks. You asked for suspects. If I were a betting man, all my money would be on him. I've sat across the table from him for hours at a time during his deposition. He's bad news."

From scanning his mug shot, I don't doubt it. But was he even on Jekyll last night? I intend to ask him in the near future but only after Scott and J.D. arrive in town. Savage is not one I want to tackle alone.

"Since you're putting things on the record, did you see anything suspicious around here last night?"

"No. I had a 9:00 a.m. docket call this morning at the courthouse in Jesup about an hour away. Needed to run into the office in Brunswick before heading over there, too. Pulling all-nighters like I did when I was younger is not too good for my health these days. My alarm was set to early, and I went to bed around ten. Woke up at five this morning and went into work."

I have too much to do and not enough time to do it. I start to stand up but sit back down again. One other point bears exploring.

"Do you know of any trouble between your brother and Meredith Bixby?"

"That state bar business? A little. Something about her approving some questionable expenses when she was treasurer two years ago. Sounded like a bunch of nothing to me—no money even went in her pockets and other people incurred the charges. She just signed the checks. But Donovan's ego wanted another year as state bar president, which is unprecedented. Just nuts. Like I said, something went haywire with him. And to the extent you're suggesting that Meredith may be the person you're looking for, forget it. Sweet lady. Tough—but she's about the nicest person around."

Raymond has spent his entire legal career doing civil work, so I excuse him for his naivete about the realities of criminal law. In my experience, sweet ladies can kill people just as easily as anyone else. Heck, even Lizzie Borden taught Sunday school. I stand to leave for good this time. He says, "One other thing you should probably know about Meredith."

"Yeah, what's that?"

"She represented Rickie Savage and the trucking company in Judy's case against them."

Interesting coincidence, I guess. But I have no idea what to do with that information.

13

The ominous skies over the ocean maintain their distance. The afternoon could go either way. I think of Rickie Savage possibly fishing off that pier, only a couple of miles away. Is he there now? And will he still be on the pier if the bad weather materializes? My Uncle Chuck—a good old boy of the best sort and an angler savant—swore that a solid rain was the best time to get the enemy to bite. But he did all his work in lakes and rivers. Does the same principle hold for a potential murderer casting lines into the ocean?

Standing between the Kessler homes, I hear my stomach gasp a sad whimper, a sign that it has pretty much given up the fight. I could skip lunch and retroactively call it a spiritual fast—the current situation needing as much divine favor as I can scrounge up.

The phone rings. Cate.

"You still golfing? Want to get something to eat?"

"Golf? Precious little of that. Something else came up. Guess who's working the Donovan Kessler case?"

"No! How did you get roped into that?"

"You do the math."

"Minton!"

Wise woman—one who understands how her Governor operates. I ask, "Don't you have a luncheon to attend?"

"Being a justice on the Supreme Court carries with it certain privileges, one of which is to skip luncheons that I don't want to attend. Besides, the murder of the state bar president has put a damper on the festivities. Weird vibe over here. I'd rather eat alone. Or with you."

We end the call with her heading to grab us a table at a Mexican restaurant between the hotel and here. I promise to hurry.

Dave Ketchum approaches from the road. Next to him in perfect march step is another state patrol officer—a baby face who looks too young to have graduated from high school, much less the police academy. They stop in unison five feet from me. Captain Dave takes the lead.

"The judge signed your search warrant, courtesy of Trooper Chad Morelli here, our newest recruit."

He offers a nod of approval to the younger man. Morelli beams. I introduce myself and shake his hand. He has a good, solid grip for a rookie. Dave asks, "What now?"

"Can you remove everybody from the house? Don't let them take anything. Have a few of your troopers guard the place to keep people out. Two of my team from Atlanta will be here shortly, and we'll search it then. I'm going to talk to the GBI down at the beach and then grab some lunch. And make sure all of your people eat. An army marches on its stomach."

Morelli exclaims, "Napoleon."

"That's right."

Captain Dave flashes a paternal grin at Morelli. I give Dave my cell number in case of an emergency and head over the wooden bridge to conference with the GBI.

* * *

Debbie Fincher, the GBI's lead person on the scene, appears tired. Her sandy-blond hair is damp with a hint of sweat, and the long sleeves of her navy pullover are now above the elbows. She and the other technicians scurry with purpose across the vanishing beach. The march of the tide in my absence is almost complete—the separation between the water and Donovan Kessler's body now only ten feet. Debbie, on her knees sifting through the sand, sees me but doesn't stop to socialize.

I ask, "Going to finish?"

"Barely."

A nearby stretcher with an empty black body bag on top rests crookedly on the uneven ground, ready to receive its freight. Two guys hover in the vicinity of the stretcher, waiting to be told when they can deliver Kessler's body to their boss for an autopsy. I return my attention to Debbie.

"Find anything interesting?"

Without a break in her concentration, she answers.

"Blood. Lots. Probably all of it belonging to the vic, but we'll test it to be sure. But I wouldn't hold out any hope that any of it belongs to your perp. On the other hand, strong possibility that some of the vic's blood ended up on the perp. We tried to find a blood trail leading away from the scene but came up empty. Also had to bag your brick in an evidence pouch or risk the murder weapon floating out to sea. Collected some hair fibers from it, probably the vic's."

"We have a search warrant for the victim's house right over the dune. Can you guys do a full forensic analysis and search for latent bloodstains? A meaningful chance exists that the killer is in residence there."

She doesn't stop to think—continuing to multitask, blending the persona of a person in a hurry who can nevertheless maintain intense concentration while juggling three or four balls in the air. A lot of people try to pull off that feat and end up doing nothing particularly well, except annoying everyone else around them. Something tells me that Debbie is the exception to that rule. Everything she does smells like competence.

"Can we do it tomorrow? Doing a thorough job requires a lot of time."

"Absolutely. Take all the time you need. The longer I can keep everyone out of that house the better."

"Good. Right now, I really need to finish what I'm doing."

The words are an invitation to end the conversation, and I decide to accept while I'm ahead. But before I get too far away, she calls out, "Hey, you want your brick to store somewhere as evidence?"

"Can you hold it for me? Otherwise, it goes to my hotel room."

Debbie shrugs without much excitement, which I treat as a reluctant yes. At that moment, a new question for her pops into my head. I decide to risk her annoyance and ask away.

"One last thing. Did you pick the brick up? Could a woman have done that damage to the victim's head?"

This time she pauses and gives me her full attention. After a couple of seconds, she peers over at Kessler's dented skull.

"Yes. The brick did most of the work. Any normally fit woman could've inflicted those blows, especially in a high state of agitation. And I really need to complete my work."

I make myself scarce. Enough sand is left for me to take the beach to meet Cate at the restaurant, and I start that way. A few steps in, my cell rings from a number I don't recognize. Probably spam, but I answer it anyway.

"Hello?"

"Chance—this is Dave Ketchum. Miss Foxx won't leave the house. She refuses to move off the couch and says that if I touch her, she will scream rape. She is also demanding to see you."

Damn that Sadie.

"What about everyone else?"

"There was some talk of lawsuits and one mention of the Gestapo, but they left. The whole crew went next door to the uncle's house. What do you want me to do about Miss Foxx?"

Never negotiate with terrorists. Besides, I'm starving and my beautiful wife is waiting for me. Choosing Cate over Sadie is one of the easiest decisions of my life.

"Inform her that she has ten seconds to exit the premises or be arrested. If she resists, get out your handcuffs and remove her by force. Park her in the backseat of a state patrol vehicle on the street. Leave the cuffs on. Give her some alone time to meditate and reflect. Tell her I'll talk to her when I get back. And make sure you film the whole exchange. She's liable to say anything. Does that work for you?"

"Most definitely."

14

Cate sits at a table on a covered deck—the ocean close by and getting closer by the second. Her auburn hair dances slightly in the gentle breeze. I sneak up behind her, put my hands on her shoulders, and bend over to kiss her cheek from the side. She purrs in appreciation.

Calling off my fast, I sit down and grab a tortilla chip to dunk in a waiting bowl of cheese dip. Pure decadence. I go back for seconds. A question forms on Cate's lips.

"Italy?"

"Told Minton that trip was our honeymoon and non-negotiable. We're getting on that plane Monday afternoon no matter what. Eighteen days. You and me alone—with orders that I'm not to be disturbed. Scott and J.D. will be landing in Brunswick within the hour. Come Monday, the baton will be in their capable hands."

The relief in her face touches me so much that I'm compelled to reach over the table and kiss her again. We order, and I savor the normalcy of the moment after the onslaught of abnormalities faced since answering the Governor's call. Cate asks, "Want to talk about it?"

Not really. But the concerned tone behind the question implies that I look as bad as I feel. So I talk to her to eject some of the poison out of my system. Narrating a rough overview of the facts and personalities of the case boosts my mood. For most speedbumps in life, a sympathetic ear can do wonders. The food helps, too. During my telling, I devote special emphasis to the antics of Sadie, including my order that she be detained in the back seat of a police car for trying to delay me from this lunch.

Cate deadpans, "Bet she's mad now and won't try to show you her hoo-hoo again."

"No more hoo-hoo from Sadie. Chalk that up as a win."

We laugh and attack our food. The steam rises right off the plates when the waitress sets them down. Cate licks some salt from the rim of her margarita glass. The drink is a rare lunchtime cocktail for her, an understandable change-up with murder on the day's menu. She says, "Why do you think Sadie Foxx—I still can't believe that's her real name—acted that way with you? Some bizarre manifestation of sorrow?"

"Doubtful. I don't get the sense that she's too grief-ridden, and all indications are that Sadie acted in similar provocative fashion long before this morning. But one thing I keep remembering—the last woman who was that sexually aggressive with me out of the blue acted that way because she was hiding something and wanted to distract my mind away from her secret."

"The power of the hoo-hoo."

"Something like that."

"And you learned your lesson?"

"Yes, ma'am."

She reaches across the table and gives my hand a squeeze. When the two of us started to become serious, I made sure to confess the sordid affair that led me to walk away from the courtroom forever. Coming off her divorce from a cheating husband, she deserved to hear the unvarnished truth about the new man in her life. Cate chose to love me anyway, and the merging of two broken things created a stronger thing in its place. Us.

I say, "You know our first date was at a Mexican restaurant."

"How could I ever forget that? You picked the place."

"Did I ever tell you why I picked Mexican?"

"No—why?"

"Because if I couldn't carry my end of the conversation, I could just gorge myself on tortilla chips as a defense mechanism."

Cate smiles. Not knowing when I might eat again, I take a chip and scoop out all the remaining remnants of the cheese dip to shove into my mouth. My phone alerts me to a text message while I chew.

From Scott: "Here. See you soon."

"Scott and J.D. just touched down. I should probably head back."

The thought depresses me. Cate offers to take care of the check in exchange for a hug, which is the best offer I've had all day. Wrapped in my arms, she asks, "See you when I see you?"

"Afraid so."

After a last kiss, she says, "Be careful." I head back up the beach.

***

Captain Dave stands in the driveway, gnawing on a juicy cheeseburger, taking the utmost care to ensure that the meat's drippings don't sully his uniform. I've yet to see him actually sit down anywhere. Maybe it's against regulations. I approach and ask, "So did Sadie pick door number one or door number two?"

His mouth full, he jerks his head up the street to a blue state patrol car. Through the rear window, I spy the back of Sadie's head. Good. I would've been disappointed in any other outcome. Putting little children in time out corrects behavioral issues more often than not. The hope is that Sadie may be similarly teachable. But I have my doubts.

After washing down his food with some water, Dave says, "Filmed her like you suggested. You probably should see it."

He waves a hand over to Trooper Chad Morelli and orders, "Show him." Morelli hands me his phone with the video already teed up. I push play.

Sadie smirks when Dave gives her the ultimatum to leave the house or face arrest. The sneering stops as Dave and another officer move in. When they reach for her, she kicks at their arms and starts slithering around like a snake with its head chopped off. Her high-octane slipperiness leads to their hands touching her all over while trying to get a grip, leading Sadie to shout, "Sexual assault! Sexual assault!" But once Dave grabs a hold of her arm, the show is close to over. With little regard for her comfort, he forces both arms behind her back, leading her to yelp in pain. Curses flow out of her during the slow walk to the patrol vehicle. Dave's parting words to her: "Mr. Meridian will speak to you when he returns." She tells him what I can do to myself. The suggestion is impolite.

The video is beautiful from my perspective because it gives me something helpful to any murder investigation. Leverage. If I need Sadie's cooperation and she doesn't want to play ball, the video is a one-way ticket to send her straight to jail. And something tells me that Sadie wouldn't like it there. Call it a hunch.

I hand the phone back to Morelli and ask, "How long have you been on the job?"

"One month."

"Any other days like this one?"

"No, sir. A lot of firsts these last few hours. Eye-opening."

The enthusiasm with which he speaks is almost contagious. He's a good kid and reminds me a lot of J.D., who is probably only a year or two older. I address Dave.

"Time to talk to the prisoner."

15

Sadie Foxx is not happy to see me. The window on her side of the car is down, allowing us to talk. She takes the opportunity to hurl more rude advice my way, most of which strikes me as anatomically impossible. I wait with my best bemused expression for the storm to pass. It takes a while.

When she finally loses steam, I ask, "You want to get out of those handcuffs or not?"

"You like me in handcuffs, don't you? Is that how you want your women, submissive and chained up? You could've just asked me. I might have said yes."

Trooper Chad Morelli's eyes go wide. His new job keeps getting more interesting. Welcome to law enforcement. And if Sadie wants to go to jail, so be it. This is America. A person is free to choose. I start to walk away and tell Dave, "Take her to a cell."

"Wait! Wait! Come back!"

I keep walking. When I almost reach the front door of her house, she shrieks, "I take it back! I'm sorry! What do you want?"

When I turn around, her body is balanced on the car window—half inside, half outside—her shape twisted and contorted so that she can look backwards toward my direction. The perch appears unsteady. With her hands still cuffed behind her back, the posturing is almost comical for its bizarreness—much like a circus freak. The face I see has lost its defiance. Rather, alarm now seems to be the flavor of choice.

The stroll back to the car, with hands in my pockets to evoke a casual air, is slow and deliberate. Sadie grimaces in discomfort while adjusting her body to something more sustainable. I stop near the trunk of the car instead of continuing to the side, which forces her to remain in the same awkward, backwards-facing position to see me. The torment figures to keep her a little more focused.

"Why didn't you tell me about Rickie Savage?"

"That loser?"

"You know him?"

"Not personally. Do you think he killed Donny?"

"Why don't you tell me everything you know about it?"

She wiggles some more in pain. To reward her growing cooperation, I head up to the side of the car. She maneuvers back into the vehicle through the window and lands hard on the seat. Another yelp follows. She'll be sore tomorrow. The handcuffs must hurt like hell.

"Can you take this these things off?"

"Not yet."

The response receives a dirty look, but Sadie holds her tongue. Progress. My hands remain in my pockets, and I wait.

"What do you want me to say? I don't know much. Rickie's the one that hurt Judy in that wreck. Someone knocked off Rickie's daughter after that. Rickie blamed Donny and talked about getting revenge. But that was months ago. Honestly, I had forgotten all about him. That's why I didn't mention anything."

"Did you ever see Rickie hanging around here?"

"How? I don't even know what he looks like. Donny mentioned seeing him lurking about once but nothing recently."

I take out my phone, find Savage's mug shot, and hold it out to Sadie through the open window for her to see. She makes a face.

"Is that him? Yuck."

"Ever see him?"

"If I did, I erased it from my mind."

She might be on the level. But with her, one will never know for sure. Her body shrinks a little. The detention doesn't agree with her. Tiredness is creeping in.

"Was Rickie Savage right about Donny killing his daughter?"

"Are you nuts? Donny was over seventy years old. Do you think he would really sneak around to shoot a young woman in a Brunswick parking lot? He didn't even own a gun as far as I know."

Sadie has a point. Septuagenarians don't commit many killings, especially ones who serve as the president of their state bars. But most murderers aren't serial killers. Ending someone else's life is almost always out of character for the person who pulls the trigger, stabs with the knife, smashes a skull with the brick. Murder is never normal. But part of her answer still feels off.

"How did you know Savage's daughter was killed in a Brunswick parking lot?"

"Donny told me."

I analyze her for veracity. Good luck with that. I change the subject.

"What do you know about Donovan's relationship with Lucy?"

She looks stupid with surprise, as if I asked her to solve a differential calculus equation. All I get out of her is her one word.

"Lucy?"

"Anything inappropriate?"

For the first time that day, Sadie looks at me with an attitude approaching seriousness. She thinks over the question in quiet deliberation. The change in her face when she comes to some realization is visible—like the scales falling from her eyes. I don't believe the performance to be an act. Drama is not her forte. Bad acting in soft core porn, maybe. But not drama. I let her work on whatever she's figuring out. She'll tell me when ready.

"The two of them? Having a hard time wrapping my head around that. But right after moving in, I overheard them talking in Donny's office and Donny said, 'No, Lucy. I can't do that to Sam.' I never go in the office. That's his private sanctuary. But that time I walked right in and found them real close together. Nose to nose. She stormed out and shot me a nasty look. Donny explained to me, 'Lawyer business.' I had no reason to doubt that. Then a couple of months ago, they came into the kitchen from the beach, late at night, all bunched up close to each other. Everything about them was disheveled. But the wind does that to you when walking on the beach after dark. They were surprised to see me, and Lucy had a little sly smile when she hurried past me. I still didn't give two seconds of thought to it. Why would he even be interested in her? He had me."

She appears genuinely perplexed.

Sex isn't everything, child. Sometimes a person just wants to be cherished and adored—appreciated. Living to merely rut around with a willing body makes for a poor existence. Pigs can do that. And intimacy is impossible when sex is nothing more than a transaction. But fat chance of successfully explaining all that to Sadie. Only experience can teach people who are too stubborn to learn otherwise. I follow up with her.

"Anything else?"

"Yeah, yesterday. Lucy was stomping around like a maniac all day, shooting hateful looks both at me and Donny. You know what I mean? Not normal at all. I assumed she was mad for Judy's sake because Donny had told the family about the divorce. That was nothing new. The whole lot of them were always giving me the cold shoulder anyways. Now I think there may have been more to it with Lucy yesterday. Intense eyes like that—only something really personal could cause something so … evil."

Lucy's earlier reaction of storming down the stairs and repeatedly calling Sadie a bitch starts to take on a new meaning. "Maniac" is the exact vibe Lucy presented when she learned that Donovan Kessler left the house to his young girlfriend. Not normal behavior for a daughter-in-law. Maxwell let slip that Lucy was in love with Donovan. And now Sadie has added more kindling to that fire. The odds are low that Maxwell and Sadie concocted the story together, meaning that this tangent of the investigation has the aroma of credibility to it. That leaves Sammy. Did he know about the infatuation—or perhaps something more—between his father and wife?

***

I beckon to Captain Dave to huddle with me for a little chat. We find a shady clearing under an ancient oak tree that is covered in Spanish moss. I say, "My preference would be to release her, but she attacked you and provided enough material for you to charge her with numerous violations of our penal code. I'd like to keep holding those charges over her to ensure her continued cooperation, except it wouldn't be right for me to make that call under the circumstances. Only fair to let you decide. What do you think?"

"Release her. I'd rather not deal with her anyway."

He tosses over the keys to the handcuffs. I return to Sadie and open the car door to allow her to exit, helping her out to make sure she doesn't fall. After I remove the restraints, she inspects the deep red imprints on her wrists and rubs at them repeatedly, squirming a little as she does so. I lay out the state of things to her.

"In light of your willingness to cooperate, Captain Dave Ketchum has graciously agreed not to press charges, as thing now stand, for your earlier violent resistance to lawful orders. But you have to remain available to us should we need to talk to you. If you get salty again, you will be arrested. Do you have somewhere else to stay tonight?"

"Why?"

"We need the house."

"You can't take my house."

"Not taking. Borrowing. Did you read the search warrant?"

"What do you think?"

I take the question to be rhetorical and ignore it. Now that she is out of the car and upright again, the toll that being in custody took on her—a grueling hour and a half in an air-conditioned car—is more obvious. The hair is wild, the wrists swollen, the attitude humbled. The short shorts are even more scrunched up on her thigh, the halter top askew. She almost looks hung over.

"You never answered my question. Do you have a place to stay?"

"I'll crash at the Jekyll Island Club Hotel."

Color me surprised. The Club Hotel is part of Jekyll's historic district, located on the marsh side of the island, and not the place where one goes to crash. Built in the late nineteenth-century, the Club was the most exclusive of its kind for the time. Names like Morgan, Rockefeller, Vanderbilt, Field, and Pulitzer spent their winters there while consolidating their control over the country. In 1910, secret meetings on the property led to the creation of the Federal Reserve—America's national bank.

But times change. Today, the Club Hotel is much more democratic than its elite origins, except not so egalitarian as to welcome the likes of a barely-clothed Sadie.

"You sure you can get a room?"

"A friend is the manager there. He'll hook me up."

Fine with me. The Club Hotel is two minutes away. She'll be close if we need to follow-up with her about something. As a concession, I decide to allow her to pack a suitcase to take with her, provided someone observes the packing and that the suitcase is searched on the way out. She doesn't like it, but the offer is the only one on the table. I give her some parting advice.

"The Club Hotel is a nice place. You might want to switch outfits."

"Oh, yes sir. I'll go up and change right now. Do you want to watch?"

Barely out of the handcuffs, she's back to the nonsense—much as a dog returns to its vomit. Scott and J.D. walk up just in time to hear Sadie's offer to me. From behind her, Scott grins his widest smile and raises his eyebrows in mock questioning. He then checks her out up and down and gives me a thumbs up. I ignore him.

Sadie asks, "Can I go pack?"

I agree to let her go, along with instructions to J.D. and Morelli to watch her. Two witnesses are always being better than one. When they depart, Scott walks up and asks, "Who was that?"

"Sadie Foxx."

"Is that her stripper name?"

***

"Lawyers. Why does it always have to be lawyers?"

Scott's reaction to my sparse rundown of the facts while Sadie packs is no surprise. His disdain for lawyers is typical of most cops, and Scott is a cop's cop. Much of our recent work together has put us neck deep in a sea of lawyers. Now we're smack in the middle of the largest annual gathering of attorneys in the state. He's right to be twitchy.

I respond, "Killing lawyers is a growth industry."

"Don't try to cheer me up."

Sadie—who has changed into a sundress appropriate for polite society—emerges from the house lugging a large suitcase, followed by a red-faced Morelli. An amused J.D. brings up the rear. I take the suitcase and lay it across the hood of the nearest state patrol vehicle to commence the search.

She packed a lot of clothes and cosmetics. Mostly standard but some risqué lingerie that I assume is her attempt to be funny, knowing that the suitcase would be searched. The confirmation of this impression comes when I find a pair of furry, pink handcuffs. I hold them up to her. She shrugs and responds, "I told you I might be into that."

But the stuff I can see is of little concern. The lingerie and handcuffs are diversions. I check out all the pockets in the suitcase with great care, not even knowing what I'm looking for. Scott watches my work. Sadie asks him, "Who are you?"

He answers, "I'm his boyfriend."

A couple of seconds later, he orders, "Stop." The command is directed to me, and I halt what I am doing. He moves to the suitcase and runs a hand along its side. His eagle eyes, one of the reasons he's so adept with a gun, must have found something. They usually do.

After a little more maneuvering and exposing a gap in the lining, he removes a Ziploc bag full of marijuana joints. Sadie's face tries to play innocent, but she's out of practice. She resorts to words instead.

"I didn't know that was in there."

Sure, that's the ticket. Scott zips up the suitcase. Everyone—Sadie, Scott, J.D., Dave, Morelli—focuses on me to see what happens next. Heavy is the head that wears the crown. I remember Dave's earlier wisdom: "*Release her. I'd rather not deal with her anyway.*" Winner winner, chicken dinner. Sounds good to me.

"Get out of here."

She doesn't waste any time, hustling away without saying another word. The sundress flutters in the breeze as she loads up her black Ford Mustang convertible for a quick getaway. The rest of us watch her leave in silence.

When she's safely away, Morelli—who appears as if he's about to burst—begins talking rapidly.

"Do you know what she did? We went up to supervise her packing and the minute we all walk into her bedroom she just starts removing clothes without warning. And she didn't have many clothes to take off before she was standing there as nude as the day she was born. Like we weren't there at all."

He quickly adds, "I turned my back."

Captain Dave looks mortified on Morelli's behalf. The two of them walk away to talk about it. I pivot to J.D. and ask, "What about you? Did you turn your back?"

"You told me to watch her."

Exactly. If my supposition is right that Sadie uses sex to divert attention away from things she'd rather keep hidden, her naked romp could've afforded her the perfect opportunity to play a game of sleight-of-hand, if not for J.D.'s dogged diligence.

"Learn anything interesting from your laser-like focus?"

"There's nothing under that sundress. And once she knew that I was watching, she became more deliberate and remained naked much longer than necessary, giving me looks from all her angles."

"That's our Sadie."

But she's the Jekyll Island Club Hotel's problem for the immediate future. I slap him on the back and say, "No big deal anyway. You've seen a hoo-hoo before, right?"

"What's a hoo-hoo?"

16

Scott and I search the house together. The one thing I would like to find has little chance of being discovered under this roof—the killer's bloody clothes. Debbie Fincher spoke of a *"strong possibility that some of the vic's blood ended up on the perp."* Having seen the scene, I tend to agree. But if one of the five people who slept in this house last evening is the murderer, then that person had plenty of time during the night to dispose of the incriminating evidence elsewhere.

J.D.'s impossible task at the moment is to try and put a net over that *elsewhere*. Dave and Morelli offered to help, and the three of them are off on a quest to quarantine as much trash as they can. The plan is to start at the state bar conference and expand to every publicly-accessible waste disposal site on the island. Real needle in a haystack stuff. I gave J.D. a blank check to find as many off-duty cops and sheriff's deputies as he can to sift through whatever rubbish is collected. That figures to be expensive, and the Governor's going to have to find the funds somewhere at the end of this.

One bit of good news. Dave explained that garbage pick-up on Jekyll is on Thursdays. Since today is Friday, the trash tide is at low ebb. Still, I'm not holding my breath.

All this effort rests on the hope, probably forlorn, that any bloody clothes that do exist remain somewhere on the island. Once on the mainland in Brunswick and beyond, the telltale clothing might as well be on Mars. That despairing reality brings the mind back to Rickie Savage, the best suspect as things now stand and the only person connected to the case who lives off Jekyll. We'll see him soon enough.

First—the house.

The search is quicker than optimal given our time and manpower constraints but thorough enough. We go through each room together, double-checking the other's work. I use the opportunity to provide Scott a mosaic of each person connected to the home—Maxwell's hostility and pent-up lust, the drug-aided depression of Katherine following her mother's accident, Sammy's mousiness tinged with violent outbursts, the growing evidence of Lucy's coziness with her father-in-law.

He's already met Sadie.

By the time we reach Maxwell and Katherine's bedroom, the next-to-last place to be searched, the whole endeavor feels pointless. The urge to move on to other things overtakes me, and I'm glad that the room is a small one. While I half-heartedly comb through the dresser, Scott lays himself on the floor to reach his hand under a nightstand. Almost immediately, he says, "Eureka."

"What is it?"

My first thought is a gun, perhaps the gun used to kill Becky Savage. But Scott's hand holds something much different. A small pink journal. He opens the flap. Peering over his shoulder, I see a title written in perfect feminine handwriting: "Diary of Katherine Matheny." Scott gives it over to me.

"You read while I finish searching."

After planting myself on the living room couch, I speedread from the beginning, which starts shortly after Judy Kessler's horrific accident. Ten minutes later, Scott again joins me. I ask, "Anything?"

"Nah—except confirmation that Katherine takes a wide range of prescription medications. She could open her own pharmacy. What about you?"

"Plenty."

His interest perks up. Earlier I had ripped a page out of Sadie's celebrity magazine to create homemade bookmarks to tag key passages in the diary. I flip back through the journal to find the relevant pages to share with him.

"Ready for a literary reading?"

"Put some feeling into it."

"First excerpt—from one year ago. 'A woman died today. The daughter of that awful man who took Mother from me. Funny how the murder of a woman I never met could increase my faith in God. As the Lord promises, the sins of the father shall be visited upon the sons. Or in this case, a daughter. Becky Savage paid for her father's sins with her life. God is good.'"

I flipped forward in the diary.

"Six months later. 'That woman that everyone has seen Father around town with is actually moving into my childhood home! Disgusting! I truly believed that she was a prostitute! When did Father become a whoremonger? Poor Mother!' Lots of exclamation points to give you a fuller picture of her state of mind."

"She seems nice."

"Yesterday's entry. 'Father is divorcing Mother to marry that common whore! The vulgarity appalls me! Mother does not deserve this injustice! Father and his roadside slut deserve to rot in Hell! I'm boiling mad!' More exclamation points."

"Of course."

"Last but not least—earlier today. 'Father is dead. I suppose I will miss him, but God will not be mocked. The Lord punishes the wicked.' All matter of fact."

Scott whistles. That's his default reaction when words are inadequate to express his incredulity. After a period of contemplation, he observes, "She strikes me as more of an Old Testament kind of gal."

"You should read the whole thing. Not a lot of talk about Jesus and love. I almost feel sorry for Maxwell."

"Three possibilities as it relates to our case. One—take what she wrote at face value, which would exonerate her for both the Becky Savage and Donovan Kessler murders. Two—she is the murderer and crafty as hell. The diary entries are purposely deceptive to prove her innocence. Three—she's a bona fide psycho and killed both of these people, except she doesn't remember it."

Damn. Speaking of not remembering things, I forgot something important until this instance that I should've already told Scott.

"Did I mention about her sleepwalking?"

17

After leaving a couple of Captain Dave's men to guard the house, I point out to Scott the flower bed that is now missing one of its bricks from the borders.

He observes, "Hell of an idea to pick that as the murder weapon."

"Worked, didn't it?"

We cross the wooden bridge to the crime scene but don't descend the stairs to the beach. The tide is near high—the water touching the first step at the bottom with a few more steps to go. I hand him my phone with the photos of Donovan Kessler in his natural state. He takes his time to process everything. I give him room and wait for his impressions.

"What I'm about to say falls under the important caveat that I haven't met most of these people. But my opinion—either Savage wandered along at the exact right moment and seized the opportunity when he saw Kessler going to the beach, or it's someone from the house. The murderer knew Kessler was headed over here, followed him, and picked up the brick on the way. That's why I don't buy the Bixby lady you mentioned. She had left the party already. How did she know Kessler was at the beach?"

"Maybe she stewed in her car for a spell, saw him head for the water, and decided to follow."

"Flimsy, but not impossible. More Ring footage would help. Everything in the area—who went where and when."

He's not wrong. But going door to door like that takes a helluva lot of people and time, not to mention tracking down the make and models of the cars driven by the people we might be interested in. I remind myself that investigations don't solve themselves overnight and that my impending trip to Italy is an artificial deadline. Scott and

J.D. are here to run point when I leave. Plus, Scott is a much better investigator than I am anyway. I'm just "*a lawyer playing dress-up as some type of fancy cop.*"

* * *

The insult is fresh in my mind as we make our way back to the house. After we cross the bridge on our return trip, Maxwell—the author of the taunt—stands a few feet from us in Raymond's backyard. The sneer he wore earlier in the day now assumes more vitality in the afternoon sun. He asks me, "Is this one of your goons?"

Insulting me is one thing. The only real way I have to injure a person is to shoot him, and I've only done that once in my life. Odds are that Maxwell will never qualify for that honor. But insulting Scott is much more likely to be hazardous to one's health. He knows where to punch, what to kick, and how to grab a suspect's arm in a way to make him beg for mercy in record time. Introductions appear to be in order.

"Chief Detective Scott Moore, meet Maxwell Matheny, Attorney-at-Law."

No handshake follows. The easy smile that Scott shows on his face is proof that he is unperturbed by Maxwell's insolence. Maxwell rocks on the balls of his feet—another beer bottle in hand—seemingly eager for us to escalate the situation. But I don't want a fight. At least not yet. I prefer information.

"Glad you're here. Need to circle back with you on something you said about Lucy. I know the two of you are law partners, and you don't want to speak bad about her but—"

"Partners? That's a joke. Sure, on paper the three owners of the firm are Lucy, Sammy, and me. But how many times do you think I've ever been on the winning side of a 2-1 vote? Never. Those two are lockstep all the way, always at my expense. I might as well be their damn junior associate. Get this—they are having a big family conference right now with Uncle Raymond about this Sadie situation and actually asked me to leave. Can you believe that? Lucy's an in-law just like me, but she got to stay. If I had a grenade on me, I'd roll it into that meeting and walk away from this family forever."

"They kicked you out?"

"Hell yes."

He takes an angry swig of the beer. The decision to exclude only him says that the others don't view Maxwell with much in the way of affection. The feeling appears to be mutual. The grenade comment, while probably in jest, reveals a deep-seated grudge that began long before today. Did that animosity lead Maxwell to head to the beach with a brick in his hand last night? I'm open to the possibility. But the more pressing need of exploiting his bitterness to drive a bigger wedge between him and the family wins out for now.

"You told me earlier that Lucy was in love with your father-in-law but refused to share any more than that. Other information has come to light confirming your account, and I need the full story from you."

"What information?"

"Let's just say that she's a person of interest."

The answer intrigues him. A growing gleam of happy malice rises in his expression. Of course, he's also a person of interest, but good manners prevent me from pointing out what should be obvious to him. He finishes off the bottle of beer and lays it next to him on the manicured grass.

"Understand—I never saw Donovan and Lucy ever going at it or anything. The situation between them was more subtle than that. But I have a good eye when it comes to reading women. I can tell when a woman is into someone, and Lucy gave off that vibe whenever she was around him. Hanging on his every word. Too much smiling at his bad jokes. Brushing against him when she didn't have to. That sort of behavior kept getting more open and obvious ever since Judy left the scene, as if Lucy started to believe she might have a chance. And Donovan clearly enjoyed her company. Liked being admired and the center of attention. Who doesn't? But I never got the impression that the flirtation was as serious on his end."

"How did Lucy take it when Sadie became the woman of the house?"

"Like a bull aiming to gore someone."

He doesn't elaborate, and his manner slips back into the same pose of hostility that happens any time Sadie becomes the topic of conversation. His reaction confirms the wisdom that it's better for her to stay at the Jekyll Island Club Hotel tonight. Too many Kesslers are staying next door here. I move the topic away from Sadie to get him talking again.

"Where does Sammy fit in this love triangle?"

"Sammy? Already told you that he's a soft one. I thought for the longest time that he was oblivious to his wife's affection for his old man. Or possibly he simply didn't care. Never got the feeling that there was much loving regard between man and wife. Lucy probably only married him because he was the son of a big-time lawyer—could be she was even into Donovan way back then. Before my time, so I don't know. But yesterday, I heard the two of them arguing in their bedroom. The old house doesn't have the thickest walls. He told her to stop making idiots of the both of them by continuing to throw herself at his father. First time I ever heard Sammy raise his voice to her. Lucy yelled at him to stick his head into an oven and stormed off."

The mental picture of Sammy waging battle against his more domineering wife is a hard one to visualize. But even a mousy man can snap if bent too far. And I still haven't forgotten that he almost struck Sadie with me only a few feet away.

Back to Maxwell. I decide to make another run at seeing if he'll volunteer his activities of last night. Katherine offered that he attended a cocktail mixer at the bar conference in the early evening, but that still leaves a lot of time for other mischief.

"That's helpful. I still need to pin down what you were doing last night. It's for your own good."

His mistrust is evident. I can't blame him. His *own good* is not a priority of mine, and he knows it. He shoots me a hostile glare, laced with violent intent.

"If you keep pushing me on that, then you're going to push me too far one time."

Scott—who has played the role of patient observer up to this point in the conversation—asks, "What happens if we push you too far? I'm curious."

When Maxwell and I were alone together earlier in the day, he told me, "*My money says you don't even know how to handle that gun.*" I wonder whether he's willing to lay any action on that same bet with Scott. I don't have to wait long for an answer. Maxwell goes a little white around the gills—his lust for violence giving way to the instinct of self-preservation. A growing realization seems to dawn on him that Scott is not to be messed with. Trying to save face, Maxwell makes a scoffing noise that convinces no one. He turns around and calls out to us over his shoulder.

"I'm going to join the family conference."

But if Maxwell hopes that scurrying back into Uncle Raymond's house will rid himself of our disagreeable presence, tough luck. That's our next destination.

18

Raymond invites us into his living room. Sammy, Lucy, Katherine, and Maxwell are all present—as far away from one another as possible within the logistics of the space, as if each of them picked their own corner and retreated to it to be alone. The mood is downcast, more than when I talked to them earlier today about the murder. On a coffee table, legal papers are scattered all over. From my vantage point, I guess it to be a deed. That might explain all the sulking. If Donovan Kessler truly recorded a deed giving Sadie the house, getting a court to throw out that conveyance is a tall order. Hard to argue that a state bar president lacked the mental capacity to complete a real estate transaction.

Maxwell stands up to leave. His distaste with us must rank higher than the desire to participate in the family conference. Raymond says, "Max, hold on. Hang around for a second. I don't know what these gentlemen want to say, but we cannot put off the discussion about funeral arrangements any longer. What do you all want to do?"

A dead, uninterested silence ensues. Everyone looks at each other without much enthusiasm. Finally, Sammy says, "Uncle Raymond, can't you just handle everything? After Father's pulling of this stunt with that woman, we can throw his body into the sea and let the sharks have at him for all I care."

Katherine quickly adds, "I feel the same, Uncle. Can you just do everything that needs to be done? I'm not mentally capable of honoring him at this time."

The frown that Raymond displays is deep and wide. He studies his nephew and niece—almost in a state of disbelief. Heaving a weighty sigh, he responds, "Don't you want to write the obituary, at least? He was your father."

Sammy snaps, "No, I don't want to write the obituary. I don't even want to read something that would be full of lies anyway—like putting perfume on a pig. If it's that important to you, just write it and put it in the newspaper yourself. Or not. Whatever you want. But I'm out of it. Damn him!"

"Same goes for me," Katherine says.

A scan of the room shows Lucy and Maxwell nodding their heads in unison. I guess that makes it unanimous. Raymond slumps and becomes even older right before my eyes. The fight sucked out of him by his family, he gives a meek nod.

"All right, I'll see to everything. Let's plan on a Monday funeral at Delta Cove. The family plots are there. The obituary should run in the Brunswick paper on Sunday."

"Can we leave now?"

The voice belongs to Maxwell. I take that as my cue.

"Hang on a minute. I have instructions. The house next door is still under our control, at least through tonight, pursuant to a lawful search warrant. But I realize you have clothes and toiletries over there that you might need. Here's the deal—and it's not up for debate because I don't even have to do this much—but each of you are allowed five-minute turns to pack a single piece of luggage. When you leave, a state patrol officer will search your bag. Also, I need to be able to reach all of you. Is everyone staying here tonight?"

Murmurs of discontent percolate following the announcement, but I tune the complaints out. Once a consensus forms among the family that they will sleep over at Raymond's for the evening, I tell them that their individual packing trips at the other house can start in a half hour. Everyone but Raymond leaves the room in haste right after.

Alone with Scott and me, he says, "What did I tell you? Not a single one of them can handle hardship. They want to stay safe in their little snow globes with their eyes tightly closed, blind to the suffering happening in their midst. It's past time for them to grow up. Truth be told, Sammy has been a brat since birth, and Katherine has always lived in a reality all her own. I've long felt this need to protect those two because they are my brother's children, but the hell with them. I need to get out of here."

"Where are you going?"

"To tell Judy about Donovan. She deserves to know."

"Is she going to comprehend anything you say?"

"Probably not, but you never know what is happening in the mind of a person in her condition. I like to think that she understands more than we give her credit for. In any event, she's better company than the rest of the family."

He straightens his bowtie and heads for the door.

* * *

Captain Dave and J.D. are back outside when Scott and I leave Raymond Kessler's house. I provide Dave instructions about allowing the family members to pack a suitcase and further ask whether he can spare some people to go door-to-door in the neighborhood to search for relevant Ring video footage. To sweeten the pot, I promise to cover the cost of any overtime that his troopers work. The offer brings a smile to his face—the dour person I met this morning long gone. He observes, "You must have deep pockets."

"No, but I know someone who does."

With a slight spring in his step, he gathers his people together in a circle for fresh orders. As for me, it is past time to meet Rickie Savage.

J.D. says, "An abandoned aquatic research station is on the westside of the island, near the marsh. All the trash we can find will go there for a closer inspection by off-duty cops. That should start within the hour. What do you want from me now?"

I want him to find out what Maxwell Matheny was doing last night, but part of me feels that having back up when Scott and I confront Savage might be the better play. A cornered man is a desperate man, and the sad trajectory of his life could very well have Savage in that feral state, especially if he killed Donovan Kessler. I make the snap decision on the spot. J.D. comes with us. But we'll take separate vehicles.

On the way to my official use black Ford Expedition—a decked out ride with a number of handpicked, personalized features—I stop in my tracks upon seeing J.D., key in hand, head to the driver side of a small, aqua rental car. I feel compelled to comment.

"Toyota Corolla, huh? I've always been a big fan of the hatchback style. Good gas mileage, too. Very economical with the Office's money."

Scott grumbles, "I told J.D. to go get us a car. He claimed that this was the last one they had. Supply chain crisis or something. Not sure I believe that. But I'm riding with you in any event."

We start the drive to the pier, me going slower than normal to ensure that J.D. can keep up in the follow-up car. Just as I turn off the main road to a side street leading to the pier, my phone sounds. I recognize the number from earlier as Captain Dave's. I hit the SUV's Bluetooth speaker and answer.

"What's up, Dave?"

"Have a little bit of a situation here. Katherine Matheny is standing next to me screaming her head off. She claims something important is missing from the house but won't tell me what it is. What should I do?"

I wondered how she would react upon learning that her diary—now safely stored in an evidence pouch—was missing. Would she pretend that nothing was amiss or go the other way and freak out? Question answered.

"Put her on the phone."

Dead air hangs in the car until Katherine's high-pitch squeal assaults our eardrums.

"It's gone! I can't find it! Someone stole it!"

"What's gone?"

"Something personal to me! I want it back right now!"

Scott chuckles silently from the passenger seat with an expression indicating that hysterical women are my department. I pull into a dirt turn-out so as not to block traffic. Close on my bumper, J.D. does the same. Across the way, a bunch of horses stand around in a fenced ring. Tourists mill around the horses waiting to take a ride. Amber and I rode together here years ago, all the way to nearby Driftwood Beach—maybe on two of the same horses over there now. The memory feels like a different life lived by a different person, which is true enough from a certain point of view. I return my attention to the moment.

"Can you describe the item?"

"No! I don't want to! It's too private!"

"Nothing I can do to help you then. Good-bye."

"Wait!"

I wait. Katherine's excited breathing echoes throughout the Ford Expedition. Her drug-addled lethargy from earlier in the morning is temporarily gone. Finally, in an elevated whisper, she says, "It's a small journal. Pink."

"Oh, that."

The thought is left hanging. Upon figuring out that no more information is coming, she shrieks, "You know about it?"

"Sure. We took it for evidence."

She gives a quick gasp and goes silent. A small amount of static caused by the rustling of the wind is the only noise coming from her end of the call. After a long enough period of time to leave me wondering if the conversation is over, Katherine speaks again in a tight, taut voice.

"You can't do that."

"I already did."

"Why?"

"Material contained therein is probative of a possible motive to murder. '*The Lord punishes the wicked*' and that kind of thing. Anything you care to confess? I hear it is good for the soul."

A tortured scream rocks through the speaker, followed by a hard thump. Scott and I turn our heads to each other, wondering about the state of things a few miles away. The next sound we hear is an upset Dave, now back on the line.

"She slammed my phone down on the ground. The screen's cracked."

After rubbing both hands on my face and up through my hair,

I gulp a deep breath of air for the extra oxygen, thinking about the nap I would be taking right about now if the Governor hadn't interrupted my golfing. Why can't life be simple and good? The answer is above my pay grade, but I can at least do something for Dave.

"Add the damage to my bill."

19

The Jekyll Island pier is T-shaped—with the stem extending from the land a good distance before splitting off to the left and the right out over the water. I pass my phone around to give the others a glance of Rickie Savage's ugly mugshot. From the foot of the dock, Scott is the first to make the match. He points to a figure leaning over the ledge of the far-right end of the pier. I can see that the person in question is a man and that he's wrestling with a long, spastic fishing pole directly in front of him. Little chance exists that I could make a positive identification from this distance, but Scott's never wrong about these things.

He instructs J.D., "You stay here, just in case the target gets past us."

The two of us make a pair as we walk on the pier—him wearing a suit and tie, me still dressed like a beach bum. I ask, "How do you want to play it?"

"You sidle up next to him and divert his attention, pretend to watch what he's doing. You're pretty inconspicuous in those clothes. I'll sneak in from behind. Hopefully, he'll stay distracted with that fish."

The long walk to reach him gets more nerve-racking with each step. A special type of cold-bloodedness is required to smash someone's head with a brick over and over again. If Savage is that person, he figures to be ready to rumble with us something fierce. I pull my sweatshirt down to cover more of my gun to aid my disguise of non-threatening onlooker and walk ahead of Scott to get in position.

I reach the railing five feet to Savage's right and find him doing battle with a hammerhead shark on the other end of the fishing line—a cigarette nonchalantly dangling from his mouth. A sweat-stained Lynyrd Skynyrd tank top shows off his tan, sinewy frame. Cut-off jean shorts do the same for his legs. The stench he emits is an odd mixture of tobacco, fish, and rank perspiration. When I lean over the rail to get a better look at the shark, my sweatshirt catches on a nail and reveals the gun on my hip.

Within a nanosecond, Savage whips around toward me with a knife pointed straight at my belly and snarls, "You smell like a cop."

The blade in his hand appears much too sharp for comfort. I stumble backwards and make a clumsy attempt to get at my gun, only to end up with a handful of sweatshirt instead.

Scott grabs the arm with the knife and yanks it upwards to heavens. Based on the curses flowing out of Savage's mouth in the aftermath, the hunch is that the maneuver hurts like hell. The weapon slips from his grasp, and the hard clank when it falls to the pier allows me to breathe easy again.

But not for long.

Savage kicks at Scott's knee with the top of his shoe, and Scott lets loose a few curses of his own as Savage scurries on all fours toward his knife a couple of feet in front of me. We arrive at the same time. I summon all available force at my disposal and slam my foot down on the dirty fingers reaching out for the blade. The crunch of a bone sounds like a sweet melody under the circumstances.

Except Savage isn't done yet. Using his good hand to hold the other one close to his body, he scampers to his feet. A hunched-over Scott—still favoring the knee—grasps him from behind while I approach from the front. But holding on to our prey is akin to trying to grab ahold of a floppy fish juiced on cocaine. Slipping out of our combined grasp, Savage escapes and darts down the pier with more speed than an over fifty, cigarette-smoking, former trucker should be able to manage. I give chase. Scott stays in place, probably debating whether he should just go ahead and shoot the suspect or not.

By the time Savage nears the end of the pier and is about to return to dry land, he turns around toward me with an expression filled with so much scorn as to be unhealthy. Not that I can do much about it. Since the sprint started, the ground that I've lost to him is noticeable. The prospect of chasing him some more feels futile.

As Savage returns his attention from me to the path in front of him, J.D. explodes out of nowhere and hits the fugitive with a vicious, shoulder-led tackle worthy of a Hall of Fame linebacker. On a real football field, a referee would throw a yellow flag on J.D. for unnecessary roughness. But the rules are different here, and J.D. just assured a little something extra in his stocking come Christmas bonus time. Savage crumbles to the ground and does not get up.

Game over.

20

J.D. secures his catch, starting with wrapping a zip tie around the suspect's ankles to prevent a sequel from Mr. Happy Feet. I watch nearby ready to stomp on more of Savage's fingers should the need arise. But my young lieutenant has the situation under control and finishes off his work by handcuffing Savage's hands behind his back, cinching the cuffs tighter than necessary. Just because.

The lull in action allows me to catch my breath. Scott lumbers toward us, still slightly gimpy after the kick to his knee. He carries Savage's knife with him, and part of me wonders if he's going to give it back to Savage blade-first. Instead, Scott barks, "Take his shoes off."

I respond, "Why? He's not going anywhere with his legs secured like that."

"Take his shoes off!"

He's in a foul mood. To appease the bear, I approach Savage, who is still lying prone with his face kissing the pier's concrete walkway. Off come the shoes. Right away, I notice something different about them, a heavier feel than normal for a standard shoe. Tapping the top of the shoe in the toe area, I feel the hard metal underneath.

"Steel-toed. That must've hurt."

The flash of Scott's middle finger pointed toward me confirms my diagnosis. I have a pair of steel-toed boots to use when moving around heavy objects—usually a car engine block—in my home garage. The idea is that the steel will protect the toes from harm caused by falling things. Blue-collar folks wear such shoes all the time. But not sprinters. That Savage was able to run so fast while attached to such anchors amazes. The man is a freak.

Pulled back to his feet by the strong arms of J.D., Savage starts to rejoin the land of living and mouths all manner of creative insults about us.

The drawl is all redneck and reminds me of certain high school buddies from my upbringing in middle Georgia—Punk Weaver being the foremost offender in my mind. Punk married the homecoming queen and opened a liquor store, only to lose both when he drank too much of his inventory. His ex-wife is Taylor Diamond—Executive Administrator to the murder squad and Scott's girlfriend. Circle of life.

But Punk on his drunkest day doesn't compare to Rickie Savage. The man J.D. now leads to the Expedition might as well be a wild animal. The rabid kind. Onlookers in the parking lot of the pier watch our march to the car, and Savage unleashes his vitriol on many of them—taunting some and spitting on others—all the time doing his floppy fish act to wrench away from J.D.'s control. One mother uses a hand to cover her daughter's face. Another woman has her phone out to record the spectacle, a helpful tonic to tamp down any eagerness to show the suspect what we really think of him.

Par for the course, Savage battles like a madman to avoid getting into the back of the SUV. Scott helps J.D. with the problem, and I position my body to block the cell phone from recording them. They finally wrangle the prisoner into a sitting position and buckle a seatbelt over him. An undeterred Savage lunges forward and takes a bite out of J.D.'s neck.

That aggression will not stand.

Scott rams the crown of his head straight into Savage's ear. The headbutt does the trick, and Savage takes a temporary pause from the burden of consciousness.

Let's call that a teaching moment. Scott reads him his Miranda rights as we pull out of the parking lot.

* * *

"Alligators live all over this island. I know their hiding places. Sprinkle some salt and pepper on our friend back there, and the rest is history."

Scott grunts—in no mood for my humor. Sweat collects on his bald head, along with a trickle of blood from where he used it as a battering ram. When I point out the slight gash to him, he mutters a word unprintable in most newspapers.

Back on the main road with J.D. again behind us in the Corolla, I pull into the first turnout available, a gravel parking area adjacent to a small graveyard. J.D. parks next to me. Scott asks, "Why are you stopping?"

"Because I don't even know where to go. I have to call Dave to get directions to the nearest jail cell. Probably would also be a good idea for us to get out of the car and cool our heels for a bit."

He doesn't appear to have much interest in cooling anything but exits the car with me all the same. Dave answers on the first ring, and I explain the problem.

"Rickie Savage needs a new home for the immediate future—one with an uncomfortable bed and steel bars. Does the Georgia State Patrol Station on the causeway have a room that can fit that order?"

"Did he confess to murdering Kessler?"

"Haven't even had a chance to ask him that yet. Without so much as a hello, he lunged at me with a knife, kicked Scott with a steel-toed shoe, and pretended he was a vampire on J.D.'s neck. Whether he killed Kessler or not, I'm going to charge him with every criminal offense possible under the sun, including fishing without a license if I can make it stick."

"Sorry to hear about that. People are crazy these days. My wife worries about me getting shot every traffic stop. Can't say I blame her. But yes, we have a holding cell out on the causeway. You can keep Mr. Savage there until you find a permanent home. Sergeant Brooks is at the station now and can arrange things. I'll give him a heads up."

He ends the call. I peek back inside the SUV to check on Sleeping Beauty, who is still out cold. J.D. meanders over to join Scott and me. I ask him, "Do you need a rabies shot?"

"Seriously? Is that a thing?"

An inkling of worry crowds around his eyes. I pop open the back of the Expedition and remove a couple of water bottles from a small ice chest I took to the golf course. Scott says, "Do you have anything stronger?"

"Not at the moment."

The two of them gulp the water while I return to the SUV and retrieve a first aid kit. For the next couple of minutes, I play Florence Nightingale to Scott's head and J.D.'s neck but only after taking pictures of both wounds for later use as evidence. When finished, I join them with a bottle of water of my own.

J.D. asks, "What now?"

"Scott and I are going to beat a confession out of Rickie Savage. You are going to find out where Maxwell Matheny spent his time last night before he came home stumbling drunk. Start with a cocktail mixer held at the hotel last night and then branch out to surrounding bars from there."

He finishes off the water, collapses the plastic bottle into a stump with one hand, and throws the remains in the backseat of the rental car.

"Why do you want me to go so hard after Matheny? You don't think Savage is our guy?"

Fleeing from the cops is what prosecutors call, "Consciousness of guilt." And Rickie Savage's performance on the pier demonstrated a whole lot of guilt about something. Evidence like that—a soft confession of sorts—can be powerfully persuasive, especially to a jury. But a man like Savage reckons to have a great many things to feel guilty about. And even though making him for the Kessler murder would bring me great satisfaction after all his brawling, I haven't quite reached the point in my life where I want to see a man go to prison for a murder he didn't commit.

"Doesn't matter whether I think he's our guy or not. We need evidence and until we get it, I refuse to be married to any one suspect. And Maxwell requires a more thorough investigation. We have him on film heading toward the backyard and the beach around the time of the murder. I want to know what he was doing the rest of the night."

The Corolla drives off in search of that answer. Scott and I stand side-by-side contemplating the marsh in the distance. I ask, "Ready?"

"You know, I've never watched an execution in my life. Seven men I've arrested for murder have received the death penalty, but I've never had the urge to go watch any of them die. Until now. If that son of a bitch in the car is the guy we're looking for and if the jury sentences him to death, I'll be watching in the front row. With popcorn."

"South Carolina is going back to the firing squad as its method of execution. Maybe I can get the Governor to have Georgia follow suit, and you can actually pull the trigger."

"Don't tease me."

He stifles a grimace while getting back in the vehicle. His knee must hurt more than he lets on. I take a last, lustful look at the marsh and shake off the remaining shivers from having Rickie Savage's knife that close to my stomach. Cate could've been a widow. I've borne the unbearable pain of a spouse murdered much too young and grieve the thought that Cate might have to carry a similar weight after everything else she has been through.

But today isn't that day.

21

The Jekyll Island Causeway runs through the marsh and connects the mainland to the island. Sergeant Theodore Brooks unlocks a small room containing a single jail cell. A desk with two chairs sits about six feet from the bars, completing the drab and sparse space.

The absence of any outside light heightens the box-like atmosphere. Fluorescent bulbs illuminate the entire area with a disorienting brightness. The smell is antiseptic, a nauseating blend of cleaning chemical agents. Savage's foul scent is almost refreshing in contrast. But only almost. The only visible colors around are black and gray—the dark gray stone that comprises three sides of the cell, the black bars that keep prisoners in place, and a seasick shade of gray that coats the walls.

The overall effect is of a burial chamber, a place where people go to die.

Savage, still groggy but coming around, lies face down on the bed. Scott removes all the restraints. If Savage is playing possum, he doesn't take the opportunity to show it. The slamming of the cell door reverberates like a bazooka in the confined space. Savage flinches but pretends not to—the first sign that he might be better than what he's letting on. Sergeant Brooks departs and leaves us alone with the inmate. Having noticed that Savage might be well enough to listen to our conversation, Scott texts me from a few feet away that we should give him something good to hear. He begins in a loud voice.

"Any aggravating circumstances so that we can get the death penalty on Savage for the murder?"

"Sure. The statute allows for death in cases of 'torture, depravity of mind, or an aggravated battery to the victim.' The murder scene was a bloodbath. Rickie here is a sadistic guy. Death penalty case, easy. Allow one year for a conviction, one year for an appeal, and another year to kill him. Three years from now, this piece of filth won't be among the living anymore."

"Good riddance."

Just as Savage pretends not to listen to us, we pretend not to watch him. But the signs are there that he's hearing every word we are saying. A tenseness in his body exists that was previously missing. His breathing, too, has quieted down, as if he's suppressing the sound so that his ears can work better.

Scott asks, "Why do you think Savage did it?"

"Revenge—what else? A motive as old as time. Clearest case I've ever had. Let's just go ahead and take him to Brunswick and let him rot. Nothing he says can possibly get him off the hook anyway. We have better things to do."

"Don't even talk to him? Shouldn't we at least give him a chance? Hear his side?"

"What for? Hard to believe any words coming out of his mouth anyway."

"If you say so."

The unscripted dialogue represents an impromptu role reversal for us. Usually I'm the Good Cop to Scott's Bad Cop. But after this exchange, I'm now playing the heavy. We go through the motions of starting to leave—putting chairs back in place, gathering the assorted items on the desk that we took from the prisoner's pockets, talking about where we want to eat dinner. Savage's loud cough stops these efforts. Scott stares at him for a few seconds and wonders aloud, "Think he's waking up?"

"Nah. Probably not for hours. Let's go. I'm hungry."

Savage rustles some more, coughs again, and drops his feet to the floor with the slow speed of a Jekyll Island sea turtle. We stop what we are doing to pay him some more attention. In a continuation of his bad acting, he moans, "Where am I?" With all the derision at my disposal, I continue my performance as Bad Cop.

"You died. This is Hell."

"Wha ... what?"

He stumbles to his feet and approaches the black bars. He grasps the bars with both hands but swiftly pulls back the one with the smashed fingers and releases a pitiful squeal. No acting there. The hand I stomped on to stop his knife grab is blue with pain. Probably broken and I didn't even need to use a steel-toed shoe. Something to celebrate later. But now is the time to make him hurt some more.

"Do you like the view? Because it's the only view you'll ever see again after what you did."

His dirty eyes squint at me. I hold the line with a withering stare. He swings his head around to Scott and asks, "What's this guy talking about?"

The weariness in Scott's response, punctuated with a slight dip of the shoulders, is worthy of Olivier. He pretends to be the prisoner's friend.

"Don't be dumb, Rickie. It's the wrong play."

"What are you talking about, man?"

I yell, "Donovan Kessler, jackass. Heard of him?"

"Sure, he's the sumabitch that killed my daughter. What about him?"

His attention is back toward me. I roll my eyes and say to Scott, "He's getting on my nerves. You deal with him."

"All right, I'll do the talking. Rickie—you got one chance in a million to get this thing right. We know you were on Jekyll yesterday. You need to fill in the gaps from there."

We don't actually know that Savage was on the island yesterday but no harm in making him think otherwise. One quirk of life in America—you lie to the police, that's a crime. The police lie to you, that's good detective work. Govern yourself accordingly.

"So what if I was on the island? Is that a crime? I'm here every day—trying to eke out a measly living by catching a few fish. Got nothing else to do. No family. No friends. No job."

"Whose fault is that? The Kessler family, right? Bet you weren't struggling when you were driving a big rig, were you? But that was before you got in a wreck with Judy Kessler and before Donovan Kessler killed your daughter. The two lowest points of your life. And all because of one family. Makes sense that you would kill Donovan Kessler to even the score."

Savage's tan face goes ghost pale.

***

"Can I have one of my cigarettes?"

A panting of lust consumes a jittery Savage as he gawks at the Marlboros on the desk. Scott takes a cancer stick out of the pack and picks up a nearby lighter. He holds the cigarette out to a greedy hand jutting through the prison bars, but I intercept the exchange. After taunting him by holding the cigarette out of his reach, I drop the object of his desire to the floor, grounding it to bits with my shoe much as I did his fingers out there on the pier.

Savage whines, "What the hell did you do that for?"

"Smoking is bad for your health."

The angry tirade I expect to follow doesn't materialize. Whimpering instead takes its place. That's a good sign. A defeated man is more likely to spill his guts. Scott says, "You know, I don't even blame you, Rickie. I have a daughter, too. After what Kessler did, I would've done the same thing to him. Any father would."

"You keep talking about me killing Kessler. Why?"

"You know why."

"I don't know nothing."

"Hard to believe that, Rickie. You ran. Guilty people don't run. You want to tell us about it."

By the looks of him, the answer is no. He again devours the Marlboros with his eyes. Scott notices and asks, "Will you tell why you ran away from us for a cigarette?"

Savage nods. Scott points at me and says in a stern voice, "Behave." I shrug. Soon, the prisoner is sucking on the tobacco like a man dying of thirst. The moment drags as Savage savors each puff. Finally, Scott says, "Your turn, Rickie."

"I'm thinking a lawyer might be a good idea for me."

Scott threatens to explode on the spot—and right after he gave Savage a cigarette. The last word that anyone from law enforcement wants to hear out of a suspect being interrogated is "lawyer." Asking for a lawyer means the questioning must cease until counsel is present. Technically, Savage didn't actually ask for an attorney. Same as technically Scott read him his Miranda rights, even if Savage wasn't awake enough to hear them. But aggressive reliance on technicalities is an open invitation for a judge to throw out a bunch of evidence.

Playing along, I ask, "Do you even know any lawyers, Rickie?"

"Meredith Bixby. I talked to her yesterday on the pier."

My face is indifferent to that revelation, but the furious wheels in my head pounce on the new math. Two enemies of Donovan Kessler met together yesterday, and Kessler received a brick to the head shortly thereafter. That plot twist wasn't one I foresaw, but new possibilities start to branch out in my fertile imagination.

"What did the two of you talk about? Donovan Kessler?"

"Why do you keep thinking I know anything about him? I'm not saying another word until I speak to Meredith."

And that's that for the moment. I look to my partner and visualize a volcano on the verge of erupting—the pressure of rising tension that has no place to go until nature forces its own opening. The Good Cop role doesn't suit Scott anyway.

Back in his cell, Savage is more interested in his cigarette than us. If one could get lung cancer from a single smoke, that instance would be now. We have no choice but to play it his way, and I tell him as much on my way out the door.

"I'll convey your request to speak to Meredith personally."

22

Food is the first priority. The both of us are too jacked up as it is to go charging into the state bar conference on empty stomachs. The concept of "hangry" is a real thing. Being hungry can turn the nicest person into the Incredible Hulk. And while I could push off dinner an hour or two because of my late lunch with Cate, all Scott had on the plane was peanuts and pretzels. He's starving. And that's not good for anybody. A call to invite J.D. to join us goes unanswered.

We land at a seafood restaurant on the river side of the island, across from the marsh. Like most of Jekyll, the place is casual, not stuffy. The seafood is as fresh as the day's catch. The waitress comes over for our drink orders. Scott asks, "Do you mind if I have a beer?"

"Mind? I insist."

"Good. Because I was going to drink one anyway. Not sure why I even asked."

For the first time since crossing paths with Rickie Savage, Scott smiles. We both need a break from the case for a bit and talk about other topics to pass the time—including an extended discussion about Atlanta Braves baseball, Scott's second favorite interest after shooting a gun. When we finish the food—catfish for him, buffalo shrimp for me—I steer the ship back to more pressing matters.

"How's the knee?"

"Functional."

"Any updated thoughts about our case? You've met all the known players now except for Meredith Bixby."

"You mean whether we can ever solve this thing? Prognosis negative. No witnesses. No physical evidence, unless J.D. pulls the Houdini of all Houdinis and digs up the bloody clothes somewhere, assuming they even exist in the first place. Savage running looks bad for him but not enough for a conviction. What we need is a confession from somebody. And if Savage lawyers up, any confession won't be from him. Might as well bang our heads against the wall. We'll accomplish more. Our best bet is to put on some gloves and go dumpster diving."

Nothing Scott says rings a false note. I kinda had the same sinking feeling in my gut but couldn't quite verbalize it. His analysis also shows the need to expand our operations to Brunswick. If Savage is our guy, we need those bloody clothes. I make a mental note to expand J.D.'s garbage radius to every location between the island and Savage's home on the mainland. And that sparks a new thought.

"We need to search where Savage lives."

"Tonight? Without a warrant?"

I didn't say that, although I might have been thinking it. I say, "Let's see how we do with Meredith first. Maybe she'll confess and spare us the trouble."

"A conference full of lawyers is your territory. How do you want to handle it?"

"One lawyer at a time—starting at the top."

* * *

Meredith Bixby stands on stage and addresses a banquet room full of intoxicated lawyers. I recognize her from the Ring video. Scott and I stand at the back with the wait staff. The mood is subdued in all corners. Meredith matches the atmosphere by being appropriately serious.

"The tragic and senseless murder of Donovan Kessler reminds us that we live in a broken world, a heartless world where people do bad things to one another. As lawyers, we fight against that inhumanity every day. More than any of us, Donovan dedicated himself to the legal profession—to the law, to the community, and to his fellow attorneys whom he faithfully served for years through his leadership in the bar. His example inspired so many in this room to be the best lawyers that we could be."

Scott rolls his eyes. Meredith is not finished.

"The State Bar of Georgia will never forget our slain president. We are already planning ways we can honor him, starting with a special remembrance luncheon on Sunday to close out this conference. But for now, please raise your glasses. I propose a toast: 'To Donovan Kessler, may his memory be forever etched in the history of the State Bar of Georgia.'"

Glasses clink, and shouts of "here, here" ring out. With the speech over, the wait staff rushes forward to serve dessert—chocolate cake with raspberries to the side. Meredith makes her way down off the dais and settles into a chair at a front-row table. Walking up unannounced and plucking her out of the crowd would set too many tongues wagging for my taste. Lawyers are worse gossips than middle schoolers.

But a solution to the logistical problem of getting close to Meredith appears one table over where Cate sits with a number of other Supreme Court Justices. The chair next to her, mine presumably, is empty. I turn to Scott.

"Wait here."

"Gladly."

The event is first-class—suits at a minimum, but black ties and tuxedos for many. If I could feel self-conscious about being underdressed, I would. Except I'm temperamentally incapable of feeling any such thing. But my sweatshirt, jeans, and sneakers ensemble does make for a unique fashion choice in a room filled with so much formality. Even the stubble on my chin seems out of step with the clean-shaven cheeks in the room. I stroll through the circular dinner tables and make my way up to the front as if I owned the place, receiving a number of curious stares for the trouble. Cate watches my approach, and I slide into the seat right next to her.

"You look like absolute hell."

Her frankness is one of her most appealing virtues. When the former Chief Justice of the Georgia Supreme Court—a vile man who needed a good killing and got one—propositioned Cate to join him in his hotel room during a previous state bar conference a couple of years ago, she refused the offer on the grounds that she had no interest in his "limp, wrinkled dick." That told me right there that she was a keeper.

"Glad to know that my appearance so perfectly captures how I'm feeling on the inside. It's been tough sledding since we parted. You almost became a widow."

"Don't joke about things like that."

"Not joking."

"I told you to be careful."

"And I carefully avoided the knife that an angry man tried to plunge into my stomach."

Cate freezes in place and studies me a with an expression mixed with seriousness and slight fear. I hold her stare and make myself vulnerable—to let her know that she isn't the only one scared about what happened. She rubs a hand through my hair and kisses me lightly on the lips.

"You caught him? The murderer?"

"Caught the guy with the knife. Not sure yet if he's the murderer we're looking for."

She frowns. Waiters drop chocolate cake in front of both of us. It looks even better up close. We pick up our forks and dig in. After a few bites, I say, "Need a favor from you. Can you introduce me to Meredith Bixby?"

"Now?"

"After we finish the cake."

The only response I receive is a scoff. We clean off our plates and head one table over for the introductions. When the pleasantries are over, Meredith looks at me with bright eyes and a wide smile. She asks a question.

"What took you so long?"

23

Meredith agrees to meet with me in a conference room down the hall as soon as the dinner ends in a few minutes. Cate walks me back to Scott. She gives him a hug and says, "Don't you lead him into something foolish."

"It's usually the other way around."

She stands back and assesses the both of us before observing, "Not sure I believe that, but not sure that I disbelieve it, either." After a hug for me, Cate asks, "Should I wait up?"

"Not tonight."

Scott and I leave the banquet to loiter in the hall. A minute or two later, a mass exodus of lawyers follows. Burt and Lois Pressley pass a few feet in front of us. When Burt sees me, he takes a detour straight my way. Lois reluctantly follows. He says, "How's the investigation going?"

I explain to Scott, "Burt and Lois. Lawyers from Bainbridge. They found the body on a morning walk."

Burt sticks an eager hand out in Scott's direction. Scott considers the offer for a full three seconds before reluctantly accepting. I turn my attention to Lois.

"We need to talk to everyone at the party last night—all the past state bar presidents and their dates, you said. Can you organize it?"

"Sounds easy enough. We have a group text. When?"

"Tomorrow morning at eight. Right here."

Lois promises to do what she can. The two lawyers from Bainbridge trot off with Burt seeming a little miffed, probably because he never got an answer as to the progress of the investigation. But that's one of the consequences of being indiscreet. People don't want to talk to you.

Meredith—still wearing a big smile—strides up to us with confident steps. She asks, "You fellas ready to do this?"

***

Perky and full of spunk. That's my first impression of Meredith—a ball of fire unafraid to tackle any obstacle in her way and to do so with an infectious, positive, can-do attitude. More than one person has already vouched that she's the friendliest person in the world. I have no cause yet to disagree. The second impression of her is that she's short—maybe five feet, maybe not. The diminutive size might explain all the pluck she seems intent on dishing out in spades, a signal to everyone that she will not be ignored. I'm curious to find out what the curmudgeon next to me thinks of her but think I already know the answer.

Scott hates spunk.

After the three of us find a quiet room so we can talk alone, Meredith opens her arms and proclaims, "I'm all yours. Ask me anything." Because Scott avoids talking to lawyers whenever possible, I take the lead.

"You seem to think that we have good reason to talk to you. Why?"

"A Ring camera caught an argument between Donovan and me last night. If you guys are half as good as everybody in the state thinks, you have seen it. Naturally, I realized that you would be talking to me sooner or later—probing my possible motive for wanting to see Donovan dead. Took longer than I thought. Made me think that you already caught the person who did it. But now you're here, late at night, wanting to talk to me. To put your mind at ease, I didn't kill him."

She smiles, as if a wide grin counts as a character reference. Is the niceness all an act? Hard to tell. But if it is, she's perfected the performance. Loud lawyers parade down the hall outside the room, probably on their way to a hospitality suite filled with all manner of alcohol. I pause to let them and the noise pass.

"But you concede that you had a motive?"

"No, I said that you would want to know about my '*possible motive*.' The truth is that I had no reason whatsoever to want Donovan dead. You know from the Ring video how little I thought of the allegations he was harping about. Just a whole lot of nothing. Desperate even—because he had this weird desire to serve another year as state bar president, which was never happening. But Donovan was all bark anyway. He didn't have the balls to cross me for real. He was bluffing. That was the kind of guy he was. A bluffer. Boast a little here, backstab a little there. Huff and puff. Yada, yada, yada. But at the end of the day, he would back down. Especially against me. He once believed that because I'm short, nice, and a woman, I would wilt under his stupid threats. I disabused him of such silly ideas."

A common misperception equates niceness and weakness. Meredith appears to be the living embodiment of that false equivalence. Underestimating her, as Kessler apparently did, strikes me as a profound error. I remind myself to keep that fact at the foremost of my mind.

"The dead person you're describing sounds completely different than the person you were eulogizing on stage a few minutes ago."

"Everyone lies about people right after they die. That's just basic manners."

She smiles again. The hour is much too late for that kind of nonstop friendliness. But I return her smile in response anyway, a small proof of the theory that smiling is contagious. Perhaps Meredith internalized that belief long ago, and now it constitutes a core part of her character. *How to Win Friends and Influence People*—that kind of thing.

"You mentioned thinking that the person who murdered Donovan might already have been caught. We actually do have a person in custody."

"Who?"

"Rickie Savage."

And there departs her smile, replaced with stunned silence. My smile vanishes, too. I try to make my face unfriendly—to probe for weakness, panic, anything. The room is deathly quiet all of a sudden. No more boisterous lawyers hover in the vicinity. Everything is still. The quiet doesn't bother me, and I won't be the first one to break it. Meredith speaks up.

"He used to work for a trucking company that is a former client of mine. I saw him just yesterday afternoon around dusk."

"You saw him?"

"On the pier. Every time I'm back on Jekyll, I go visit the pier to breathe in the sea air and look out toward St. Simons. He was there fishing. I didn't recognize him at first, but he called out my name and walked over to me. We talked for five minutes or so. Tops."

"What on earth did you talk about?"

"He asked me if I knew that Donovan had murdered his daughter."

Her conversational tone belies the spectacular nature of the admission, and her face gives nothing away. She's not quite back to smiling, but the manner is pleasant enough—her look conveying the message that the ball is now in my court.

"That's a strange topic of conversation."

"Yes and no. I met Rickie a couple of years ago defending a lawsuit against his employer for an accident involving him and Judy Kessler, Donovan's wife. So simply mentioning Donovan to me did not rise to the level of unusual. He's our only shared acquaintance. The part about Donovan's killing Rickie's daughter, though—yes, that was strange. I hadn't known about the murder but flat out told him that he was barking up the wrong tree with that idea. For one thing, Donovan lacked the nerve. After that, we said our good-byes."

"How would you describe Savage's state of mind toward Kessler?"

"Bitter, resentful, frustrated. The man thought Donovan murdered his daughter, after all. Wrongly, in my view, but his feelings were perfectly sincere. When I heard about Donovan, that's where my mind went—Rickie. Did he do it? Did Rickie really kill Donovan?"

"Well, you obviously made a big impression on him yesterday. Maybe you can ask him yourself. He's looking for a lawyer and requested to see you."

She bursts out laughing, a hearty and full-throated guffaw out of keeping with her little frame. I turn to Scott to take his temperature and wish I hadn't. Meredith's spunk is getting to him. The misery on his face makes me feel bad for dragging him down here in the first place. But we can both blame the Governor for that. I should swipe a beer for him from the lawyer's hospitality lounge, at least. After she finally stops with the laughing, Meredith shares her thoughts about Savage's request for representation.

"That's the silliest thing I've ever heard in my life. I don't even do criminal work. Please politely decline on my behalf. And besides, I would be conflicted out from being his attorney anyway. You would put me on the stand as your witness, wouldn't you? All that talk about his state of mind and such."

Yep. Any hope that Savage had of Meredith's representing him died when she described their conversation yesterday. She's a witness and a strong witness at that—smiling at the jury about how a few short hours before the murder, Savage was ranting about Kessler's killing his daughter. Combined with his fleeing from law enforcement, Meredith's testimony would just about sink Savage's chances at an acquittal, if only we possessed any concrete proof he actually smashed Kessler's head with a brick. I study Meredith's amiable face one more time and try to think of any further questions.

"You said the trucking company is now a former client?"

"They dropped me because of the Judy Kessler case. I wanted to take our chances at trial. Some evidence existed that the wreck happened when Judy strayed too far out of her lane—that the wreck wasn't Rickie's fault at all. But Raymond Kessler was on the warpath and his reputation spooked the client to settle for way more than I advised. They worried that the jury would bankrupt the company. Of course, the client still blamed me for the bad outcome when they forked over that settlement check."

The thought of Meredith doing battle against Raymond Kessler in the courtroom intrigues me. Raymond is the best for a reason, but something tells me that Meredith would have had a fighting chance of holding her own, except for the tough sell of trying to persuade a jury to side with Rickie Savage over a brain-dead Judy Kessler. The trucking company was right to be scared out of its wits.

When informed that I'm out of questions, Meredith bounces out of the room like a kangaroo. Where does she get the energy? I turn to Scott.

"You thinking what I'm thinking?"

"That seeing Meredith yesterday made Rickie remember how much he hated Donovan Kessler? And that we should go ahead and search his house?"

We message J.D. to see if he's available to join us but again get no response. I grab Scott that beer from the hospitality lounge on the way to the Expedition.

24

"Why are we doing it this way again?"

Scott raises an excellent point. Searching Savage's place without a warrant is stupid—inexcusably dumb. The exclusionary rule prevents illegally obtained evidence from ever being presented before a jury. And a magistrate judge is always on duty to sign warrants at odd hours. With enough effort, we could get permission to search in due course. I try to explain my reasoning in short-circuiting that process.

"Because I'm tired and stuck in a foreign land where even the simplest task back home is outside my area of expertise here. I don't even know how to get to the courthouse. I've imposed on Captain Dave and the state patrol all day and believe they deserve to rest. The possibility of finding anything that implicates Savage for the murder is nil. What could that evidence possibly be? The bloody clothes? Could he really be that foolish? We've caught some brainless murderers in our time, but that would take the cake. What's left? Not a dang thing. But not searching where he lives is investigative malpractice. That box has to be checked off. So that's what we're doing—checking off the box so we can move on to other things."

"You don't have to convince me. I like it when you think like a cop instead of like a lawyer."

The GPS takes us to a rundown trailer park in what I take to be a bad part of Brunswick. An hour before midnight on a Friday night, the place appears dead. I'm not sure what I expected, maybe a party or two. Far as I can tell, we attract no attention when pulling up to Savage's place. But the whole vibe gives me the creeps—pitch-black, foreboding, and no doubt plenty of guns in the unlit trailers that make up the community. The quicker we can check off this box, the better.

From his investigation bag, Scott removes rubber gloves, flashlights, and a large circular keychain that contains just about every key known to man. He fiddles with the lock while I scan around for potential boogeymen in the night. The small staircase leading to the front door sways under our combined weight. The night wind carries with it the rotten-egg smell of Brunswick's paper mill, and the nauseating stench is worse than I've ever experienced down here. The pulp plant must be nearby.

Scott opens the door and shines his flashlight.

Right away, I feel dropped into one of those bizarre television shows about hoarders. Boxes, fishing gear, trash, and other odd assortments cover floor to ceiling and everywhere in between. The two of us crowd together beyond the doorway, trapped by the multiple roadblocks impeding our path to anywhere. Our flashlights barely help.

An added treat is that the smell isn't much better in here than outside, probably worse. I laugh to keep from crying. Scott's response is more poetic. He unleashes a string of profanity positively Shakespearean in its lyrical quality. I turn on the lights and complain, "So much for the subtle approach."

The clutter comes into better focus. Five feet away, an ancient stuffed marlin—dusty, chipped, discolored—rests on top of a pile of newspapers from last century. The sword of the great fish retains its sharpness and sticks out into what appears to be the most natural trail to travel the house. I imagine being impaled on it and think that such a punishment might be just for neglecting my constitutional duty to get a search warrant. With my imagination running amuck in such fashion, the whole misadventure feels cursed at this point. A search of these premises is impossible anyway. I share my thoughts with Scott.

"I'd rather dumpster dive all the trash on Jekyll than plough through this mess. What do you want to do?"

"Not as hard as it might appear. Most of what you see hasn't been disturbed in years. Let me peruse the lived-in areas. Shouldn't take long. You just poke around and try not to knock anything over. And watch out for that damn marlin."

Even wearing gloves, I have little desire to touch anything under this roof and put my hands far down in my pockets to fight any urge that would move me otherwise. Scott wiggles through a small crevice like a well-trained cave spelunker and disappears into the back of the single-wide. I wander into the kitchen afraid of what might live there. A mutant roach the size of a small mouse crosses in front of me with little regard for my superior physical presence. I give him a wide berth. One glance at the stove—crusted with an oily, filthy grime—convinces me that Rickie eats out most nights. Trash collects in a corner, as does a foul, vinegar-like odor. I might gag.

The Governor doesn't pay me enough money to open the ancient refrigerator, so I let it be. If Savage hid any bloody clothes in there, congrats to him. He outwitted the murder squad.

Off the kitchen sits a dilapidated washer and dryer. The appearance suggests disuse, but duty compels me to at least peek inside. Maybe Savage tried to wash the blood out. I open the doors to both machines, but no spin cycles have run around these parts in eons.

A movement to my right catches my attention, and I damn near jump out of my shoes upon seeing a racoon scurry outside through a hole in the kitchen floor. Coastal Georgia is home to its own special species of racoons, and I just got a taste. When my nerves are about settled from that surprise encounter, I startle again when Scott disturbs the nocturnal quiet with a whistle followed by a yell.

"Come back here."

"Do I have to?"

"Yes."

I worm my way through the traffic jam, pass what may be a bathroom, and find Scott at the far end of the trailer. Call it Savage's sleeping quarters for want of a better description. The twin mattress on the floor gives it away. The rest of the room is stuffed to the gills much like everywhere else, including a 1950s-style juke box that doubles as a table for the mountain of clothes packed on top of it.

Scott stands next to a camouflaged foot locker. The top is open for my inspection. At the bottom are three trays of drugs—one devoted to weed, another for opioids, the last for heroin. Scott quips, "For when the fish aren't biting, I guess."

"Wonder that he fishes at all."

"What do you want to do?"

"Ask Dave to get a search warrant tomorrow and have some of his officers search the place. They'll find what needs to be found. We'll pretend to be surprised when they find it."

He agrees and starts repacking the foot locker. I ask silent forgiveness from the poor souls that will carry out this sad assignment. I slither back up to the front—my eyes peeled for any and all strange creatures of the night. The thought of taking a cleansing shower at the hotel fills me with anticipation. Back outside, Scott works on relocking the door, and I gladly take a deep breath of the paper mill-infested air.

Readjusting my eyes to the dark, I spot an elderly African-American gentleman standing ten feet away with a shotgun laying across his chest.

**

"Are you the po-lice?"

I answer, "Close enough. What's your name?"

"Otis Harper. You look like po-lice."

"Nice to meet you, Otis. I ask that you make no sudden movements and keep that shotgun pointed away from us."

Scott stands beside me—his pistol already in hand and held behind his back out of sight. Otis laughs, which would be disconcerting if not for the friendliness of the chuckle and his grandfatherly demeanor.

"A black man in south Georgia doesn't live to eighty-four years of age by going around pointing shotguns at the po-lice. Where's Rickie?"

"Friend of yours?"

"Hell naw. He's a racist piece of ... piece of scum. But he is my neighbor, and neighbors should look after each other. Wanted to make sure nobody was stealing from him. Is he in trouble?"

"A little. Maybe a lot. Do you happen to know what time he got home last night?"

"11:59 p.m."

The answer throws me for a loop, and I pause to contemplate it, trying not to rush the conversation just so that I can jump in that shower. The moonlight illuminates Otis Harper's figure and the shotgun but not much else—making it hard to get a read on him. I answer.

"That is oddly specific."

"Every midnight I watch *Perry Mason* on the TV. You can set your watch by it. Rickie got home right before the theme music started playing. A little later than normal. Usually he gets home around 11:30 p.m., right when *Mr. Ed* begins."

I consumed *Perry Mason* reruns like candy while growing up and dreamed of one day forcing a confession on the stand from a witness powerless in the face of my withering verbal assault. That day eventually came. But the long-sought dream turned into a nightmare, like a dog who chases cars and finally catches up with one.

"Perry Mason? I love him. Which episode was on last night?"

"'The Case of the Moth-Eaten Mink.'"

"Who's the murderer in that one?"

"Sgt. Jaffrey. A bad cop murdering another cop. Better than a bad cop murdering an innocent black man. Mind if I head on home now? I'm missing *Mr. Ed*."

"My favorite talking horse. Thank you, Otis. You've been more helpful than you know."

He shuffles back to the neat single-wide next door and slowly takes the steps to the front door one at a time. Sgt. Jaffrey was the culprit in the "Case of the Moth-Eaten Mink," which is one of the best *Perry Mason* episodes of them all—at least in my opinion as a connoisseur. The more immediate point is that every word Otis spoke rings the bell of truthfulness. I turn to Scott.

"You don't see that every day."

"What?"

"An honest man."

25

The Ring camera on Donovan Kessler's front door caught him and Meredith arguing at 10:56 p.m. last evening. The trick now is to figure out whether Rickie Savage had a window of time to commit the murder after that point and make it back to his place a minute before midnight. And that requires a test drive. I turn on the SUV's sirens to do a Speed Racer impression to determine how quickly one could travel from Point A to Point B. That this endeavor accelerates the moment I can hop into the shower is only a happy byproduct.

Scott starts the clock. The path out of the trailer park has potholes big enough to swallow the SUV and is not the place to try and set any land speed records. But once we reach smoother ground, the pedal hits the floorboard. After making sure that no oncoming traffic is approaching, I even run all the red lights—reasoning that a fleeing murderer eager to get home might do the same. Scott remains quiet. He tries to reach J.D. again but strikes out for the third time. The part of my brain adept at constructing worst case scenarios begins to grind into gear.

The only thing to slow me down is the toll plaza on the causeway to get onto Jekyll, a hindrance that one does not experience leaving the island. The state patrol station now housing Rickie Savage for the night is adjacent to this area, and I mentally send negative energy his way for his role in making a bad day much worse.

Once on Jekyll, I lower the speed considerably, and we pull up to Donovan Kessler's house in short order. Scott checks the time. Thirty-six minutes and nineteen seconds driveway to driveway.

He says, "Enough time. Barely. But factor in the following—you still have to account for however long Savage took to walk to the beach, murder Kessler, and walk back. Kessler didn't go outside right at 10:56, either. Add at least a few minutes there. Doubtful Savage ran the red lights like you did. Doubtful that he would drive that fast and risk attracting the attention of the cops. Probable that he also would've stopped on the way to do something about the theorized bloody clothes. Doesn't leave a lot of time. Tight. Real tight."

"But possible."

"Only if Kessler headed to the beach pretty soon after the Ring video. If he stayed in the house for any appreciable amount of time, all bets are off. Let me see your phone again."

I hand it over and make the short drive back to the hotel. Scott swipes at my cell. I ask, "What are you looking for?"

"Want to see if Kessler was wearing the same clothes when he was arguing with Meredith as when he was dead on the beach."

Good thought. I find a parking spot and wait for the verdict. Scott tosses my phone back to me.

"Same shirt. Same pants. He removed a sweater he must have worn for the party, put on that UGA letterman's jacket instead. Couldn't see his footwear on the Ring video, but he's wearing old shoes on the beach. Almost certain he switched those out. Not a full-bore outfit change, likely took a minute or two."

"Meaning Rickie is still in it?"

"Rickie is still in it."

* * *

As we exit the SUV on road-weary legs, I ask a question that is starting to occupy a greater percentage of my mind.

"When do we start worrying about J.D.?"

"He's probably asleep in the room, which is where we should be. It's been too long of a day."

Fine by me. If he's not worried, I'll try not to assume the worst. As we head toward the hotel, Scott stops and peers over toward a collection of shops and restaurants, all of which must be long closed by now. He starts walking that way without any explanation. I hesitate but eventually hurry to catch up. Maybe he'll need back up. When I reach him, he gestures with his head and says, "There goes J.D. right now."

A street light gives me enough illumination to confirm the identification. The person with him is another matter—young, blond, and leggy. Scott mumbles, "Somebody isn't tired."

"I thought he was seeing that musician."

"They broke up."

J.D. and his mystery date head toward a parking space in front of the stores. I see the aqua Corolla in the distance and wonder whether that will be a deal breaker with her. Scott continues in their direction, picking up his pace. I call out after him.

"Are we really going to accost him?"

"Might be fun."

The closer we get to the couple, the more obviously gorgeous the young woman becomes. Figures. While I was constructing terrible scenarios in my head, J.D. was keeping time with Miss Georgia. A good gig if you can get it. The boss side of me grumbles internally that this is a work trip, not a vacation. The human side reminds me that I was once young, too.

Scott walks up to J.D. and his new friend, as if it is the most normal thing in the world to cross their path on the dark side of midnight. I straggle behind but soon reach the three of them. J.D.'s face lights up when he sees us, and he speaks in an excited voice.

"Guys, glad you are here. I tried reaching you, but my cell didn't have service. Anyway, I have news. Meet Cecilia Franklin. She's a waitress at the Shore of Shadows—that English pub on the other side of the parking lot."

Introductions are made all around. The woman is polite enough but not exactly enthused at meeting two middle-aged men at this late hour. I don't blame her. Truth be told, not much enthusiasm exists for meeting her on my end. I should be back in my hotel room by now. J.D. continues.

"Cecilia just finished a long shift and is starving. We're going to grab a bite to eat, and she's going to tell me again in one sitting how Maxwell Matheny spent his time at the pub last night. Based on what's she told me so far, you need to hear it. Want to come with us?"

Framed that way, the offer is an impossible one to refuse.

26

We all climb into the Expedition. Jekyll Island is not a late-night kind of place, which means another trip across the causeway. Once again, we come within spitting range of Rickie Savage's jail cell. But this time I cannot even blame him for keeping me from my sleep. That honor belongs to Maxwell, who is probably snoring away in Raymond's house at the moment.

Once we reach the mainland, I pull into a Waffle House next to the interstate that offers 24-hour service. The four of us cram into a tight booth—Scott and me sharing a side that is one size too small for the both of us. A couple of truckers sit at the counter, but otherwise the place is empty. Cecilia orders hashbrowns scattered and smothered but not covered. J.D. opts for the namesake waffles. Figuring that the witness will be more comfortable if all of us dine along with her, I go with scrambled eggs and raisin toast, although part of my stomach rebels against the prospect of eating so soon after emerging from Savage's trailer. Scott orders a steak without a second thought.

Since this is J.D.'s party, I wait for him to start the fun. While Cecilia sucks on a straw that leads to a glass of sweet tea, he begins.

"Picked up Maxwell's tracks last night at the state bar cocktail mixer. He had a few drinks, socialized with other lawyers, ho-hum stuff. After that, I fanned out to all the other places he might've gone to do more drinking. Got his picture from his law firm website and started showing it around. Came up empty at the first couple of places but got a hit when I went to the Shore of Shadows, where Cecilia works. He came into the Shadows around ten and sat in her section. She can pick up the story from there."

His full-of-encouragement grin aims to put her at ease but doesn't quite accomplish the mission. She gives a tentative, half-smile in response. In the bright light of the Waffle House, her youth is on full display. Working in a pub, she must be at least twenty-one, but one wouldn't blink twice at seeing her at UGA freshmen orientation in the fall. Turning her head from J.D. to face Scott and me, she takes a deep breath that puffs out both of her cheeks.

"Yeah, Max—he told me to call him that—came in around ten. He ordered a Bloody Mary right off and said that we would be great friends. I smiled, of course, but took an instant dislike to him. He stayed in that seat all the way to closing time. Kept ordering drinks and bragging about being an important lawyer. I played along because that's the job. What I didn't like was him groping my ass and rubbing the side of my breast. I'm used to the customers getting a little handsy, especially after a few drinks. Most don't mean anything by it and keep it within tolerable bounds. Usually means a bigger tip, too, so I live with it. But Max became more aggressive as the night went on, even trying to feel up my muff. I slapped him and told him another move like that and he'd hit the pavement with his ear. Charley—the bartender—would do it, too. Max pouted a little but then started asking about taking me home. Promised to show me a good time and even throw some money my way if that's what I wanted. What a joke. He turned out to be a cheap-ass tipper on top of everything else. I was happy to see the clock strike midnight."

The sharp dichotomy between her world-wearied words and fresh-as-snow face reminds me that I sometimes don't like humans all that much. That she describes sexual assault, even the low-grade variety ubiquitous in most bars, as "*tolerable*" only worsens my mood. Sadie Foxx made a business decision to lean into the lechery of older men, but I hope that Cecilia chooses a different path for herself—that she actually chooses herself. J.D. says, "There's more."

"Yeah, never had a customer hang around in the parking lot after we close before. Until last night. Once everybody is out of the Shadows, all of the employees help tidy up some so that the lunch shift doesn't get to work and find a tornado. Last night, Charley and I were the only two still there when I left him. Charley always stays behind to lock up.

In other places, I would normally have a man walk me to my car that late. But not here. I mean, it's Jekyll Island. Safest spot on earth."

She pauses—the first signs of difficulty start to crowd around the bridge of her nose, the unnatural lines spoiling some of her vibrant youth. The waitress brings the food to break the spell of the tense silence. Cecilia digs into the hashbrowns with vital concentration. The men pick up their forks. I play around with the scrambled eggs and put them into my mouth with the same energy as a man on death row walking to his execution. The memory of Rickie Savage's nauseating kitchen is too fresh to enjoy the food. I attempt to drive that revulsion from my mind and succeed only in dwelling more on that very thing, like trying not to think about a pink elephant. I set my plate to the side.

Cecilia devours the hashbrowns with greedy speed, almost licking the plate when finished. I offer her my raisin toast and watch it soon disappear. The waitress refills her sweet tea, and Cecilia chases the carbs with gulps of sugar—the kind of feat that only a young person can successfully pull off.

With the food finished and the plates cleared, the time for the rest of the story arrives. Cecilia frowns but presses on through.

"When I walked out to the parking lot, he was out there waiting with a sick look on his face. Smirking, drunk. He asked, 'Miss me?' I ignored him and hurried to my car. I tried to open my door, but he slammed it shut with the heaviness of his body, wedging me between him and the car. He started putting his hands all over me. On my breasts. Up my skirt. Forced his mouth on my mouth. His breath smelled terrible. I tried to scream but nothing came out. When I squirmed away, he grabbed my arm and jerked me back to him. I have a bruise."

She lifts up a sleeve to reveal her blackened arm near the shoulder. A horrified J.D. says, "You didn't show me that."

"Didn't have time. Too busy serving drinks."

I ask, "Can we take a picture?"

Cecilia tentatively nods, and I instruct J.D. to capture the injury from a couple of different angles, hopefully for later use in court. She completes the story.

"He kept at it. I started crying and thought I would be raped right there in the parking lot, but Charley pulled Max off me and shoved him to the ground. Max began calling me vile names and making threats about what he was going to do to us. That we didn't know who we were dealing with. Charley could've killed him, but I stood between the two of them to keep that from happening. Working people can't go around attacking lawyers and get away with it. Max staggered to his car and drove away. Is he really that important?"

The question is directed to me. I answer, "Not so important that you need to worry about him. Being a lawyer ain't what it used to be. But he sexually assaulted you and needs to be held accountable. Would you be willing to testify against him? Would Charley?"

A couple of tears run down her cheeks. She rushes to the restroom, and the three of us watch her with growing protectiveness. I ask, "Has Maxwell taken the lead over Rickie in the race for people we don't like?"

Scott says, "They're running neck and neck."

Charging Maxwell with sexual assault is the starter course. Can we hook him for murder, too? The timing of Cecilia's story fits. The Shore of Shadows closes at midnight, she cleans up the bar a little, Maxwell attacks her in the parking lot, and he arrives—drunk, angry, his bloodlust unfulfilled—at Donovan Kessler's front door at 12:39 a.m. according to the Ring video. Eager to lash out at anyone to feel better about himself, he stumbles across Kessler heading to the beach and kills him.

As a theory, I like how the pieces fit. The timing would mean that Kessler went for his beach walk a lot later than what we assumed, but that quibble is hardly fatal to the hypothesis. While I keep playing with various scenarios in my head, Cecilia returns and stands next to the booth. Any sign of tears is gone, replaced instead with eyes blazing with fire.

"I'll testify against that bastard."

27

The alarm on my phone beeps on a regular loop and keeps on beeping until the wall of resistance that is my consciousness finally crumbles. Long ago, I decided never to hit the snooze button. The risks of perpetual punching said button are too great. A corollary to this practice requires placing all alarms out of arm's reach, which means my cell phone now taunts me from a table across the room. I blunder toward the noise and finally make it stop. I check the time and do the math in my head. Four hours of sleep. Some vacation.

Cate is gone. She mentioned the night before last about possibly doing sunrise yoga on the beach together on Saturday morning. I laughed at her. She stuck her tongue out at me. But now the thought of stretching on the sand next to my wife sounds positively glorious compared to the day I have planned. The fun starts with a shower—my second one in the last five hours. Cold water works even better than coffee as a stimulant, and I need octane whatever the source. I prepare myself psychologically for impact and jump in for as long as I can endure it.

The freezing jolt does the trick. A new mental acuity snaps into place, even as I shiver to raise my body temperature. Opening the bathroom door to go and put my clothes on, I feel like a new man. My wife greets me bearing a gift.

The Starbucks coffee that she holds in her hands is almost as alluring as her figure in yoga pants. Almost. But I only have time for the coffee. She hands me a Pike Place Venti with a smile on her face, better than any barista. I give her an appreciative kiss and pat her bottom.

She says, "Looking better this morning. Thought you might end up pulling an all-nighter."

"Came close. We made two separate trips to Brunswick after I saw you. Today figures to be more of the same, running in all directions hoping some miracle drops out of the sky to solve this thing. Scott's not hopeful that we'll ever crack the case."

"Any suspects?"

"Too many—that's part of the problem."

"No one else pulled a knife on you, did they?"

"Thankfully, no. Although one gentleman did approach us with a shotgun slung across his chest."

"Chance!"

"Don't worry. That guy was the salt of the earth."

Cate doesn't seem so sure. She gives me another admonition to be careful as I walk out the door.

***

Captain Dave is alert and wide awake when we meet in the main hall of the state bar conference. Today he doesn't even bother to notice the informality of my polo shirt and jeans, much less the sneakers. When I explain my desire that the state patrol obtain a search warrant and then search Rickie Savage's place, he promises, with a big smile on his face, to lead the expedition himself. His excitement for the assignment is an extra twist of the knife in my guts. I know what's on the other side of that rainbow, and it isn't gold. He walks away exuding purpose in each stride with Chad Morelli joined at his hip. Searching Savage's single-wide can only add to Morelli's ever-growing ledger of new and unique experiences.

J.D. could use some of Captain Dave's energy. He should've had at least four hours of sleep like me but looks like a man who might not have gone to bed at all. When I ask him about it, he launches into a complaint.

"Have you ever stayed in the same room with Scott? He snores like a Yeti. I couldn't sleep because it was so loud. Can I get my own room tonight? Please. I'll pay for it out of my salary."

"You guys got the last room in the hotel."

"Maybe I'll just sleep in the car."

Having once shared a room with Scott, I feel J.D.'s pain. His bad luck continues when I explain the need to search all the public trash bins between here and Rickie Savage's home for bloody clothes. By the blank stare on his face, I question whether he even comprehends what I am saying. But J.D. understands well enough.

"That's impossible."

"Not impossible. Highly labor-intensive with little prospect of success, yes. But not impossible."

"What if he threw them in the water somewhere?"

"Scuba divers are the next phase."

He doesn't know if I'm kidding or not. Me, either. But I don't have to guess at his true feelings. The irritated expression says plenty—first Scott's snoring, now another futile search for trash. Like a good and compassionate leader, I try to cheer him up.

"Look, you don't have to do the search yourself. Hire more off-duty cops. Get whatever help you need and delegate the responsibility."

"Should I start pulling bodies from Florida? We've already engaged most of the police in the area."

"Keep it in Georgia for now."

That's just good politics. If I'm going to spread the Governor's money around everywhere, I can at least make sure that it goes into the pockets of his constituents. Also figures to be good for the murder squad's reputation in the area. J.D., though, appears dubious. He slouches away in near dread at the task now on his plate.

Scott shows up—still a little gimpy in the knee. He sees J.D.'s sad walk from afar and asks, "What's eating him?"

"Apparently he couldn't get any sleep because of the hideous racket coming out of your nostrils."

"You got the wrong guy. I don't snore."

***

Scott and I spend the next couple of hours interviewing all the past state bar presidents about the party at Donovan Kessler's house shortly before the murder. We break up into two rooms to speed the process along and promise to fetch the other one if we learn something important. I start with Burt and Lois. Her company again proves delightful, his not so much. But together they don't add anything meaningful to my understanding of the facts. The rest of the interviews provide the same boring description of a garden-variety dinner party filled with a lot of drinking and the telling of old war stories.

The only divergence from this monotony comes from former state bar president Bill Barwick—who narrates for my benefit an X-rated tale about a past state bar conference involving a drunk elephant that somehow ended up in the hotel pool. That momentous event in Georgia legal history happened in Florida, which strikes me as fitting.

When finished with my group, the urge to hop back into a freezing shower for another round of instant energy runs strong. If I were better at multitasking, I could've napped while doing the questioning. Maybe Scott is having better luck. I grab a Coke from a beverage table out in the conference hall and wait. Ten minutes later, he emerges from his makeshift interrogation room looking much like I feel. He doesn't hesitate to let me know how things went.

"Lawyers! That's two hours of my life I'll never get back. What about you? Anything?"

I tell him the uncensored version about the elephant in the pool, which at least earns a chuckle. He asks, "What now? Rickie Savage or Maxwell Matheny?"

"None of the above. No Rickie until we hear the results from Dave Ketchum about the search of Savage's premises. I would like to have some extra leverage with which to smack Rickie upside the head and have a strong premonition that the state patrol will fulfill that order. We also need to nail down the time of death first. If Kessler was still alive at eleven-thirty, Savage isn't our guy. Same thing holds true for Matheny on the other end. If the autopsy shows that Kessler died before twelve-thirty, Maxwell is in the clear for the murder."

"Yeah, I know. He was too busy trying to rape Cecilia. That's one hell of an alibi."

"With our luck, the time of death will be between eleven-thirty and twelve-thirty and absolve both of them."

"That happens and you're on your own. I'm walking back to Atlanta."

Not on that knee he isn't.

28

A person needs a scorecard to keep track of all the law enforcement fiefdoms in this area. Brunswick—located in Glynn County—has its own city police force. Glynn County, like every county in Georgia, has its own Sheriff's Department. But Glynn also has its own County Police Department, a perplexing duplication that only exists in five of Georgia's 159 counties. Like Brunswick, Jekyll Island is in Glynn County. But because Jekyll is owned by the state, jurisdiction on the island is the province of the Georgia State Patrol. Not to be left out, the GBI has its own regional investigative office in Kingsland, forty-five minutes to the south. Except the GBI's coastal lab is in Pooler, which is one hour north. The cherry on top is that the headquarters of the Federal Law Enforcement Training Centers is located in Glynco, a part of Glynn County on the northwest edge of Brunswick.

And despite all these options, the Atlanta murder squad somehow ends up with the Donovan Kessler case. The checkbooks of millions of taxpayers weep at the waste. The bright side is that J.D. has a ready supply of cops in the area to assign trash duty.

The immediate puzzle that Scott and I must solve is which of these agencies has possession of our dead body. Scott takes charge of the search while I drive. By the time the SUV reaches the end of the causeway, I have to pull to the side of the road because we still don't have an answer and need one so I can know whether to turn right or left. After five more minutes, Scott solves the mystery.

"Best I can tell, the medical examiner for Glynn County performed the autopsy."

"Where?"

"In the county elections office."

He's not kidding, and I stare at him like he is an alien. Once the GPS tells me which way to go, I make a right turn and head to Brunswick. The drive is short, and five minutes later we pull into the parking lot of the most nondescript building imaginable—a colorless stone, rectangular hunk of nothingness. A morgue has more personality.

The front door, the only entrance visible to the eye, is locked. Not surprising for a government building on the weekend but a huge problem under the circumstances. I ask, "Weren't they expecting us?"

"Yeah."

"You could try your keys. Worked on Savage's place."

The suggestion isn't taken kindly. He makes a call and talks to somebody. The weather is much warmer than yesterday, and with the heat comes the humidity. Scott already looks uncomfortable in his standard suit and tie—another item to put on his list of grievances since arriving in the area. The islands of Georgia are called the Golden Isles, but given his last twenty-four hours, I don't think he will be returning in the near future for a vacation. A scruffy-looking kid of about fifteen wearing a Metallica t-shirt unlocks the door and waves us in.

"Hey, I'm Tripp. My dad is the medical examiner. I'll take you to him."

Good thing we have a guide. The byzantine maze of offices could double as an obstacle course—the type of nonsensical design that could only ever come from the mind of the government. When we at last reach our destination, I kick myself for not leaving a trail of bread crumbs to lead me back to sunlight.

Like most autopsy rooms, coldness permeates the air. The chill attacks my exposed arms, and goose bumps rise up in bodily defense. A brown-haired man, graying at the temples, stands before a steel table that holds Donovan Kessler's ghost-like body. When the man looks up from his work, his plastic frame glasses slide to the perch of his nose. He pushes them back into place and introduces himself.

"Dr. Abe Ridgeway. Nice to meet you."

We return the favor of the introductions, but no handshakes are exchanged. The debris of Kessler's organs on the doctor's plastic gloves is a healthy deterrent to completing that ritual. Ridgeway continues.

"Being the medical examiner is only a side passion of mine. My main practice is family medicine, which means I end up doing most of my autopsies on the weekend. I got two other bodies on back order that I have to complete today. But they told me yours had priority so I moved it to the front of the line. Almost done. You met Tripp. He tends to hang around and has taken a deep interest in my work. What father could ask for more?"

Tripp offers a single nod to confirm the accuracy of his dad's account. Despite the t-shirt, the cold doesn't appear to bother him at all. Although I used to crawl the corridors of the State Capitol while my father attended to political business, hanging around at a young age to watch dad cut up dead bodies strikes me as a whole different level of Take Your Kid to Work Day. The future trajectory of that path for Tripp is ending up either as a surgeon or a serial killer. Flip a coin.

Ridgeway says, "What do you want to know first? Time of death, I bet. Do you want the whys and the hows or just the bottom line? You look busy, so I'll cut to the chase. Bottom line is this—the deceased met his end anywhere between eleven at night and one in the morning. Given the condition of the corpse, that's the best range I can give you. Based on the lividity of the body, he wasn't moved if you are wondering about that. He died on that spot. Questions?"

The speed with which he talks makes me pay attention if I want to catch it all. I manage to keep up and digest the information. The doctor's timeframe for the murder keeps both Rickie Savage and Maxwell Matheny in the conversation, which suits me fine enough because I personally want to put the screws to the both of them. The information also spares Scott from a long walk home. He asks, "Cause of death?"

"The blows to the head—definitely the blows. Indeed, the killer was thorough. Used more strikes than necessary to get the job done. Had the deceased somehow survived the brick attack, the cold and possibly drowning would've got him anyway, but he died soon after the blunt trauma to the head. Good thing for him, too. Staying out there all night in his condition with the temperature dropping and the water rising would've been torture. Better to go quick. Fortunate thing."

Looking at Kessler's dead body stretched out a few feet in front of me, not sure I would go so far as to count him as being lucky. Scott studies the smashed head at close range. With the blood and brain matter cleared away, the dents in the cranium are more noticeable. The room's harsh light heightens the general ghastliness of staring at something so unnatural.

Ridgeway sees thoroughness in the murderer's repeated blows to the deceased—the good sense to make sure that the deed is done.

I see something else. Rage.

29

We only get lost once on the way back from the autopsy room to the SUV. I chalk that up as a win. In the parking lot, my cell rings. Captain Dave.

"Have you ever seen that TV show *Hoarders*? That's what we have out here. Never seen anything like it. Junk, trash, everything piled sky high to the ceiling. I thought those shows were fake, staged or something. I guess not. Gonna take a while for us to go through everything, but we'll get it done. Another funny thing—a neighbor said two FBI guys were out here last night scoping the place. Know anything about that?"

"FBI? That's interesting. Thanks for the information. I'll check it out. Let me know if you need anything."

Scott hates the FBI more than he hates lawyers. Both groups fall under the general heading of often wrong, never in doubt. When I end the call, he snaps, "Don't tell me the feds are in this business now. I can't stand those guys."

"Big development. Apparently, a neighbor reported to Dave that two FBI agents were hanging around Rickie Savage's home last night."

"Otis Harper thought we were feds?"

"When he asked me if we were the police, I told him '*close enough*.' Guess his mind made the jump from there."

"As if."

While Scott works out whether it is funny or an insult that we were mistaken for FBI agents, I come up with the idea to talk with the lead detective investigating the murder of Becky Savage. Except I have no idea who that person is, although I'm fairly certain the case would belong to the Brunswick Police Department. Scott works to find the answer while I search for some lunch, landing on Chick-Fil-A once

I spy the red sign in the distance. When lost in a strange land, experiencing the comforts of home can ease some of the terror of the unknown. We order, and Scott makes calls.

"Lead investigator is named Leslie Hamrick. She's off today. I left her a message."

While we eat in the car, I use the time to do a Google search about Becky Savage's killing. According to press reports, she was coming off her Thursday night shift as a waitress at Briscoe's Seafood when someone put a gun to her temple and fired. Becky died on the spot in the parking lot, right next to her car, at the age of twenty-three. The internet is scant on any other details, which likely reflects police efforts to keep information about the case close to the vest.

With lunch finished, I drive to Briscoe's Seafood for want of anything else to do while giving Leslie Hamrick a chance to call us back. The restaurant has some renown locally, topping many lists as having the best seafood in the area.

Amber and I once ate there around a decade ago. I recall that the food was excellent but not much more than that—no moments, no images in my mind. Everything else about the evening has faded away, like a lot of my time with Amber and Cale. With each passing year, I lose a little bit more of them, a realization that sometimes produces an indescribable feeling in me. Not guilt. The happiness that Cate has brought into my life is a story of redemption, not remorse. More like some weird version of imposter syndrome—that the person living my life now is not really me. The real guy remains stuck somewhere back in the past.

These thoughts dissipate once I pull into Briscoe's parking lot and scan the terrain with an investigative eye. Not a lot of detective skills are necessary on the front end. A small cross in the back of the lot, near the dumpsters, sticks out of the ground next to an empty parking space. An orange cone blocks off the space, and messages of love dot the landscape around the cross. Unless this parking lot is one of the most dangerous places on earth, the spot where the murder occurred is right before my eyes.

The weekend lunch crowd is out in full force, and I park as close to the parking space with the cone as possible. We exit the vehicle and take in the scenery. The cross bears Becky Savage's name all right. Seems strange for all this fanfare to still be up a year later, but maybe she was a popular girl. Scott pulls himself up to peek inside the dumpster, one of the few in the area not within the parameters of J.D.'s search for trash. The thought is an interesting one. Assume the perpetrator murdered Becky and Kessler. Would that person really come back here to dispose of the bloody clothes? That's serial killer pathology right there. Scott jumps down off the dumpster.

"Anything?"

"Bunch of garbage bags. Can't see the bottom."

"Should J.D. add it to his list?"

"When you're searching for a needle in a haystack, you should probably check out all the haystacks."

I text J.D. the good news.

A dirt pathway starts ten feet from where the murder happened. Scott and I follow the trail and travel twenty yards through a dense thicket of trees. The footpath dead ends at a parking lot for a long-abandoned establishment, one of those old daycares with the red pyramid on top. The spot is hidden from the nearest road—hidden from most everything, unless ghosts lurk about in the abandoned building. The perfect place to stash a getaway car.

Scott asks, "Do I need to draw you a picture?"

"No, I can put two and two together."

We walk back to Briscoe's on the path. When we reach the other side, a stout older man—his skin rawhide from a lifetime on the coast—stands in the parking space with the orange cone. He asks, "Can I help you gentlemen with anything?"

"My name is Chance Meridian. We're investigating Becky Savage's murder. Did you know her?"

"You're Lieutenant Governor Meridian's boy—the spitting image of him, in fact. He and your momma used to eat here all the time when they were in town. I'm Barry Briscoe, the owner of the restaurant. Hated to hear about your dad passing away. How's your momma doing?"

"Same as ever. Fairly indestructible."

A healthy laugh jostles his oversized belly, like a jolly Santa Claus. He responds, "That she is. Always orders the catfish. She might've eaten here a hundred times and nothing but the catfish. Can't blame her. Best catfish in the state. Why are you investigating Becky? Have something to do with Donovan Kessler getting killed? Saw the news in the paper and immediately thought about Becky."

"You hit the nail on the head."

The lightheartedness in him seeps away, replaced by melancholy. Barry stares at the cross memorial and shakes his head. Instead of the earlier laughter, he emits a mournful sigh.

"Just came upon the year anniversary a couple of weeks back. Some employees put up that cross to commemorate the occasion. I keep a cone in this spot where her car was parked that night. Doesn't seem right to let anyone else park there. She was right at her car door, keys in hand, when it happened. Most senseless thing I ever saw."

Scott's phone rings, and he walks away to take the call. I stay focused on Barry and ask a follow-up question.

"Any theories on who did it?"

"No one could've ever had any reason to kill Becky personally. She was the sweetest kid you'd ever want to meet. She had to be a random victim of some depraved mind, killing for the sake of killing. A gang initiation thing is my guess. I never bought the Donovan Kessler idea. Her daddy kept trying to get me on board with that notion, but the idea doesn't appeal to me."

"You know Rickie?"

"Sure thing. Knew him through Becky. He sells me fish from time to time."

"When is the last time you saw him?"

"Yesterday morning. Around seven. He had a bunch of fish for me in a cooler."

I study the dumpster with renewed interest. If Rickie didn't dump the bloody clothes on the way home after killing Kessler—and he probably didn't given the tight time window—he would've made damn sure to get rid of them first thing the next morning. Scott ends his call and rejoins Barry and me.

"That was Leslie Hamrick. She's at home now and has invited us over to talk about the case."

"She's going to have to wait a spell."

30

J.D. slams the door to the Corolla and walks over. He whines to me, "More trash?"

"You mean growing up in Dunwoody you didn't dream of being the garbage king of the Georgia coast?"

The petulance covering his face suggests the answer is no. At least he brought friends. A couple of off-duty sheriff's deputies, dressed in their absolute worst clothes, exit a monster truck. I give them their instructions, and they make quick work transferring the trash bags in the dumpster to the bed of their jacked-up ride.

Their uncomplaining willingness to do the task makes me wonder how much J.D. agreed to pay them. When the Governor gets the bill, I hope his enthusiasm for pushing the murder squad to set up camp in south Georgia wanes considerably.

Barry Briscoe oversees the unloading of his dumpster with growing uneasiness. He motions me to the side and whispers, "I know what you're getting at. You think Rickie had something to do with Kessler getting bumped and are searching for evidence since he was here yesterday. I know you probably don't go much in for character references, but he's not a murderer. Yes, he's had a rough patch—a real rough patch. That doesn't mean he would snap and kill a man. Just can't see that."

The friend to my parents is a hard man not to like, and I hate to burst his bubble about Savage. People rarely believe the worst of those around them, and that bias makes all of us poor evaluators of the awful things friends and family might do under the right mix of conditions. But a man like Barry deserves to know the truth.

"Rickie Savage pulled a knife on me yesterday. He attacked Detective Moore's knee with a steel-toed shoe, and he took a bite out of

Lieutenant Hendrix's neck, all while trying to run away from us as fast as he could. I'm not saying he killed Donovan Kessler. Maybe he did, maybe he didn't. But the man is capable of deadly violence and acted guilty as hell about something."

He digests the news in silence and chews on it for a good minute. With a sad shake of the head, he turns towards the direction of the restaurant that bears his name.

"I'm going back inside now. Nice to meet you, Chance. Say hello to your momma for me."

Barry departs, and I return my attention to Operation Garbage. The bags of trash emptied from the dumpster take up all the room in the truck. The off-duty deputies use rakes to sift through the remaining debris in the dumpster. Scott and J.D. provide extra pairs of eyes to inspect the potential evidence. After five minutes, all parties concur that no hidden gems are buried in the rubble. The deputies take off to go through the bags one-by-one at a local landfill in Brunswick. We now have two base stations for all the trash we're collecting—one on Jekyll, one on the mainland. I'm beginning to think that might be excessive.

J.D. asks, "What's the next rabbit you want me to pull out of a hat?"

"Two things. First, check the records of the Jekyll toll plaza to determine if any of the people we're interested in left and came back on the island yesterday. Second, go through the Ring videos that the state patrol collected yesterday from the houses near the scene of the murder. See if anything interesting pops up."

"Good, no more trash duty. My computer is in the trunk of the car. I saw a Starbucks near here and will set up shop there."

The Corolla speeds out of the parking lot before I have a chance to change my mind.

***

Leslie Hamrick sits on her front porch in a rocking chair, sipping a lemonade. She's probably pushing sixty and appears much too relaxed for a person who presumably has spent most of her life in law enforcement. The ranch house is clean and modest—the type of place that attracts retirees who want to live close to the water. She tells us to call her "Leslie."

"What do you fellas want to know?"

On the way over, Scott and I decided that he would take the lead in talking to Leslie since they are both cops. He answers, "Who killed Becky Savage?"

"You and me both want to know that, buster. You and me both. I saw you give a talk about how to perform a proper police interrogation at a law enforcement conference in Valdosta about eight years ago. I came away quite impressed. Ring any bells?"

"My first and last trip to Valdosta, except on my way to Florida."

"Can't blame you. Although I met the late Mr. Hamrick there forty-two years ago at the Governor's Honors Program at Valdosta State, so the place holds a special place in my heart."

"Was he a cop?"

"Good gracious, no. A painter—the artistic kind. Too much of a sensitive soul to see the things that we do. Died two years ago of a heart attack at the other end of this porch with a paintbrush in his hand."

"Sorry for your loss."

She waves the condolences away with her left hand—the fourth finger still wearing a diamond ring. My mother still wears her ring, too. I figure the both of them always will. I took another route. After Amber's murder, I stuffed my ring in a box and left it there, eager to suffocate anything that might remind me of what I had lost. The bill for that strategy eventually came due with crushing force. Leslie's method seems healthier. She begins to tell us about the case.

"We don't have a ton of murders in Brunswick. Usually two or three annually. One year we had eight, and gun sales shot up by 200%. Over the course of my career as a whole, I've probably investigated thirty or so killings. And I know less about Becky Savage's death than any of them. The case is a total black hole. Have you been to the scene?"

Scott nods.

"Then you probably know as much as I do. Perp parked on the other side of the trees behind the old day care. Did the kill and made a clean escape. Used a .32 with a suppressor. No signs of a robbery. Her purse was wrapped about her arm in a funny way—could be the perp tried to take it, got thwarted, and decided not to hang around to try again. No physical evidence anywhere about anything that points to anybody. A big bag of nothing. That's all I got."

"Gangs?"

"Not a big problem here. I get what you're saying—an initiation kill, execution-style. Would be a first in this area. No chatter about anything like that, either. A gang killing, multiple people are in the know. Somebody would get loose lips. Rumors would spread—not with the name of the perp necessarily, but some murmurings. But a big fat zero on any of that."

"What about Donovan Kessler?"

Leslie scoffs and takes another drink of her lemonade. I follow her example and raise my glass to enjoy the cold tart sweetness on my lips. By the smell of it, I'm guessing freshly-squeezed. She maneuvers in her chair to get more comfortable before answering.

"Becky's father raised hell about that. We looked into it, of course. Not a lick of any suggestion on that front. Honestly, the idea of a seventy-year old corporate lawyer traipsing about in the dark trees to shoot someone point blank in the head never appealed to me. Start with motive. Why? If Donovan Kessler was that upset about Becky's father injuring his wife, wouldn't the better response be simply to kill the father? And—just among us friends—I'm not entirely sure that Kessler was even that distraught about what happened to his wife. Upset, sure. But he bounced back pretty damn quickly given the situation. I talked to him and came away with the impression that he barely knew Rickie Savage existed. Just not interested. Indifferent people don't go around killing folks."

I think again about her wedding ring. Leslie would figure to have a good feel for the intensity of someone's grief in the wake of a spouse suffering unimaginable calamity. And Kessler's shacking up with Sadie doesn't indicate a lot of concern for his still-alive wife in a care facility. But then again maybe Sadie is evidence that Kessler simply snapped.

That's the view of his brother Raymond, including Raymond's fear that Donovan did kill Becky Savage. Leslie continues.

"You want my theory? That girl was killed by a person who didn't even know her. The victim could've been anyone else in that parking lot around that time. Becky just had the worst luck of her life at exactly the wrong moment. Do not ask for whom the bell tolls. It tolls for thee. Poor girl."

"The hardest cases to crack are the random ones. The perfect murder is killing someone you don't know for no reason whatsoever in a place you have no connection to. Pull the trigger, disappear into the woods, and get away without ever being seen. No murder weapon, no physical evidence, no motive. Impossible to solve."

Two old cops talking about the intricacies of the trade. Unsolved murders are the perpetual nightmare for homicide detectives everywhere—the ones that keep them up when they are trying to sleep. Leslie says, "The fact that you're sitting on my front porch already answers the question, but do you boys really think my murder links up with your murder?"

Scott turns toward me—an invitation to join the cop talk. I drain the rest of my lemonade and hold the perspiring glass up to my eye for further study while I process the question, wondering both whether Rickie Savage is really my guy and if I will ever get enough evidence to prove it one way or the other. All I learn is that the solution to my mystery isn't in that empty glass.

"Depends on what you mean by *'links.'* No question that Rickie Savage is one of our top suspects, and his motive would be his belief that Donovan Kessler murdered Becky. The belief itself is the key. Doesn't really matter whether Kessler pulled the trigger or some nobody. Only that Rickie believed that he did, which is beyond dispute. Rickie told me himself that Kessler was *'the sumabitch that killed my daughter.'* So linked in that sense—yes, if Rickie is the perpetrator. But linked in that the two crimes were committed by the same person—that I don't see, unless you know something about Rickie that I don't."

"Can't help you there. We looked into that, of course. He's rough around the edges but appeared to love his daughter well enough. Checked out all of Becky's other acquaintances, too. Co-workers, customers. She was bisexual. Had some old boyfriends and a current girlfriend but nothing popped on any of them. To a person, everyone thought the world of her. The killing shocked the community."

Leslie stares off her front porch toward her green lawn and pretty flowers. Something comforting exists in a front porch, especially one sprinkled with memories of love. The guess is that sitting near the place where her beloved husband passed away supplies a lot of contentment in times of loneliness. She returns her gaze to us and delivers a final epitaph.

"Damndest case I ever saw. Like the murderer was a ghost."

31

We decide to head back to Jekyll and shake the trees some more on the Kessler family. Before we hit the causeway, my cell rings and Captain Dave's number pops up on the computer screen of the SUV. I can tell right away that he's excited.

"You're not going to believe this, Chance."

"That's a bold statement. I can believe a lot."

Dave laughs—obviously in high spirits, which doesn't strike me as his typical work personality. He says, "Well, whether you believe it or not, what I'm about to tell you is the God's honest truth. We found a stash of drugs in Rickie Savage's bedroom. Some dope, pills, and heroin. Looks like a dealer's stash, too. No one person could consume this much. We're talking drug trafficking. Big time. What should we do now?"

"Drugs, huh? Good work. As for next steps, you should call the GBI. They'll be interested and will want to visit the scene to collect the evidence. Y'all find anything else interesting? Any bloody clothes?"

"No. Just a bunch of personal items packed in the mobile home like a can of sardines. A lot of trash. Those hoarders don't pick up after themselves. The kitchen was nasty."

I pretend to be surprised and offer words of condolences to him and his team for having to navigate all the garbage and clutter. His response astounds me.

"No need to apologize. We don't get to search many houses, and the change of pace has been nice. My guys are really excited about discovering all those drugs. That's the highlight of some of their careers."

"I have more excitement to offer if you're up for it. Can you leave someone there to meet the GBI and come to the Kessler property with one other trooper?"

He doesn't like the idea of leaving Savage's place before the GBI arrives but agrees to the request. After we hang up, Scott asks, "What do you need him on Jekyll for?"

"To squeeze a rat."

***

Debbie Fincher and her lab team occupy Donovan Kessler's house when we arrive. I meet her at the front door, but she waves me off.

"Too busy to chat. It's a big house, you know. We've discovered nothing earthshaking so far. If that changes, I'll let you know."

She retreats back inside before I even have an opportunity to respond. I leave her to it.

Scott and I move toward the beach and find Raymond Kessler tending to flowers in his own backyard. Even while gardening, his attire is formal beyond the norm—seersucker pants and seersucker jacket. The only concession to the weekend is a white polo instead of dress shirt and bowtie, plus a straw hat to keep the sun out of his face. A salmon-colored rose is tucked neatly in the buttonhole of his suit jacket. The heat is bearing down, and I'm hot just looking at him in that outfit. But my mother dresses the same way, covered top to bottom no matter the temperature. Maybe it's an age thing.

Upon seeing me, Raymond points his garden shears my way and complains, "I'm out here because I can't stand being indoors with those people you forced into my home. Their company is intolerable."

"Your family, you mean."

"Don't remind me."

He returns to trimming some rose bushes. A half-filled bucket sits next to his side with all his cuttings. I ask, "They still giving you a hard time about planning the funeral?"

"Not in the slightest. All of them still categorically refuse to discuss any issue related to the death of Donovan, except for plotting how to void the conveyance of the house to Sadie. I remain unsure whether they'll even deign to attend the funeral or not. But that's not my problem with them. The real rub is that they are individually and collectively insufferable. Sammy grew up to be a mean little twit. Katherine, who always smiled as a little girl, somehow became a joyless, judgmental Puritan. Their spouses are even worse. Lucy is always conniving about something. And Maxwell—the less said about him the better. I've never had to spend the night in the same house with all of them until last night. An old man's nerves can only take so much. These people hate each other. I suppose I knew that before yesterday but seeing it up close, under the stress of what happened to Donovan, really crystalized the impression in a way like never before. Makes me convinced that I made the right decision in never having children. Thank God they spend most of their time in Savannah."

The disgust he feels is plain, and some prickly thorns on one of the rose bushes pays for it. His work is methodical and reminds me of my labors on old cars in the garage behind my house. Everyone should have a physical hobby. For thousands of years, humans were an outdoor, blue-collar people. Work and survival went hand in hand. These days, too much sitting, too much wasting away indoors.

I could never go back to being just a prosecutor because being chained to a chair now strikes me as a poor excuse for living. Crazy people may lunge at me with knives these days, but at least I get some exercise. I steal a glimpse of the sun and try to savor some of the Creation.

"How did it go with Judy yesterday?"

"The same as every other day. I talk and pretend that she can hear me, despite all contrary evidence. Honestly think she's getting close to the end now. No discernable responsiveness on any level. But I told her about Donovan. Whether she understood or not …"

He shrugs his shoulders in uncertainty and attacks some more of the roses, cutting off a long-stemmed red one and handing it over to me. Raymond says, "Give this one to that beautiful wife of yours. The Governor did a good thing putting her on the Supreme Court. I liked her opinions when she was on the Court of Appeals. She upheld a $55 million verdict in one of my cases."

"Thank you. She'll love it. But I need to ask you something distasteful that may offend you."

"Son, for nearly fifty years, the nastiest lawyers across the country have been calling me names unfit to print—slurs that would make a skeleton blush. While I may very well exercise my constitutional right not to answer your question, I can assure you that nothing coming out of your mouth will offend me. Ask away."

"Sounds fair. Multiple sources indicate that Lucy may have had some type of romantic entanglement with your brother. Care to comment?"

The shears start to work overtime, like the baton of a maestro conducting a high tempo symphony. Each rapid movement married to a particular purpose. But not a drop of sweat sullies any visible aspect of Raymond, despite the heat and the exertion and his being dressed for court except for the want of a tie. I'd be dripping oceans in similar circumstances. I'm forced to wonder whether he's ever sweated in his life. Surely in the jungles of Vietnam—no man could escape unscathed in that sauna. I let him finish what's he doing, content to give him all the time he needs to compose an answer. At last, he momentarily stops pruning.

"What do you want me to say? That my brother whored around more than I let on to you yesterday. Well, he probably did. I heard rumors. Picked up on little signs. Donovan never flaunted his adultery before me because he knew I didn't approve of such behavior. I'm too much of a traditionalist. He had a wife at home, and Judy deserved better. But I still knew. One doesn't rack up the jury verdicts I have over the years without being a keen observer of how human beings interact with one other. As for Lucy and him, I never caught them *in flagrante delicto* if that's what you are asking. But I have two eyes that always are attuned to the people around me. And I have little regard for the morals of each of them. Your question doesn't surprise me, but I wouldn't swear an answer to it in court—one way or the other."

"So you suspected?"

"I've talked too much already. What about Rickie Savage? You know, the man who actually threatened Donovan. Did you find him?"

"Right on the pier, like you said. He pulled a knife on me and is now cooling off in a jail cell. But we're still not convinced that he killed your brother."

"Sounds pretty convincing to me."

He goes back to trimming his roses. The waste bucket is now almost filled to the brim. Pruning—to make something stronger through destruction. That's a hard process to trust, whether applied to flowers or our own lives. The idea that sacrifice will lead to greater bountifulness—that subtraction can actually lead to addition—is so foreign to our linear, mathematical brains. For us, less is less and more is more. But Jesus fasted in the wilderness for forty days for a reason. When we make ourselves smaller, we create more room for God.

"You going to be okay?"

The question gives him pause. Raymond puts the cutting tool down and uses a handkerchief to wipe away perspiration that isn't there. He finds a nearby garden stool and collapses his weight on it, the ocean and the roses at his back. He cranes his head up at me and sighs.

"Am I going to be okay? If you had asked me that yesterday morning when I was arguing against a motion to dismiss in Jesup, the answer would've been different than the one I'm going to give you now. But then I got the call from Sammy about Donovan. I rushed back here because that's what people do in a time of crisis. They hurry home. To what end? To be close to the ones that they love. What I've learned over the course of the past day is that I am all alone. Donovan was the closest relationship I had left, and now he's gone. Where does that leave me? An old man, without a brother and a law partner. I have my cases but little else. Today, that type of existence doesn't seem to be enough. Except for me it's too late. Chance, you want some advice?"

"Sure."

"Stay close to that pretty wife of yours."

"That's the plan."

Raymond grabs the shears again and stands back up—the creaks of his weary body cracking under the strain. He observes, "I have my flowers at least."

The comment brings forth a fit of dark laughter, followed by coughing. He points the blades toward his brother's backyard.

"Sorry—some gallows humor. Just realized that I've lost half my flowers, too. After Judy's accident, I maintained Donovan's yard for him. He didn't really care, but I thought, 'What the hell?' The movement would do me good anyhow. But I'll be damned if I'm going to be Sadie's gardener."

Another laugh. He trims one last flower, and I notice the perfect symmetry of the roses as a result of his labors. He picks up the waste bucket, turns in the direction of a garden shed at the back of the property, and leaves us with one last lament.

"Loss is the universal condition of life."

32

The last twenty-four hours have not been kind to Katherine Matheny. I figured that last night she would take more sleeping pills than healthy and sleep for two days. Appearances suggests she went the opposite route. Her tired eyes are almost begging for rest. Scott and I find her alone in one of Raymond's bedrooms, drooping in a white wicker chair. *The Brothers Karamazov* rests unopened in her lap. A weathered, yellow bookmark sticks out around page 800 of the novel, near the end.

Upon seeing me, Katherine reacts as if her brain issued a warning that I was a hostile predator. She tries to morph into an angry, aggressive posture, but the effort proves too draining. Her body slumps back, almost resigned to the inevitably of being devoured. Nothing is wrong with her mouth, though. Her lips curl into a sneer, and she snaps, "What do you want?"

"To talk about your diary."

The droopy eyelids inch a hair wider, which is no surprise. Distrust has a way of focusing one's attention. But she doesn't seem inclined to talk about it, so I give her a little push.

"Interesting reading. You were quite angry at your father."

"Wrong. I was praying to save his soul. The prophet Isaiah proclaims, 'Woe to the wicked! It will go badly with him. For what he deserves will be done to him.' I wanted to save Father before it was too late."

"Save him from what?"

"Eternal damnation."

The words are all fire and brimstone, but the voice is a timid whisper. Her body is frailer than yesterday, and she gives off the illusion of vanishing in real time. Hatred can have a Gollum-like physical effect on a person—shriveling up their insides and leaving sunken, sallow skin that is tar-stained with bitterness. The disease has metastasized in Katherine, and the drug companies have yet to invent a pill that can ameliorate that condition.

Loathing always cannibalizes its host.

"Your idea of prayer and mine must be different. Granted, I'm only a Baptist. But when I read in your diary that '*Father and his roadside slut deserve to rot in Hell!*', the first thought to come to mind was not intercessory supplication. Rather, my imagination leapt to something more violent. Do you remember when you wrote that?"

She doesn't answer and shrinks away into her cocoon a little more. Thinking is visibly a chore for her in the moment. Chalk it up to fatigue, the pills, the stress, the weight of self-righteousness. Take your pick. Seeing that she's still not ready to talk, I do the talking for her.

"Two days ago, the same day someone murdered your father, you wrote that he deserved to burn in Hell. Do you see why that would be interesting for me? Why my mind might jump to certain conclusions about your involvement in your father's death?"

More silence. Her eyes refocus—perhaps pushed by some innate, evolutionary realization that such focus is the only chance for self-preservation. Little good that will do her, though. Her need for rest is so strong that I will easily outlast her in any test of stubborn endurance. She'll cave because tired people talk. Carpet bombing suspects with questions all through the night is a universal police tactic for a reason. I throw out another question to remind her of how exhausted she really is.

"Sleep much last night?"

"Hardly at all … I'm … not myself."

"You told me yesterday that you were a good sleeper. What happened?"

"I … don't know. Father's death was quite a shock."

Scott chimes in, "Afraid you might sleepwalk?"

The impact is immediate. That's the first time she has ever heard his voice, and the effect of hearing him—when up to now he has been nothing but a silent beast standing by my side—frightens her.

Panic crouches around her forehead. The fact that both Scott and I are standing while she sits in the wicker chair only adds to the intimidating atmosphere. He keeps up the pressure.

"Tell me everything you remember about the night someone murdered your father."

"Nothing, I swear. I was … reading my book—"

"After that."

"I … I went to bed."

"Did you?"

"Mm-hmm."

"You don't sound so sure."

Katherine doesn't look so sure, either. The sleepwalking angle didn't excite me before now and still doesn't. I gravitate toward solutions that I can understand. And murderers who kill while walking about asleep doesn't fill that order. But her apparent concern at such a simple question suggests some type of guilty mind. Unless the whole response is a work—a charade to give her a legal defense should events go sideways for her. Scott keeps at it.

"Well? Did you go to bed?"

"I … had dreams."

"What kind of dreams?"

"About the book that I'm reading."

On the strong assumption that Scott has not read *The Brothers Karamazov*, I interrupt to fill in a critical gap.

"The book where a father is murdered by one of his own children?"

"That was my dream. Fyodor's being beaten by his son Smerdyakov—or was it Dmitri? The son kept hitting the father with a heavy object. It was terrible. I woke up sweating all over and didn't want to go to sleep last night in case the dream returned. I'm so tired."

Scott looks at me, and I return the favor. Almost as if in a trance, Katherine stares out beyond us and over our heads. The feeling in the room is stilted—eerie, unnatural, dream-like even. A rising headache in my skull, which is acutely authentic, breaks the unreality of the moment. Since the topic is Dostoevsky, I assume that Scott's impulse is to surrender the lead to me. A tilt of his head toward her confirms the premise. I take a deep breath.

"Are you sure that this episode was a dream, Katherine?"

"I think so, although it felt more real than my other dreams."

"Maybe you were sleepwalking again."

That thought grabs her attention. She starts to shake, much like when she learned that her father had deeded the family home to Sadie Foxx. In that moment yesterday, I moved toward her fearful that she might make a play for Sadie's throat. This time, the possibility of violence appears off the menu. A mental breakdown is the better bet.

"Do you think that I don't know what you're implying? You think I killed Father. The mere suggestion is abhorrent!"

"*Father and his roadside slut deserve to rot in Hell!*' Could be you decided to speed things along."

Katherine starts crying—a jagged, gasping for breath, the world-is-ending type sobbing. She pushes her weight down on the chair to lift herself up, except the wicker isn't strong enough to do the job. Scott offers her a hand. She considers whether to accept it before allowing him to help. Once on her feet, she sprints on wobbly legs to the bathroom and slams the door shut, fiddling with the lock until we hear it snap into place. We leave her be.

***

"Sleepwalking? Are you kidding me? Please tell me that wouldn't get her off in court."

The sun continues it assault while we wait outside for Sammy Kessler to join us, and I make no assurances in response to Scott's comment. We're swimming in uncharted waters now. If Katherine is on the level, then shrinks would have a field day psychoanalyzing her. With her family's money, she could afford to hire ten expert witnesses to say whatever needs to be said for a not guilty verdict. That doesn't mean a conviction would be out of the question, only that we would have to fight like hell to secure it. But is she on the level? I throw yet one more curveball Scott's way.

"You want another fun wrinkle? In *The Brothers Karamazov*, the son who murders his father fakes an epileptic fit as part of the murder plot. Coincidence or inspiration? Figuring Katherine out is like unpacking one of those Russian babushka dolls—opening one doll reveals another and so on. Too many layers. Sleepwalking. Fake sleepwalking. How do we prove any of it?"

"Fortunately for you, you're going to Italy and leaving the whole mess to me. I hope your conscience bothers you the entire trip."

"It won't. But every day at noon I will turn toward the western sky in your direction and meditate on your wellbeing, including the success of this investigation."

He tells me where I can stick my meditations.

33

Last time I questioned Sammy, Lucy sat across from him. That won't do for the second time around. Separating husband and wife is a far better method to mine for truth. When I explained that we needed to speak privately with him, he didn't protest. Quite the opposite. Claiming a desire to get out of the house, Sammy suggested that the three of us talk while walking on the beach. He joins us now, and we make our way to the sand over the same wooden bridge that the murderer traveled shortly before rearranging Donovan Kessler's head.

The tide is receding, and we have plenty of beach to walk. Sammy asks, "Which way?" I scan both directions and opt to head south toward the hotel. We walk astride with each other—Scott and me bookending the witness in the middle. I let the silence linger for a bit to see if Sammy has anything he wants to get off his chest. He does.

"When can we go back to our house?"

"You sure it's your house?"

"Lawyers are drawing up the papers right now to reverse that travesty. First thing Monday morning, we will be seeking an injunction to get her out of our family home."

"Criminal law is the only thing I know, but how are you going to prove that your father was not in his right mind when he executed the deed?"

"We don't need to show that. Illegal contracts are void against public policy."

"Illegal?"

"Prostitution. Sadie traded sex for the house. That's illegal. The deed will be thrown out, and the house will go into Father's estate to stay in the family. Crisis averted."

Sammy flashes a sickly smile, full of malice and perversion. Despite the warmth in the air, he wears a windbreaker that almost devours the entirety of his thin frame. He'll be bald sooner rather than later, and the visible flesh on his head appears like a pink, worn down pencil eraser in this sun. I bet he experienced some prurient elation when his lawyer presented him with the prostitution angle. But I'm not convinced that argument will carry the day.

"How are you going to prove prostitution? Only two people would've been parties to that transaction. Your father can't testify as to the nature of any arrangement he had with Sadie. And Sadie sure isn't going to agree that she sold herself."

"Father admitted it to Katherine and me. Lucy and Maxwell were there, too. Said he deeded the house to her for sexual favors."

"That's some feat. Especially since none of you knew about the deed until I told you yesterday—after your father was dead. Remember the scene in the living room? You walked toward Sadie with clenched fists. Dave Ketchum of the state patrol thought you were going to hit her. That's how upset you were when you learned about Sadie getting the house. And yet now you claim already to have known about it. Lying to law enforcement is a crime, you know."

"We forgot."

"Another lie. You're racking up quite the tab."

"Well, that's the truth. He told us."

I laugh out loud. Sammy stiffens in response but keeps walking straight with a pout on his pointy face, the effect of which is to make him appear even thinner. If these bozos go forward with this prostitution nonsense, then chances are that I would be called as a witness in the case on Sadie Foxx's behalf. That prospect is as appealing as a root canal. Out of self-interest, I try to talk some sense into Sammy about the stupidity of his legal strategy.

"Your father didn't tell you that. We both know it. But go ahead and lie about it. The thing is—that lie doesn't even help you. Your father's make-believe statement is hearsay. It's inadmissible in court. You'd be risking a perjury charge for nothing."

He tells me in choice terms what he thinks about my legal advice. I pretend to be a good sport.

"Don't be so touchy. I'm only asking the questions that Sadie's lawyers are going to ask you. You need to think about these things. I'm actually doing you a service."

"You're not doing anything for me. Raymond has already raised the exact same points as you."

"Well, he and I are both experienced trial lawyers—some of the best in the state if you forgive me for a little self-conceit. You'd do well to listen to us if you want that house."

He sneers at me full of meanness and makes a dismissive noise. I remember what Maxwell said about his brother-in-law: "*The man's a mouse. Does bond work because that's all the conflict he can handle. He once got assigned a pro bono criminal case, and the experience nearly broke him. He shrinks from confrontation.*"

I know the type. The world is full of soft men whose privileged upbringing allows them to pretend to be tougher than they are. The same might have happened to me if not for some rough-and-tumble uncles who kept me grounded and made me strong in a rural, redneck way. Football helped, too. On the field, everyone is equal and stands the same risk of getting their head knocked off. If you're going to play the game, the first rule of survival is to get tough or die.

Sammy never played football. I'd bet a large sum on that. And if he shrinks from conflict as much as Maxwell says, he should stop lying to me. I grab his arm and shake him a little.

"Listen, Sammy. I don't give a damn who ends up with your house. Someone murdered your father, and I'm going to find out who. But you spewing stupid lies really puts me in a bad frame of mind. Makes me think you're lying about a lot of other things—such as whether you are the person I'm looking for. Einstein once said, 'The difference between genius and stupidity is that genius has its limits.' You're proving him right. Trust me, you won't be thinking about who's sleeping in your precious childhood home if you're killing time on death row. So my question for you is pretty basic. Are you ready to start telling the truth?"

He stares at me with his mouth wide open. A decent possibility exists that no one has ever touched him with a hostile hand in his life.

I stand taller and crowd into his personal space to heighten the effect. Sammy pretends to want to make something out of it. You can almost see the blood working its way up from a simmer to a boil in his face. But the moment is too big for him. He slumps and makes himself even smaller. The sound that comes out of him is almost a squeak.

"What do you want to know?"

34

The walk on the beach resumes. What do I want to know? That's a good question. The fight between Sammy and Lucy over her too fond feelings for her father-in-law is the main cave to explore with him. But after dragging him down to that level, he might decide that talking to us is bad policy. Other questions must come first before asking about wife and daddy. I start by taking a blind shot in the dark.

"You told me that you didn't leave your bedroom after your shower the night of the murder—those twenty minutes when Lucy was in the bathroom."

"That's right."

"Are you still sticking to that story?"

Sammy, Lucy, Katherine, and Sadie all claim that they were upstairs around the time a brick was hammering Donovan Kessler's head. Except for Katherine's possible midnight sleepwalk, I have no basis to doubt any of these statements. But Sammy doesn't know what I don't know.

"Why wouldn't I stick to that story?"

"Maybe your memory is a little bit better today than yesterday. You've already changed your story once, remember? Maybe your memory works better without your wife in the same room. Maybe a thousand other things. You're running out of chances to do the right thing. A failure to tell the truth now will land you in a cell. And just between us girls, I don't think being in prison will agree with you."

He sighs and says, "You know about Lucy, right?"

Scott and I exchange looks over Sammy's pink head. We know some things about Lucy but not necessarily all things. And no need exists to educate Sammy about which pieces of knowledge fall into which bucket. He's the one that should be educating me.

"Forget about what I know. I need to hear it from your lips."

"Fine. You remember how she told you yesterday that she didn't leave the bedroom when I was taking my shower?"

"I remember."

"That wasn't exactly true. I went back into the bedroom to get a robe, and she wasn't there. I didn't want to contradict her in front of you, but I guess you found out anyway. She probably went downstairs for a water bottle. When I dried off and came out of the bathroom five minutes later, she was there."

The disclosure informs on multiple levels. That Lucy lied to me is obviously a good poker chip to play when interrogating her. But Sammy's selling us on his wife's dishonesty is a curious response to a question that directly asked about his own mendacity. A neat trick. I circle back to the original issue.

"What about you? Did you leave the bedroom when she was showering?"

He actually appears hurt that I would ask that follow-up, probably figuring that betraying Lucy would've bought him a lot of credibility with me.

"Just like I told you yesterday, never left. Went straight to bed and was asleep in five minutes."

"That's the story you're sticking to?"

"I am."

His facial features scrunch up and make him look like a mouse nipping on a giant piece of cheese. Or maybe a rat—the untrustworthy kind. Even this version of Sammy's story contradicts yesterday's account.

"Let's make sure I have the correct picture. You're done with the shower. Lucy goes in the bathroom after you. You immediately crash and are out like a light."

"Correct."

"Except you told me yesterday that Lucy didn't leave the bedroom after her shower. How on earth could you know that if you were asleep?"

He stops walking in his tracks, like a frozen deer in the headlights of an approaching car, which is a common enough sight in the area.

Jekyll Island is around nine square miles and has a deer population approaching 1,000. Plus one if you count Sammy. The notable thing about deer is their sheer stupidity, another thing they have in common with the nervous man now in front of me. He fumbles for a response.

"I just assumed …"

We peer down at him with hostile glares and wait with bated breath to hear what he just assumed. He struggles with the zipper of his windbreaker before zipping it as high as it will go. With that task complete, he scans down the beach in search of the next diversion but comes up empty, leaving him little choice but to finish the incomplete thought.

"Of course, she came to bed afterwards. I've been married to her for over twenty-five years. I know her habits. Stop trying to be so clever. Where else would she go?"

"To meet your father for a secret rendezvous. Word on the street is that they were close."

Sammy takes a step toward me. I don't flinch. Sweat collects at his unkempt sideburns. He is close enough that I can smell the coffee on his breath. After making some type of inarticulate grunt, he pivots around to make the journey back to Uncle Raymond's house. I say, "Good call. About time we start to head back."

We take up our positions again by his side. Scott's gait is more pronounced than when we started the journey. His suit and dress shoes are a poor match for a stroll on the beach. He must be sweating rivers under his armpits. Sammy tries to speed up on us, but we keep pace with him. I throw another haymaker at him.

"Tell us about your fight with Lucy on the day your father died."

The statement isn't phrased in the form of a question. On this point, I want to show him all my cards—to make his chest tighten with worry. He abruptly stops walking again, apparently dumbstruck that I possess that piece of intimate knowledge. I wonder whether he will be dumb enough to deny it.

"What fight?"

Close enough. I put on a disgusted face that doesn't require much acting. Catching Scott's eyes, I ask him, "What do you think? Book him for false statements? I'm kinda getting tired of being jerked around."

"You have more patience than me. I would've arrested him a couple of lies ago. Some people need to learn the hard way."

"Hold up! What are you guys talking about? I'm—"

"What am I talking about? Georgia code section 16-10-20 makes it a felony to lie to law enforcement. You've been doing a lot of lying to me. One to five years in prison. Except I'm not sure you'd survive three months."

Scott counters, "Nah. He wouldn't make it two weeks."

Sammy whines, "Come on! I'm doing the best I can here. A lot has happened in the last couple of days. It's too much to process. I'm grieving, and my brain isn't working quite right. What fight with Lucy are you asking about?"

"Did you have more than one?"

"Not really."

"Then I'm asking about the one you did have. Seems simple enough."

"Did Lucy tell you about the argument?"

That's a curious question and indicates that Sammy has a deep suspicion of his wife. Putting myself in his shoes, that distrust would appear to be a healthy supposition. If Sammy didn't kill his father, then someone else did. And from his perspective, Lucy would make a fine candidate. The announcement of Kessler's impending marriage to Sadie obviously put her in an agitated state, enough so that even Sammy felt compelled to challenge her about it. That he might now be fidgety by the prospect of possibly sleeping in the same bed as a murderer is fertile ground to plow with him. I start by being coy.

"I don't think she'd want me to tell you."

He nods as if he knew it all along, again showing that he didn't graduate at the top of his class. Sammy should realize well enough that his wife wouldn't be the one spilling family secrets to the likes of me. She told him just yesterday in response to one of my questions, *"Don't answer that, Sammy."* But small-minded men think small. He begins to tell me about it.

"Fight is too strong a word. More like a spirited discussion. Everyone was on edge with Father's bombshell about wanting a divorce to marry Sadie. Lucy, especially, worked herself up about it. I told her to calm her down, and she took issue with my tone. But that's the gist of it. Just a normal husband-wife squabble on a day when everyone's emotions were out of whack."

Maxwell told a wildly different version of what he heard, and I decide to smack Sammy in the mouth with it.

"You ordered her to stop making idiots of the both of you by continuing to throw herself at your father."

"She told you that?"

The response rises to a yelp. I give a slight shrug and feign innocence. Sammy starts stomping back to the house, enough to create deep impressions in the sand all the way up to his ankles. We hurry to keep pace with him.

He whines, "Why would she tell you that?"

"Maybe she thinks you killed your father."

"Me?"

"Look, I don't want to get into your personal business. But your wife fooling around with your own dad is messed up on too many levels to count. You had every right to be steaming mad about it. Anyone would. Knowing how angry you were, Lucy probably believes you took it out on your father. Someone killed him. Why not you?"

"Ludicrous."

I give my innocent little shrug again. As we cross the bridge back over to Raymond's house, Sammy is still stomping. The loud thumps ricochet off the wood like the beating of drums. In the lead, he halts and swings back toward us right before the bridge gives way to the path that runs between the homes of Donovan and Raymond Kessler. He jabs a thin, manic finger at the both of us.

"Listen to me. Only one reason that my wife would try to throw the blame my way, and that's to get it off herself. That's where you need to be looking. You don't know her like I do. When Lucy found out that Father was marrying Sadie, she snapped and started acting like a lunatic.

You know how women sometimes get crazy eyes? That was her. And I already told you that she lied to you about leaving our bedroom. The whole thing makes me sick. My own wife and father."

Sammy whirls around and hurries to his BMW parked in the street. I catch up to him and ask, "Where are you going?"

"No idea. Somewhere to find a cold drink and get drunk. Don't think I can go back in that house right now. Not sure if I'll ever be able to be around Lucy again. But I doubt I have much choice. The ties that bind are their own form of prison."

The tires squeal as he speeds away.

35

We knock on Lucy's door at the end of a long hallway. A sharp voice calls out from the other side, "It's open!" Taking the words to be an invitation, Scott and I enter a long, rectangular bedroom built over the garage below. Lucy lounges on a daybed in front of windows looking out to the ocean in the distance, her back supported by a number of pillows, a MacBook on her lap. She is not happy to see us.

"What the hell do you want?"

"Needed to follow up with you on a number of things."

"I'm not talking to you."

"That's your prerogative, but you might want to listen to what I have to say and decide whether to provide your side of the story before your silence backs you into a murder indictment."

She doesn't even commit to that much but does continue to stare at me, which I take as a cue to continue the conversation.

"Here's the deal, Lucy. You had a motive to want Donovan Kessler dead and don't have an alibi. Strike one. You lied to me about leaving your bedroom around the time of the murder. Strike two. On the day he died, you were mad as hell at your father-in-law for deciding to marry Sadie. You even had a screaming match with your husband about it, which some would say is evidence of your emotional volatility. I caught a peek of that explosiveness myself when you darted down the stairs like a road runner after I told you about Sadie and the house. Kept calling her, '*You bitch*!' That's strike three. But I'd really like to hear your side of it before taking any action."

Silence in the face of accusation is unnatural. Something innate in humans compels us to want to defend ourselves—to justify, to explain, to make people see things from our point of view. Lucy fights the urge. Her lips wrestle with each other in funny, twitch-like movements to stop her from saying the wrong thing. The rest of her doesn't fare much better. Her body is stiff and locked in a "L" position. Just like yesterday, she is shoeless. Her oversized feet dangle over the daybed's edge. She closes the laptop and lays it to the side. I hit her with another cattle prod.

"You know what your husband told me? We just shared a walk on the beach, and he confessed a lot of your sins. Let me see if I can remember it word for word. I'm pretty adept at the power of recall. Comes from years of close listening to people testifying in court. But speaking of you, Sammy said, *'That's where you need to be looking. You don't know her like I do. When Lucy found out that Father was marrying Sadie, she snapped and started acting like a lunatic. You know how women sometimes get crazy eyes? That was her.'*"

I pause before adding, "As you can see, he was pretty passionate on the subject of whether you murdered his father. Let's call that strike four. Response?"

"You're lying. He wouldn't dare."

A sad shake of my head indicates that dog will not hunt. I turn to Scott, who is already holding out his phone. One practice that we have internalized on the murder squad is recording all our witness interviews—sometimes on the sly, sometimes not. The recording of Sammy was on the sly. Before confronting Lucy, we anticipated that she wouldn't take our word for what her husband said about her. So Scott stands with cell in hand, ready to push the button that will replay Sammy's impromptu diatribe. He presses play, and Sammy's high-pitched voice fills the room. Listening to it play back, I nailed the monologue verbatim.

Not that Lucy is going to give me any credit for the feat. She goes pale in the face but only temporarily. A deep red soon replaces the white, and I get a glimpse of those crazy eyes that Sammy mentioned. She slides off the daybed and stands on her bare feet. The intensity rivals her anger when informed of Kessler's gift of the house to Sadie. She snarls out a question.

"Where is that son of a bitch?"

"Off getting drunk somewhere. He's unsure if he'll ever come back. But you have more immediate problems than your domestic troubles. You lied to me about not leaving your bedroom. The question is why. I figure you went for a walk with Donovan and didn't want me to know about it."

"Why do you believe what Sammy says?"

"Is there a reason I shouldn't?"

Lucy snorts out a pig-like oink. Unlike the day before when she was dressed in her lawyer clothes, the outfit of the moment is more pedestrian—red sweatpants and a green, baggy t-shirt. Almost like a Christmas tree. Now that she's closer to us, I can discern bags under her eyes from crying, lack of sleep, or a combination of both.

"Don't you see what's happening? Sammy's pointing the finger at me because that's part of his plan. He and I didn't have a screaming match. He's the one that did all the yelling. He hated his father for a whole bunch of reasons and killed him. Now Sammy's trying to frame me, and you're falling for it. That's a win-win from his point of view."

To credit her response, Sammy would have to possess special, hidden skills as a thespian that are not obvious from being around him for repeated viewings. But you never know.

"What reasons did Sammy have to hate his father?"

"Because Donovan was strong, confident, and the kind of person everyone liked. Sammy could never be that kind of man and resented his father because of it. People admired Donovan, including me. Sammy turned that admiration into something ugly. He hated his father because of me and burned with jealousy that Donovan, even at his advanced age, could satisfy a woman like Sadie. All of it pushed him over the edge."

Her eyes shine. On the Sadie front, she could just as easily be talking about herself. I decide to test the hypothesis.

"A woman like Sadie could make a man like Donovan feel young again. How much sex do you think the two of them were having?"

She grabs a wineglass and hurls it toward my head. Her aim is so poor that I don't even have to flinch. The glass careens against the wall and shatters with a loud boom. I remember the last time an angry woman threw a glass at my head. On that occasion the warhead did hit its target, fueling both a possible concussion and a murderous rage on my part to get even. I reclaimed my sanity a step before madness. Barely. But that was in another country, and besides the wench is dead. Sort of.

Lucy screeches, "Go! Just go!"

"Not yet. If you want me to believe you instead of your husband, I'm going to need a proffer of good faith. You have one shot to get this right. Did you leave the bedroom at any time?"

"Yes! From my window, I saw Donovan walking in the backyard while Sammy was in the shower. I needed to talk to him about Sadie. About his disastrous decision to marry her. But when I went downstairs and opened the backdoor, he was gone. I called out to him, but he didn't answer. No one was there. I went back to my bedroom and never saw him again. That's all I know. Now leave me alone!"

We leave her alone.

36

"Lucy might have just saved Rickie Savage's bacon."

We sit in lawn chairs adjacent to Raymond Kessler's rose bushes. Scott has a dress shoe in his hand, pouring all the sand out of it. He responds, "The timeline."

"The timeline. Sammy and Lucy got home at eleven-fifteen from a dinner on St. Simon's. Doubtful he hit the shower for at least ten minutes after that, but let's call it five. Lucy would have seen Kessler alive in the backyard at eleven-twentyish. He makes his last walk to the beach. Rickie follows him and somehow avoids being seen by Lucy. Commits the murder. Runs back to his car and still makes it home before the midnight showing of *Perry Mason* starts. That drive took me thirty-six minutes and some change. Hard to make the timing fit."

"Still possible."

"By the thinnest of thin threads."

"That's all it takes."

So true. Things happen the way they happen. Trying to fit puzzle pieces back together after the fact often runs into the roadblock of our own preconceived notions about the way things should've happened—a focus on probabilities. But in real life, the improbable is normal. In a world of infinite possibilities, long shots cash out daily. Maybe Rickie Savage drove 120 miles per hour to get back to his house in under thirty minutes. Sometimes impossible solutions are as easy at that.

With his shoes back on, Scott stretches his hurt knee out and winces. He observes, "I hate this place."

"We are strangers in a strange land."

Captain Dave and Chad Morelli come bopping into view from the street. They appear far too happy. Dave proclaims, "You won't believe the day we have had."

He takes out his cell to show us pictures from the crammed inside of Rickie Savage's single wide, complete with added commentary on the array of sights and smells that greeted his team. Morelli adds his own animated insights, too. We act appropriately shocked. No mention is made of any raccoon encounters.

I stop feeling any guilt about dumping the search of Savage's premises onto their shoulders. They are much too chipper about the whole experience, like they went to Disney World or something. They must really be bored in their everyday routine. Maybe I can give them the rest of the case, and they can call it a party.

Now that Dave and Morelli are here, we can gang up on Maxwell Matheny about his sexual assault and near rape of Cecilia Franklin. I explain the plan of action to everyone assembled.

* * *

Lucy's revelation that Kessler was alive and walking to the beach shortly after eleven-fifteen not only forces the case against Savage to fit into the tightest of windows, it also complicates the timeline for Maxwell in the other direction. The working assumption is that the murderer followed Kessler to the beach and picked up the brick along the way. Except we know from Cecilia that Maxwell's ass was firmly planted in the Shore of Shadows until midnight, which means he cannot be the killer under our pet theory. Suggestive, but not conclusive. Maybe we have the crime figured wrong.

We find Maxwell much the way I found him yesterday—in the kitchen nursing a beer. He sees the four of us and emits a soft curse. Raymond's kitchen is larger than the one next door with plenty of room for us to gather. I sit across the table from Maxwell. Scott leans on a nearby wall. Dave and Morelli take chairs behind me. Maxwell is the first to speak.

"Is this show of force supposed to scare me? The Four Horsemen of the Apocalypse? Whatever effect you're going for isn't working. The whole lot of you look like Village People rejects."

Given Morelli's youth, I doubt that he gets the reference. The comment isn't really funny, but I laugh just to play along.

"We have a problem, Max. You need to be straight with me, or we're going to take you in for murder."

"The hell you say. You told me yesterday you were looking at Lucy as a person of interest."

"True when I said it, but a murder investigation is a process of elimination. We have live video of you stumbling around outside the house at the same time someone killed Donovan. Everybody else is accounted for. That leaves one person, and you haven't exactly done yourself any favors by refusing to tell me what you were doing that night. I'm suspicious by nature. Your unwillingness to be transparent makes me believe that the truth hurts you. But I'll try one more time. Can anyone corroborate your whereabouts around midnight on the night of the murder?"

He pays an inordinate amount of attention to the bottle of beer—drinking from it, massaging it, staring at it. If he finds any good answers from alcohol, that would mark a first in human history. We wait him out. After a long interval, he brings his eyes up to me and condescends to speak.

"A waitress. From the Shore of Shadows. Little blond thing. She was throwing herself at me all night, impressed that I was lawyer. The pub closed at midnight. She told me to wait in the parking lot for her. By the time she came out, I was too tired and went straight home. Slept on the couch downstairs. And to save you the trouble of asking, I didn't see anything or anyone."

Good. He's talking. I'd have wagered the other way—that he would've told me what I could go do to myself. But I can't claim total surprise. Lawyers should know better than anyone never to talk to the cops. Law professors everywhere hammer that point home to their students. But the lesson doesn't stick, at least when it comes to lawyers talking about themselves. The right to remain silent is solid advice for clients, but lawyers need not be so constricted. We can talk ourselves out of anything.

Call it hubris—the tragic flaw of people great and small.

37

With Maxwell willing to talk, the trick is to keep the words flowing so that he can incriminate himself. I decide to start easy with some gentle jabs.

"This waitress—what's her name?"

"Camille, I think."

Cecilia. Camille. Close enough. Maxwell was drunk and no doubt paying more attention to certain other of Cecilia's features besides her name. I don't correct the mistake.

"Believe what I'm about to say. I don't really want to pry into your private affairs, but you're a married man. And based on what you just told me, you were prepared to engage in some extracurricular activities with this Camille."

The tone is non-judgmental. I don't even ask him anything. Questions, by definition, put a person on the defensive. Rather, we're just two guys talking about woman problems while he drinks a beer. The other armed men in the room put the lie to that tableau, but maybe Maxwell will become so engrossed with my company that he'll forget that little detail. He puts down the bottle and continues the conversation—proving that once the lips start moving, they don't want to stop.

"What of it? You know how long it's been since I got laid? Well, I don't. It's so long ago now that I quit counting. Katherine is not the same woman I married. She used to be a lot of fun once upon a time. Before she got all crazy and judgmental. That woman hasn't cracked a smile in years. Judy's accident only made her worse. You might be thinking, 'Well, why doesn't he get a divorce?' I'll tell you why. My whole professional career is tied up with Katherine's brother and her sister-in-law. If I'm no longer in the family, where does that leave old Maxwell? Up the creek without a paddle. Worst thing that ever happened to me was getting entangled with the House of Kessler."

He looks as pathetic as he sounds. Self-pity doesn't look good on anyone. I wonder to what extent his own behavior made Katherine into the woman that she is today. Surely his share of the blame is sizable. Causation is a two-way street, though. Living with a woman like Katherine would figure to harden and embitter even the most ebullient husband. I pretend to commiserate with his dilemma.

"Your situation doesn't sound ideal. Hopeless even. Is there any way out for you?"

"Beyond starting over? No. But being down here these past few days has clarified a lot of things for me. Time to rip off the band-aid and live with the consequences. I can't take it anymore."

Prison is probably not the fresh start he's aiming for, but that's what he deserves for attacking Cecilia. Now I have to get him to admit it.

"Honesty buys you a lot of grace with me. You're halfway home. The name of the waitress who can provide you with an alibi is named Cecilia, not Camille. We had a long talk with her last night at Waffle House, which could be good news for you if you're smart. Whatever exactly happened between y'all two is not my concern, but I do require that witnesses be straight with me. Cecilia tells a much different story about how things transpired between you and her. You need to tell me the unvarnished truth—warts and all. Lie to me, and all bets are off. My imagination will start thinking that you killed your father-in-law again."

"Can I have another beer?"

Scott grabs a fresh bottle for Maxwell and takes the cap off with his bare hands. The witness takes a long drink. My mention of Cecilia's real name got his attention real quick. Good liars are born from confidence, and such confidence comes from knowing that the falsehoods they peddle cannot be fact-checked. I just showed Maxwell that I know his story better than he does. Asking for another bottle of beer buys him time to reassess his approach.

"What did Cecilia say about me?"

"Look, I'm investigating a murder. If you got too handsy with her because you read the situation wrong or she's some kind of tease, big deal. Not my business. But I insist on the truth. I cannot do my job without it. And you need to give it to me without first being told the Cliff Notes version. If you're worried about incriminating yourself somehow, don't. You have my word that the only charge I'll ever arrest you for is murder. Unless you lie to me."

He takes another drink to do more thinking about his troubles. His body is strung tight, and a light flush that is not from the alcohol starts to change the coloring of his cheeks.

"I don't care what that waitress says, she was flirting with me hard in the bar. And not just laying it on a little thick to get a bigger tip. I know how to read a woman, and she wanted me to go home with her. Begged me to wait in the parking lot for her."

"Tell me about the parking lot. You know what happened and should also consider that Cecilia might have other witnesses to back her up."

Maxwell grimaces—probably remembering Charley the bartender. He turns his head to face a window and stares in the direction of the ocean while sipping on the beer. I take the opportunity to reflect on Cecilia's description of the attack: "'*I tried to open my door, but he slammed it shut with the heaviness of his body, wedging me between him and the car. He started putting his hands all over. On my breasts. Up my skirt. Forced his mouth on my mouth. His breath smelled terrible. I tried to scream but nothing came out. When I squirmed away, he grabbed my arm and jerked me back to him. I have a bruise.*'" The memory of the pathos in her voice washes me anew in righteous anger. I envy the fact that Charley got to lay his hands on Maxwell and hurl him to the ground. The would-be rapist begins to speak.

"We walked to her car and started kissing hot and heavy with her really grinding against me. All of a sudden, she broke away and started screaming. The bartender—he was right there. Grabbed me and pushed me to the ground. Everything happened really fast. But I knew right away that I was being set up. Either the bartender's her boyfriend, and she was trying to make him jealous. Or they were conspiring to create some rape claim to blackmail me out of money. Anyway, I didn't give them the chance. Got the hell away from there as fast as I could."

The lying son of bitch. Part of me wants to slap him across the table. Another part wants to burst out laughing at his absurd explanation. What I do instead is take out my phone and hold it up to his face—showing him a picture of Cecilia's battered and bruised arm.

"How do you explain this?"

"You think I did that? Why don't you ask her boyfriend the bartender? He probably hurt her for making out with me."

"But it's your fingerprints on her arm."

Now I'm the one lying, which is one of the privileges that comes with a badge. Fingerprints can be left on a body. But by the time we talked with Cecilia a day later, any prints from Maxwell would've been long gone. I doubt that he knows that much about forensics, though. His punch-drunk face seems to confirm my hunch. For the first time, seeds of panic line his middle-aged features.

"I may have grabbed her a little when we were making out. Guess I did. She liked it on the rougher side. I could tell. Look, I've been frank with you, Meridian. What happened to you not caring about anything except Donovan's murder? The point is that you know I didn't kill Donovan. This conversation is over."

"That's your story? That she didn't resist at all while you were pawing her all over?"

"Weren't you listening? I told you she broke away and started screaming."

"And you grabbed her arm because you could tell she liked it on the rough side?"

"Yes—I told you that, too."

He's now on record that she resisted him and that he grabbed her arm to hurt her a little bit. Combined with the testimony of Cecilia and Charley, that should be enough. Asking more questions risks giving him a chance to walk some of it back. I give a sideways glance at Scott and see his smirk. He thinks we got Maxwell, too. I switch to the murder.

"Here's my problem, Max. You had a violent encounter right before going back to Donovan's place. You're angry. You thought you were going to get laid but got beat up instead. Back at home, things don't get much better. The front door won't open. You kick it and hurt your foot. Now you're really enraged. Going around to the back of the house, what do you see? Donovan Kessler walking alone toward the beach—an old man who you already resent because of Sadie Foxx. The chance to take out your frustrations on someone else is staring you right in the face. Don't you agree that the pieces fit?"

Maxwell looks like a man that would hit me in the head with a brick if one were handy. If not for Lucy's testimony likely moving the time of death to before midnight, he would be my leading contender. But I just cannot make him for the murder in a world where Kessler walked to the beach shortly after eleven-fifteen. Of course, if Maxwell goes ahead and confesses, I'll come around.

"You lousy bastard. This conversation is over and for real this time. I didn't kill Donovan, and you'll never prove otherwise."

"The good news is that I think I believe you. The bad news is that Captain Dave Ketchum of the state patrol is now going to arrest you for sexual assault of Cecilia Franklin and related crimes."

"But you said you didn't care about that. You even gave me your word."

"One—never trust a person with a badge. Two—I didn't lie to you. Murder is my business and little else. But Dave here cares a lot. He's responsible for policing this island and doesn't like it when predators like you try to rape young women. Hurts the tourist trade."

"You son of a bitch!"

He stands up and grabs one of the beer bottles and tries to use it like a baseball bat on my head—swinging the makeshift weapon in a long arc that appears destined to make contact. But Scott is the quicker man and lands a devastating punch to Maxwell's kidney that collapses my attacker to a heap on the kitchen floor. The beer bottle drops and shatters right next to him. Assuming he's not dead, Maxwell will probably be urinating blood for a fortnight.

Dave and Morelli pick up their cargo and drag him to their squad car. Scott helps himself to one of Raymond's beers and appears well-pleased with himself, forcing me to comment.

"I think you might have enjoyed that a little too much."

"He did call me a '*goon*.' I didn't want to make a liar out of him. Also, it's a personal policy of mine never to turn down a free chance to punch an attorney."

Fair enough. Those opportunities don't come around every day. At least Scott got his money's worth. Couldn't have happened to a more deserving lawyer.

38

The afternoon sun beats down with more brightness than I can stand—harsh revenge for the recent cold front. I long to shed my jeans in favor of some shorts, but the change would be unbecoming for someone in my position. Scott's concession to the heat is the removal of his coat, but the damage to the armpits of his dress shirt is already done. He's been dripping in sweat for hours.

Debbie Fincher stands outside Donovan Kessler's house talking to one of her technicians. The GBI pullover strikes me as cruel and unusual punishment in this heat, but she shows no signs of being bothered by it. She asks, "Ready for me?" Without waiting for an answer, she leads us into the house and launches into her findings.

"No recent blood. That's the big thing you want to know. Some residue from blood droplets long past, but that's the extent of it. If the victim's blood splatter landed on the perp, then the perp removed those clothes before entering the house. We paid special attention to the laundry room in case the perp tried to wash the blood out but found nothing. The amount of splatter we're talking about, we would've found something if it existed. I don't care how good a clean-up job the killer did. No one is perfect when matched up against forensics."

I don't doubt her conclusions. An old detective once shared with me some homicide wisdom. With any murder, at least a hundred things can go wrong from the murderer's perspective. A smart murderer might anticipate half of these landmines. This math leaves plenty of room for error. The murderer cannot plan for every random scenario that may lead the law to his identity—the prying eyes of a random neighbor, the patrol car that passes at the wrong moment, trace DNA evidence. Something will go wrong. The perfect crime is a myth. Of course, not all murderers get caught. Police make mistakes, too. Debbie continues.

"We also used black lights to check for seminal fluid throughout the house. Not too much out of the ordinary. Found some concentrations in the master bedroom. The rest of the upstairs was clear. Also some trace amounts in the office on the ground floor."

"The office?"

"Yes."

"Show me."

Debbie leads us through the living room to a small hallway that snakes around to the office at the back of the house. The room is dark, and she shines her black light on the couch against the far wall. Scattered dots of semen glow brightly on the couch and surrounding floor. Sadie told us yesterday that the office was Kessler's private sanctuary and that she never visited it except that one time when she found Kessler and Lucy huddled close together. *Lawyer business*, he told Sadie. More like monkey business.

The sun assaults my eyes again when the three of us emerge from the darkened house. Debbie and her crew pack up to leave. Scott says, "We've been putting it off long enough. It's time to pay Rickie Savage another visit."

"You know he's only going to kick sand in our faces."

"And we can kick his drug stockpile right back into his. Gives us leverage to make a deal."

"What kind of deal? That we'll drop the drug charges if he confesses to murder?"

"You'll think of something."

He has a higher opinion of my abilities than I do. A screech of tires too close for comfort jars us to attention. Scott reaches for his gun as a matter of reflex. I scout for a place to hide. But the sight of J.D.'s aqua Corolla allows the both of us to stand down. The car jerks to a hard stop that gives me whiplash from just looking at it. A breathless J.D. emerges from the vehicle.

"Glad I found you. Came across something huge."

"On the Ring footage from the houses in the neighborhood?"

"What? No. I got bored with that and started surfing social media instead. Good thing, too. I tried calling you but couldn't connect. My phone doesn't work great down here. So I got in the car and hoped like hell that you were here. A state trooper even pulled me over for speeding but let me go when he realized I hired him yesterday to go sort through trash. Anyway, what I discovered can't wait."

"You identified the killer?"

"Maybe."

J.D. is not one to exaggerate, and goosebumps rise up on my arms in anticipation. He unloads a laptop from a leather messenger bag and lays the computer on the hood of the car. Scott and I crowd him on opposite sides. The sun at first makes the screen hard to see, but my eyes adjust. J.D. launches a search on Facebook. With a few more keystrokes, he pulls up a number of pictures containing unapologetic displays of public affection. Scott laughs out loud. My reaction is not so sanguine.

I moan, "You cannot be serious."

39

Sadie Foxx's long, tan body is stretched out on a flat lounge chair next to the pool at the Jekyll Island Club Hotel. The deep blueness of the water sells a message of calmness, but I'm not in the mood to buy. Sadie lies on her belly, hardly covered by anything in the way of clothing. Her bikini top is untied at the back, and the bottom might be big enough to wipe my nose. Emphasis on might.

I stand over her and despair that nothing in this case has been easy. While I have no hesitancy hauling her off to jail and intend to hold that threat over her head in short order, I'd rather she be clothed if we have to arrest her on the spot. But shock and awe are part of what makes for effective questioning. And twiddling our thumbs while waiting for her to get properly dressed would douse a cold shower on the momentum we need to put her on the defensive.

"You're blocking my sun."

The complaint contains an undercurrent of preening entitlement, and her eyes remain closed while lodging the objection. The combination of oil and sweat makes her body glisten, like a slimy snake fresh out of the swamp. I don't move.

"Better get used to it because you're going to a place where the sun doesn't shine."

Sadie opens her eyes, recognizes me, and smiles indulgently. She adjusts to a sitting position while holding her bikini top over her breasts. The coverage of the forbidden zones dangles precariously close to the line of demarcation. But no matter. I've seen nipples before and am not in the mood. She starts to speak in that taunting voice of hers.

"Not this weekend, I hope. Have to attend a luncheon tomorrow in honor of Donny at the state bar conference. That's why I'm working on my tan. To look my best. That's what Donny would've wanted."

"You're invited to that?"

"Of course. That nice lady that's taking Donny's place as president—Meredith—asked me to come. She felt that I deserved to be there with the rest of the family. Given how close Donny and I were, you know."

A sneaky move on Meredith's part, sticking a shiv right between the eyes of the rest of the Kesslers. That's quite the spiteful gesture for a person whose whole persona revolves around being excessively nice. Maybe I'll get to ask her about it. Sadie stands up and stretches out the strings to the bikini top on both sides of her body.

"Can you tie me up?"

"No."

"Meanie. My lawyer said I shouldn't talk to you."

"Raymond Kessler told you that?"

"Not him, silly. A new lawyer in Brunswick. I forget her name. She's going to make sure I get to keep my house."

Her house. How very American. We hold these truths to be self-evident—that what's ours is ours. It's right there in the Declaration of Independence. Sadie made a deal to trade herself for a $5 million piece of property on the beach. And from her perspective, she held up her end of the bargain. Fair is fair.

She re-ties the bikini top behind her back without my help. Scott walks up and gives me a slight nod. Sadie notices him and says to me, "Why did you bring your boyfriend along? I had hoped that the two of us could slip away to my hotel room and that you would strip-search me to help you find whatever you're looking for. Unless your friend wants to come along and watch. Wouldn't be my first time."

"Sorry to disappoint you, but this is not that kind of party."

"What kind of party is it?"

"The kind where you need to do a lot of talking to avoid spending the night in jail. Get up. We're going for a walk."

"Ooh, I get turned on when you talk tough."

Provocateurs live to provoke. But the problem with Sadie is that everything with her is amateur hour. Her act borders on clownish. A true femme fatale relies on nuance and subtlety to stir the imagination of her target. She makes the chase part of the fun—the tease of playing hard to get. Sadie's method is to hang a vacancy sign on a cheap motel that rents rooms by the hour. The whole charade is low rent. Or maybe I'm overthinking things. She did just inherit a $5 million house.

The caravan walks back toward the hotel. In a show of pretend modesty, Sadie now wears a thin, transparent white cover-up that doesn't do much covering. Scott's earlier nod to me signaled that he found a place for us to conduct our interrogation. He leads us through an outer door marked "Staff Only" into the hotel's basement. After a couple of right turns through maze-like hallways illuminated only by fluorescent lights, we enter a large storage room filled with spare furniture. Scott shuts the door behind him, and it clangs like the closing of a prison cell. Half the bulbs in the overhead light fixture are out, creating a shadowy effect that makes it hard to see. The whole space feels like a coffin.

The hotel's central air conditioning must be nearby because the air contains a crisp, arctic chill. Or maybe the wine cellar is next door. Sadie—who is not dressed for the change in weather—glances around and shivers a little. She proclaims, "Let me go. Whatever you're trying to do won't work. I have nothing to say to you guys."

"You either talk to us now or spend the night in jail. Your choice."

"On what charge?"

"Assaulting a police officer, resisting arrest, obstruction of justice. You recall that little scene you created yesterday by refusing a lawful order to leave the house? And if that's not enough, we have you on possession of marijuana—that secret stash in your suitcase. Cooperation was the price of your release, and it's time to pay up. Remember what I told you? '*If you get salty again, you will be arrested.*' So don't be salty. You should also know that your odds of getting bail on the weekend aren't the greatest. Two nights in jail won't be good for your tan."

I peek at her wrists. The faint outline of her hour-plus stint in handcuffs yesterday still shows. Here's hoping the lesson remains fresh in her mind. I'm cautiously optimistic. The brashness of a few minutes ago at the pool is gone, and her concerned expression shows that the game is not turning out to her liking. A complaint forms on her lips.

"Do we have to do it in here? I'm cold."

Always the gentleman, Scott removes his suit jacket and hands it to her, which reveals the shoulder holster strapped to his chest. Sadie takes up the offered jacket and puts it on with greedy fervor. I hold back a smile. The draping almost swallows all of her up. She might as well be wearing a curtain. The picture is comedic, as if all her sexiness leaked out into a puddle on the floor. What's left is ridiculousness. And that works in my favor. Negotiation is hard from a position of absurdity.

"We're not moving to another room, unless it's a police station. Look at it this way—the cold is good incentive for all of us to wrap this up as quickly as possible."

"Well, get on with it then."

That's a fair request. I take my cell out and scroll through a number of images before picking the right one. Glancing at it once more to be sure, I shake my head yet again. The genuine shock of this development still clings to my ribs. I walk up to Sadie and hold out the phone to give her a good look. The recognition is instantaneous. Her eyes go wide, and she gasps a shallow breath.

The photo shows Sadie in a passionate kiss with Becky Savage—Rickie's murdered daughter.

40

"You have a lot of explaining to do. Better make it good."

Sadie pulls Scott's jacket tighter around her body, hugging herself with her arms. Below the knees, her skin remains exposed, including her flip-flop clad feet. She stands there like a person might stand before a firing squad with trembling legs. Exposed with that vulnerability, she appears younger than her young age. But youth is no defense to murder. Motive, means, and opportunity. Sadie now checks off all the boxes. I wonder if she has a criminal record. In a normal investigation on my home turf following the usual channels, we would already have that information. But we've been chasing our tails since the beginning down here, and I'm tired of running. Sadie gathers up the courage to speak.

"Threatening me with jail if I don't talk to you is extortion. That's illegal."

"Your idea is so wrong on so many levels that it would take me two hours to explain all of them to you. Start with this one—we're from the government. Blackmail is a synonym for good police work."

The response doesn't surprise her. She played a long shot with little prayer of success, but she's not winning the lottery today. Only two choices exist. Talk or jail. The resignation on her face suggests that she has reached the same conclusion. She starts over again.

"What do you want to know? That's Becky and me. The picture speaks for itself."

"Indeed. I hear it speaking to me right now. Do you know what it is saying? The word 'revenge' keeps repeating itself over and over. Loudly. But that's not all. The photo is also telling me that you murdered Donovan Kessler because he killed Becky—the love of your life."

"Nope."

"Which part? That you didn't murder your precious Donny or that Becky wasn't the love of your life? Because I can assure you that this photograph and all the other similar pictures plastered on social media are pointing an accusatory finger straight at you. That part is definitely true. I can barely hear anything else because the screaming is so loud in my ear."

"I didn't kill him."

"How on earth do you expect me to believe that?"

She shudders and points her head down, almost perpendicular to the floor. Her body starts slowly swaying. Fainting seems a possibility, but she appears sturdy enough. Her mouth remains shut. I find another picture on my phone and show it to her. She straightens her head to stare at it.

"Recognize this man smiling with his arm around you? Bet you do. His name is Rickie Savage, Becky's father. Only yesterday I asked you if you knew him. Remember what you said? '*Not personally*.' Big mistake. Did you realize that lying to law enforcement is a crime? A felony. Minimum of one year in prison. Could be up to five. I know you fancy yourself some type of sex kitten, immune to the consequences of your actions, but you've about used up all of your nine lives. You better take it from the start. The truth this time."

Her gaze shifts from me to Scott back to me again. She looks like someone weighing the option of making a run for it, only to realize the hopelessness of the situation. Besides the two big men standing between her and the door, trying to escape while wearing flip-flops makes for a poor getaway. She straightens up her back and drops her arms to the side. The sleeves of the oversized jacket flap about, but she doesn't quite look as cartoonish as before. Attitude can cover a lot of other weaknesses. Sadie begins her story.

"Becky and I went to the same high school. Cheerleaders together, best friends, two peas in a pod. Fast forward a few years. After both of us had some bad experiences with guys, we decided that life might be better with each other than with men. The relationship worked. And then one day somebody murdered her in the parking lot of Briscoe's. That's all."

"Hardly all, and you're smart enough to realize how screwed you are. You knew Kessler murdered Becky and still moved into his house. Then boom—someone murders him. I could get a murder conviction on that sequence of events alone. You getting the house is just the icing on the cake."

She returns to her hangdog pose and stares at the dark floor. After taking a forlorn deep breath, she picks her head up to defend herself again.

"You're wrong. I didn't know that Donny murdered Becky, only that Rickie said so. He told everybody around town the same story but nobody paid him much mind, including me. After my car wreck, I hired Raymond as my lawyer because he's on all the billboards. I had no idea that he was Donny's brother. Then I met Donny in the office and knew. The moment felt like destiny. For the first time, Rickie started making a lot of sense. A few days later, I followed Donny from his office. When he stopped at a grocery store, I made sure to bump into him by accident. He asked me out. Again destiny. I decided to try and kill him."

41

That Sadie just said out loud an intention to kill Donovan Kessler is one hell of an admission. I turn to Scott to make sure I understood her right. Sure enough, the glint in his eyes confirms that we both heard the same thing. She now has all of my attention. I hold back any follow-up questions and wait for the story to continue. Moving in too soon could stunt the telling of the narrative. Better to hear everything first from the horse's mouth.

"Thought you'd be all over me after admitting that. But obviously I didn't kill him, although I guess I tried in my own way. You see, my plan was that maybe having sex with me would kill him. Give him a heart attack or something. Not really murder, but he would be dead all the same. That felt like a good use of my talents. But it didn't work. He was in good shape for an old man."

Scott bursts out laughing. I crack a smile. Of course, Sadie would hatch the bright idea of trying to kill a man by having sex with him. Homicide by heart attack. A law professor could have a field day torturing students with hypotheticals based on what she just said. Does a non-criminal act—such as sex between consenting adults—become criminal because one of the participants hopes the activity kills the other participant? What if Sadie had suggested a vigorous jog instead? Or convinced Kessler to climb the 129 steps to the top of the St. Simon's lighthouse? If Kessler keeled over from a heart attack after any of these activities, is that murder? Good luck getting a jury to ever convict someone because the victim died of the leading natural cause of death in the country.

The world is mad. I wait for Sadie to finish the story.

"But after spending a lot of time with Donny, I realized that Rickie got it wrong. Donny wasn't a killer and certainly would not become one to avenge what happened to Judy. When I unpeeled the onion, none of it made sense. And that's the truth, the whole truth, and nothing but the truth."

"You got close to Kessler to kill him but decided that he didn't actually need killing. And yet you stayed with him afterwards anyway. Something doesn't add up."

Sadie smiles.

"My plans evolved. Donny took a shine to me and started promising to take care of my financial needs the rest of his life and beyond. He was even open to marriage. Without a prenup. After what happened to Becky, I didn't feel much like living. But Donny's company was tolerable enough, especially with such a huge prize in sight. I reckoned that one day I would be ready to be happy again and having money in the bank would be a good start."

"How did Rickie feel about the way you decided to move up in the world?"

The question is a stomach punch for her—the revulsion on her face evident even in the weak light. She gives herself a tight hug to make everything better.

"He saw Donny and me out at dinner one night a few months ago and flipped his lid. Sent me a bunch of texts filled with obscenities. I met him for coffee the next day to explain how wrong he was about Donny. But Rickie wouldn't listen to reason. He called me a whore and worse names. I returned the favor and explained how pathetic he had become. Haven't seen or talked to him since."

"Did you tell him about your boyfriend's penchant for taking late night walks on the beach?"

"Hell no."

"Rickie is currently sitting in a jail cell. A visit to him is next on our agenda. If you've seen him recently, exchanged texts, or talked with him on the phone, tell me now. If he was ever a little too curious about your boyfriend's habits—such as Donny's nightly walks on the beach or even what toothpaste he liked to use—I need to hear it before we leave this room."

She sticks to the same story of no contact in months. I glance at my watch. We have just enough time to circle back to Rickie Savage before dinner. The cold in the room is getting to me at this point, and talking to her is too tiring anyway. She had said enough to avoid jail for the moment. I turn to Scott to see if he has anything to ask her.

He barks, "Who killed Becky?"

"How the hell would I know? Ask the police."

"Where were you the night she was killed?"

Sadie makes a hiss-like noise and rushes to throw off Scott's jacket but gets tangled during the effort. I try not to make the situation worse by laughing at her. When she finally manages to escape, she throws the jacket at Scott and announces, "I'm leaving now." She makes a move to the door, but I block the way.

"Answer the question."

Looking at me with enough anger to kill, she curls her lips up and sneers, "Where was I when someone murdered Becky? Waiting for her to come home. I'm still waiting. You disappoint me. I could've taken you to the moon and back. Now I can barely stand to look at you."

"I've been to the moon. It's overrated."

The comment goes unanswered. After a hard brush past my shoulder on the way out of the room, Sadie storms away.

Scott observes, "Worse ways to go than dying in the saddle. Imagine her trying to kill him that way. To be so lucky."

"Yeah, but his luck reached its expiration date when someone turned his skull to mush with a brick. Curious that Sadie wanted him dead and got her wish in the end. Maybe she's the lucky one."

"Some people make their own luck."

We begin to maneuver our way back out from the hotel dungeon and bump into an obviously lost Sadie on the way. Scott points a finger in the right direction, and she thanks him by flipping up both of her middle fingers in a heartfelt double salute. She hurries forward and beats us to the door, threatening to fall out of her clothes the entire way. Back outside, the sun is beginning its descent over the far reaches of the western horizon. Sadie runs up some stairs and into the hotel proper without so much as a good-bye.

One person who hasn't seen the sun today is Rickie Savage. I ask Scott, "What kind of state do you think Savage will be in after spending a day in a cell?"

"Ornery, smelly, and stupid—just like any other day."

42

"I don't like the knife."

Scott and I debrief on the way to the Expedition. His curious words are barely loud enough for me to hear over the swoosh of a stout wind that kicks up out of nowhere. Not that I am complaining. The temperature is still too hot for comfort. Besides, the fresh breeze feels good on my skin after the stale, claustrophobic, tundra-like air in the bowels of the hotel basement. Unsure of his meaning, I ask a follow-up question.

"What knife?"

"Savage's knife."

"Having been on the wrong end of it, you'll get no argument from me."

"You don't get what I'm saying. The knife bothers me because it wasn't the murder weapon. That knife is glued to his side, like a security blanket almost. Assume Savage is out for a late-night stroll outside Kessler's place. He sees the man who he thinks murdered his daughter walking alone toward the beach. He decides the time has come for that man to die. What weapon is Savage going to use? A brick that borders a flower garden? Never. He probably wouldn't even notice it in the dark. Besides, he doesn't need a brick. The perfect tool for the job is already at his side. He's gonna fillet Kessler like a fish with his trusty knife. Remember how fast he whipped it around on you? That's his weapon of choice."

The reasoning makes too much sense. But I'm not willing to give up on Rickie Savage quite yet, especially given his connections to Sadie and Meredith Bixby. I try to answer Scott's objection.

"Here's the thing—no one is likely to use a brick as a murder weapon. Except someone did. The brick is a neutral fact that doesn't convict or exonerate anyone. It just is. As for Savage, maybe he only wears the knife when he's fishing and stores it in his tackle box at all other times. Maybe he forgot about it in the delirium of deciding to kill Kessler. Maybe he didn't want to throw it away after the murder and decided to use something else. Maybe Sadie or Meredith Bixby paid him to commit the crime but told him to use a weapon that couldn't be traced. Maybe a thousand other possibilities. You know better than anyone how random some murders are."

"All true. And I'm telling you from my innermost policeman's gut that I don't like it."

The both of us are practically shouting at this point over the din of the ever-rising wind. We take in the disappointment of the other person. A world in which Rickie Savage didn't kill Donovan Kessler is not our preferred reality. But I stop arguing the point with him.

Truth be told, I have no clue who the murderer is.

* * *

Once more, we ride over the bridge that connects Jekyll Island and the causeway. I point out a pod of dolphins to our right, but Scott is unimpressed, which is consistent with his big city outlook on issues small and large. Dolphins are plentiful down here, and I have yet to lose the wonder that comes from spotting such magnificent creatures in the wild. On my last trip to the island with Amber and Cale, a large pod was grazing close to the shoreline on the beach. With Cale in my arms, I slowly walked out to wade in the water with them. Cale squealed with excitement every time one of the dolphins zipped past us. The memory is one of my happiest but always with a bittersweet tinge. Never being able to see the man he would become figures to remain the lifelong thorn in my flesh—a dull ache that never fully heals.

The phone in the SUV rings, and J.D.'s name pops up on the caller ID. He asks over the car's speaker, "How did it go with Sadie Foxx?" I let Scott handle the response.

"She admitted trying to kill Donovan Kessler by inducing a cardiac event through deployment of her most lethal skill—frantic sex. But she denied using a brick to redecorate his head."

A long silence transpires on the other end of the line. At last, J.D. asks, "You serious?"

"As a heart attack."

"Is that even a crime?"

I answer, "Don't know. I missed that day in law school."

J.D. mulls that over for a second before getting to the point of the call.

"Well, I completed those tasks you assigned me. First, except for Rickie Savage, none of our suspects left the island and returned yesterday through the toll plaza. If one of them is the murderer, we might find the bloody clothes on Jekyll, after all. The off-duty guys are still digging through the trash. Second, I combed through the Ring footage in the neighborhood and cross-tabbed that information with all the license plates I could capture. Only one thing popped out. Meredith Bixby's vehicle drove away from the victim's house at 11:25 p.m. on the night of the murder. I found that strange because the Ring camera on Kessler's front door caught her leaving there at 10:56 p.m., and the hotel is only a couple of minutes away. What was she doing during those thirty minutes?"

Excellent question and one I intend to ask her later tonight. But first we have another date with Rickie Savage.

43

Scott figured that Savage would be *"ornery, smelly, and stupid"* when we saw him. One part of the trifecta—the smell—is confirmed immediately upon entering the holding cell space. I don't know why I assumed that Savage's unique fragrance would improve after a night of sitting behind bars. Evaporation maybe. Science was never a strong suit of mine. But I certainly didn't expect the stench to worsen. Except here we are.

Rickie's appearance has taken a turn for the worse, too. The stubble on his face is a day longer. The sweat and grime from yesterday are no longer fresh but baked-on like hardened crust. He looks mean as hell, as if the time alone has given him the opportunity to catalogue a lifetime of grievances. His first words when we enter do nothing to change that perception. Savage launches into curse-laden descriptions of us that are at least amusingly descriptive. The twang is even more redneck than yesterday. I mentally check off the ornery box from Scott's prediction as being fulfilled. That leaves just one—stupid.

Scott responds to the insults in good humor, "We missed you, too."

More expletives follow in rapid succession. At the end of the tirade, Rickie bellows, "What about a lawyer? I told you I wanted one." The mention of lawyers is my cue to enter the conversation.

"Not exactly. You asked us to see if Meredith Bixby would represent you. We asked. And you know what she did in response? Laughed in our face. Told us that's *'the silliest thing'* she has ever heard in her life. She added for free that after hearing about Donovan Kessler's murder, her mind immediately went to you as being the killer. Seems her opinion of you doesn't match your opinion of her. And before you go off asking about getting another lawyer, I want you to listen real close to what I'm about to say."

I pause to allow him to calm down and fully process my next words. He grunts some indecipherable noises but gives me the full attention of his eyes, which is close enough.

"We have some bad news for you. The state patrol searched your place today and found a boatload of drugs. Dealer levels, in fact. The GBI has already confiscated your entire inventory and will no doubt be wanting to talk to you shortly. The good news is that drugs bore me. I'm a murder guy and can help you on the drug charges if you'll talk to me about my murder. But if you really want a lawyer, I have to stop this conversation immediately. Up to you. A man in your position, though, needs all the friends he can get, and I can be a good friend."

Savage stares at me blankly—his face close enough to the prison bars to reach out and touch them with his tongue. When one of his eyes begins to twitch, I interpret the movement to be the mental wheels in his head grinding to a start. It's an arduous process. Raymond Kessler told me that he actually sat across the table from Savage during a deposition for the Judy Kessler car wreck case. Trying for hours to get answers out of Rickie's slow-moving brain would have made me reconsider my career choices. It'd be like watching a snail make its way from Jekyll Island to California but going the long way through China. He readies himself to respond.

"But I don't know nothing about no murder."

"You arrived later than usual at home the night Donovan Kessler was killed. Why?"

"I'd prefer not to say."

"And I'd prefer not be talking to you right now, but cosmic bad luck has brought the two of us together. The failure to answer the question will be taken as your complicity in Kessler's murder."

"Man, you're way off base. You serious about not caring about drug dealing and all that?"

"Murder is the only thing that scratches me where I itch. Nothing else."

"Well … I had a … um … transaction that night around eleven-twenty on the pier. Once that was complete, I headed straight home."

"We're going to need the name of the buyer."

"Are you crazy?"

He's the insane one to believe that he can get away with not disclosing the name of the closest thing he has to an alibi. After more back-and-forth, I convince him that his self-interest would be best served by giving up the information. Scott texts the name to J.D. with instructions to check it out. I ask another question.

"Why did you run from us yesterday, Rickie?"

"Because of the pills in my tackle box. I thought you two were drug boys."

I turn to Scott, who looks skeptical. He swings around and exits the room. Thirty seconds later, he returns with all of Rickie's personal effects, including the knife that yesterday hovered far too close to my stomach. I stare at it again and shudder a little. So much of existence hangs on the most fragile of threads.

As the search of the tackle box commences, Savage directs Scott to a set of red and white fishing bobbers—a small earth-shape sphere used to alert the fisherman when a fish has taken the bait. After further instructions, Scott unscrews one of the bobbers and finds a stash of little white pills inside. Oxycodone is my guess. Pain relief for the masses. The other bobbers contain the same bounty. Rickie is pleased with himself.

"You see? I'm being straight with you. Mind if I have one of those pills?"

We ignore the request, but Savage is starting to make a believer out of me. And if his story about the late-night drug deal holds up, the odds of his being the winning suspect in the Donovan Kessler murder sweepstakes would take a nosedive. A drug deal at eleven-twenty would be a fatal complication in the timeline, making Rickie the GBI's problem and not mine. I decide to see what else he might know.

* * *

"Let's say I'm inclined to believe you didn't kill Kessler. Someone else did. Maybe you know something about who that person might be. The more help you give me, the more help I can give you. Becky's girlfriend moved into Kessler's house. What about her? Could she have killed him?"

"Sadie? That'd be the only way she could redeem herself in my eyes. She pimped out her body to the man who murdered Becky, like a high-priced hooker. Last time I saw her, she tried to convince me that her dearest Donny would never murder anyone. Made me sick—her disrespecting Becky like that—and I told her exactly what she was."

Interesting that Sadie's story checks out, at least the part of it that involves Rickie. But if she truly was playing a long game that involved murdering Kessler at the end of it, sharing that secret with Savage would be foolish. I switch to the other person of interest that connects to Rickie.

"Tell me some more about your conversation with Meredith Bixby on the pier."

"Why on earth?"

"Call it a test of her honesty."

He squints at me strangely, as if the thought of a dishonest lawyer is the craziest thing he has ever heard.

"We didn't say much. Meredith didn't know about Becky, and I told her that Donovan Kessler killed her. She didn't quite believe that. She admitted that he was a first-class snake but doubted that he would murder anyone himself. Is that what you're looking for? Want me to say that she talked about killing him?"

"All I want is the truth."

Savage again gives me the weird squint eyes. Thinking continues to be hard for him, and the work appears to be taking its toll. Once he cycles through all his thoughts, a slimy smile manifests itself on the prisoner.

"Now that I remember it—she did mention that it would be a nice thing if something happened to Kessler and asked me if I might be interested. I said, 'Like murder?' She just shrugged and answered, 'Why not?' I told her that was too much trouble for me to handle. She answered, 'Too bad.' That's exactly what happened, and I'm willing to testify to that in court for the right deal."

I glance at Scott—whose slow shake of the head shows that we share the same lack of faith in the veracity of the witness. Scott told me earlier that I would find a way to convince Rickie to give me something on the murder in exchange for help on the drug charges. Give him credit for that prediction. But Savage is offering to sell counterfeit goods to the wrong guy. I wasn't kidding with him. *All I want is the truth.*

"And yet you requested that Meredith be your lawyer? If she was the killer like you suggest, I'd figure she would do her best to make sure you went down for the crime. She'd take the case and lose it on purpose so that the murder stuck to you. That would put her in the clear."

The idea is too much for him. He weakly replies, "Man, I don't know. I didn't get that far in my thinking. Tell me what to say, and I'll say it. Anything to help with the drug business. Is it Sadie you're after? I might remember some more about her if you can guide me a little."

"You've seen too many movies."

It's always jarring to come across people who simply assume that you're a lot more corrupt than you really are. I leave him without another word. The Sheriff's Department, acting on the GBI's behalf, will soon arrive to transfer Savage to a county jail on the drug charges. I'll make sure that the local prosecutor adds yesterday's attack on us at the pier to the criminal ledger.

But on the mental list I keep in my mind of all the suspects, I scratch Rickie off the list.

44

The ride back to Jekyll is a quiet one. Scott and I are deep in our own thoughts after another long day. We could eat—the hour being right for dinner—but neither of us is really in the mood. The last glimpses of light fight a losing battle for survival on the far horizon. The thing to do now is find out what Meredith Bixby has to say for herself. Rickie's attempt to save himself by implicating her is of no concern. That's fake news in the current parlance. But she still has to answer the mystery of why she took so long to make it back to the hotel the night of the murder.

Tonight Meredith is set to be sworn in as the new state bar president. Pulling her away from her big moment is poor form. And while I'm generally indifferent as to what people think of me, missteps in front of an audience of the most important lawyers and judges in the state could rebound against Cate. That caution gives me pause.

Just like last night, Scott and I enter the banquet room to find Meredith on the big stage. This time her right hand is high in the air as she takes the oath of office. When the ritual is complete, a standing ovation follows. Scott—who is dressed like a lawyer at least—sighs and heads to the bar to grab a free drink. Meredith takes her position behind the microphone to discuss her plans for the next year. I pretend to listen. At one point she makes eye contact with me and holds the contact for a couple of seconds. She doesn't glance my way again.

Another standing ovation follows the conclusion of the speech. Meredith flashes her trademark grin on the way off the stage. Like a seasoned politician, she shakes many hands in the audience while working the crowd. I wait. The end of her journey through the room stops a few steps in front of where I'm standing. Another smile—this one forced—greets me. She speaks through gritted teeth.

"Your timing is impeccable."

"Murder investigations have a timetable all their own."

"Come on."

We follow her out of the banquet hall. Scott places his empty glass of beer on a tray. She leads us to the same room where the three of us talked last night. With the door closed, her smile falls right off. She snaps, "Make it quick."

"Less than an hour ago, Rickie Savage alleged that you solicited him to murder Donovan Kessler."

The allegation is obviously bogus, but it does make for a nice conversation starter. Meredith looks wounded. Her disappointment in Scott and me is apparent, like a loving mother who cannot believe that her darling kids would ever do her wrong.

"And you believed him?"

"Never said that, but I'm obliged to ask you about it."

"I suppose you are. Here's my response. Make sure you write it down for your files. That allegation is categorically false, and Rickie Savage is a damn liar. In no way, shape, or form did I ever make such a suggestion to that near worthless man."

"Your denial is noted for the record. Thank you."

She nods her head appreciatively. No one speaks for a few seconds. Noise from the banquet next door floats through the air. From the sound of it, everyone is having a good time. A wary Meredith asks, "That all?"

"One more thing. The Ring video of your argument with Kessler shortly before he was killed has a timestamp of 10:56 p.m., meaning that's when you left his house. But according to other Ring footage from neighboring homes, you didn't drive back to the hotel until 11:25 p.m., thirty minutes later. What were you doing in-between?"

For the first time, a question catches her flat-footed. She tries to smile but ends up scoffing instead. Even that comes off a little short. Flustered would be the best word to describe her. Flustered that instead of being celebrated and feted in a room full of well-wishers, she's getting caught off-guard with surprise questions from murder investigators. Composure is like a second skin for her, though. She recovers quickly.

"You guys are thorough. My compliments."

The praise falls on deaf ears. My focus is on her, not on any stall tactic. That the question so obviously staggers her makes me all the more interested in the answer. The tingle I get in anticipation of big moments in a case radiates throughout my body, all the way down to my toes. The next version of Meredith's smile that I see is a sheepish grin of surrender.

"You guys are not going to believe me, but all I can do is tell you the truth. I was meditating in my car."

Even with a million guesses as to what words would next come out of her mouth, I'd never have landed on those. The knowledge that Scott doesn't believe her is secure without any need to look at him. She has a better chance with me. I have a particular weakness that he lacks. The more fanciful an answer is, the more susceptible I am to believe it. Truth is stranger than fiction and all that. Meredith's response is of the same species.

"Meditating?"

"Afraid so. Long ago, I internalized the practice of transcendental meditation. When I first became a lawyer, opposing counsel, always older men, would patronize and belittle me. They'd make comments about my body, hair, inexperience. The whole gamut of misogyny. Anything to get under my skin, you know. Their tactics worked and brought me to the edge of depression sometimes. One day I realized that I could never change the sexist dinosaurs that still roam the earth, but I could control how I reacted to them. A strong smile to an insult is disarming to a pig. The response makes him think that I know something he doesn't. I became a happy warrior, and the change served me well."

She stops and even takes a calming breath, gulping all the air that can fit into her small lungs. Maybe my imagination is playing tricks on me, but I can almost see a wave of peace flow over her. Her narrative is only half-complete, though. I prod her to finish it.

"Interesting story, except I didn't hear anything in it about Donovan Kessler or spending a half hour in your car around the same time he was getting murdered."

"The resolve I developed over time doesn't happen by magic. It takes work—intentional meditation to center myself when the shores of life get too rocky. Becoming president of the state bar represented an important milestone in my journey. I worked a lot of years to get to this point, and now here comes Donovan threatening to take it all away through a baseless attack on my integrity. After that kerfuffle on his front porch, the anger started boiling inside of me. But I no longer allow men like Donovan Kessler to make me angry. I reached my car and decided to retake control of my emotions. Right there in the driver's seat, I closed my eyes, worked on my breathing, and repeated my mantra over and over. When I opened my eyes again, about a half hour had passed. My equilibrium had returned, and I headed back to the hotel."

"Your meditation process couldn't wait until you returned to the hotel a couple of minutes away?"

"Allowing negative energy to fester is bad for the soul."

Good grief. But maybe she has a point. This case is giving me more negative energy than I can handle. Meredith's account of her whereabouts could be perfectly true but good luck ever verifying that one way or another. The best alibi is one that can be proved. The second best is one that cannot be disproved. Meredith's falls into this second category. Approximately zero chance exists that I could ever show that she wasn't in her car mantra-ing herself to be a better person. The only hope would be a south Georgia jury's thinking the explanation so weird as to be inherently disbelievable. Scott asks, "What mantra did you keep repeating over and over?"

"Mantras are intensely personal. The leading authorities on transcendental meditation all advise that the best practice is to never share your mantra with anyone else. To this day, I've never told another soul."

"Humor me."

Meredith doesn't appear in the mood to humor anyone, but Scott's determined face—chiseled by years of chasing murderers—can persuade people to do a lot of things they otherwise would prefer not to. Meredith is no different.

"All right, you win. The mantra I repeat over and over is: 'My positive thoughts guide me to new heights.' Go ahead and laugh."

Scott doesn't laugh but he does offer an incredulous curse. For good measure, he also shoots a mean glare at me for dragging him down here from Atlanta to talk about meditation mantras. *My positive thoughts guide me to new heights*. How could anyone ever dream of making that up?

She looks at me with yet another version of her malleable smile. This one reminds me of the type my grandmother used whenever I skinned my knee or suffered some other bloody injury—kind, compassionate, sympathetic to my troubles. Meredith realizes that what she just told us is hard to stomach and is actually sensitive to the dilemma we have in choosing to believe her. Her emotional intelligence readings must be off the charts. No doubt she's read all the right books on such things.

"Am I free to go now? People are going to start wondering where I ran off to. It is my big night, after all."

The point is a fair one but part of me doesn't want to concede it. She just told me a few minutes ago about the anger boiling inside of her after arguing with Donovan Kessler—that he stood poised to steal her big moment away from her. Shortly afterwards, he is dead. And Meredith was right there, supposedly with her eyes closed repeating that mantra. I can't let go of her just yet. She must see the lingering concern on my face and takes another shot at convincing me.

"Chance, really. Use your brain. Do I look strong enough to use a brick as a weapon on Donovan Kessler's head? Have you noticed that I'm really short? I wouldn't even be able to reach him up there."

Every muscle in my body freezes. All murderers make mistakes, and the lucky break I need to solve this case may have just fallen into my lap. Only a limited number of people on this island know about the brick, and Meredith shouldn't be one of them. I specifically asked Lois if she or Burt told Meredith about the brick that first morning, and Lois answered, *"Do I look like I fell off the turnip truck or something?"*

But I have to decide pretty damn quick how to handle Meredith's slip. The snap decision is to hit her head-on before she finds a mantra to hide behind. Except she is the first to speak.

"Can I go or not?"

"How did you know that Donovan Kessler was killed with a brick to the head?"

Meredith doesn't even flinch. She matter-of-factly responds, "Burt Pressley told me."

I might as well have been tased with a stun gun. The effect would be the exact same. With hardly any control over my body, I manage to spit out, "When?"

"This afternoon. Can I go now?"

A nod is all I manage. When I do calm down, wrapping my hands around Burt from Bainbridge's neck is the first order of business. And no mantra will be able to stop me.

45

The back of the banquet room is becoming like a second home. Meredith is back smiling at everyone, probably after repeating "*my positive thoughts guide me to new heights*" to herself a few times. I scan the crowd trying to locate Burt and Lois and find them near the front, replete in their finest dinner wear—her in a sparkling evening dress, him in a classic tux. His neck is as thick as his dull-headed brain, making the possibility of strangling him with his bowtie an iffy proposition, which is a shame. I march to their table. On the way over, Cate sees me and starts to offer a little smile but stops midway when she catches the disoriented look on my face.

Just as Burt prepares to put a bite of beef tenderloin into his mouth, I lean into him and snap, "Need to talk with you right now. You can come voluntarily or be dragged."

"Hey—"

"Now."

Lois contemplates me with alarmed eyes. She whispers something to Burt, and the both of them push their chairs back from the table. They follow me out of the ballroom and into the same area where we just questioned Meredith. A bad-tempered Scott stands there already. He looks like an old-school cop from central casting who doesn't mind roughing up suspects who refuse to play ball.

An alarmed Burt whines, "What's this?"

"Did you tell Meredith Bixby earlier today that Donovan Kessler was killed by a brick to the head?"

"Me? Of course not! You told me not to."

He's almost indignant. Between him and Meredith, someone is lying, and my money is on Burt. I give him one more chance.

"Listen to me closely. I'm going to ask you the same question again.

If you give me the same answer, I'm going back into the ballroom next door and will arrest Meredith Bixby for the murder of Donovan Kessler based on the strength of your word. The stakes are fairly high, as you can surmise. Here we go. Did you tell Meredith earlier today that Donovan Kessler was killed by a brick to the head?"

Burt appears shook. His mouth twitches in uncontrolled movements that come close to turning him into some kind of deformed monster. He fights this battle with himself for a few moments before finally corralling enough composure to speak again.

"Well … when you put it that way … I remember maybe … mentioning something along those lines… Felt like she needed to know—"

Lois moans, "Honey, how could you?"

I explode—yelling with full voice and utilizing the full range of my vocabulary. Burt shrinks from the intensity of the onslaught, probably the first time since he became an important man that someone has dressed him down so viciously. Over the years in the courtroom, I grew adept at role-playing the part of an angry lawyer to emphasize a point that needed emphasis. This outburst is not that. What's happening in this room right now comes from the heart. The wild animal is loose on the range, untamed and with unbridled tongue.

When I pause to catch my breath before launching into him again, Lois says, "Enough. You've made your point."

"Have I?"

"Yes."

"You sure? Because I thought I had made my point yesterday. Someone that looks a lot like me said, *'Everything about that crime scene needs to stay secret. If anyone asks you, just say that the authorities have instructed you not to talk about it.'* Howdy-Doody standing next to you vigorously nodded his head like he understood but apparently the lesson didn't take."

An offended Howdy-Doody intercedes, "Hey!"

Lois says, "Shut up, Burt!"

He swivels toward her about to say something but stops cold when he sees the steel in the eyes of his wife. When satisfied that he intends to follow her order, she returns to me.

"You have the information you need, and you have appropriately chastised him for his screw up. Is there anything else?"

"Sure is. I'm still deciding whether to arrest him or not."

"For what? Disobeying your instructions? You're not a court that can throw people in jail for contempt for refusing to follow your orders. Burt messed up, but he didn't do anything criminal. Arresting him only makes you as big an ass as he is."

Burt wants desperately to say something in his defense but again thinks better of it. Scott continues to look tough, but Lois is immune to his charms. I bet she was a heck of a prosecutor down there in Bainbridge. Still, I'm not ready to concede the argument that her husband isn't a criminal.

"He lied to me in this room not five minutes ago. Three witnesses—and you're one of them—heard him make a false statement to law enforcement."

"You're not going to arrest him."

"Why the hell not?"

"Because you're one of the good ones. And even a dog can distinguish the difference between being stumbled over and being kicked."

I don't feel like one of the good ones. Not tonight. And using the famous example about dogs from Oliver Wendell Holmes to distinguish the legal significance of intentional versus unintentional acts doesn't really aid her husband's case. Burt intentionally told Meredith about the brick to puff himself up in her eyes—to show that he was the holder of special, secret knowledge. He didn't accidentally stumble over anything.

But Lois is right. Her husband is just an ass. And if I started arresting everyone who acted like an ass, there wouldn't be too many people left to vote for the Governor. I say, "Get out of here before I change my mind."

Lois grabs her husband's arm and hightails it out of the room. When they're gone, Scott notes, "You're too soft. A night in the county jail would've done wonders for his outlook on life."

"Probably."

"But I did hear you use a bunch of words I've never heard come out of your mouth before. That was worth the whole trip down here. I'm rubbing off on you finally after all these years."

I mumble something to myself that Scott doesn't quite catch. He asks, "What did you say?"

"*My positive thoughts guide me to new heights.*"

"Good luck with that."

46

The banquet is breaking up. I decide that if all those lawyers in their fancy clothes deserve to be fed, then we do, too. Scott texts J.D. and arranges for the three of us to meet at the Shore of Shadows for a late-night meal. As we make our way to the exit, I notice a lonely Raymond Kessler ahead near the doors. He stands far apart from the crowd, just staring out the windows into the dark night. Our approach jostles him out of his reverie. He bows his head in a courtly greeting and starts to talk.

"I hate these things. The only ones I attend are those on Jekyll every few years. Hard to avoid when the event is only a quarter of a mile away. Donovan always leaned on me to come—good for the firm and that type of rigmarole. Don't know why I attended tonight. Habit, I suppose. Should've stayed home. Too many people patting me on the back and speaking in hushed tones. I feel as out of place as a priest in a brothel."

That's an interesting analogy given all the sex scandals in the church world these days. But I appreciate the sentiment all the same. Playing dress up and going to the ball isn't really my cup of tea, either. The last high-end party I attended ended up with a man collapsing dead at my feet after someone decided to poison him. No one's dead tonight at least. Raymond goes on.

"Had a chance to speak with your charming wife tonight. Count yourself fortunate. Not everyone is wired to be alone like me. And if a man can't help himself and decides he has to get married, he better make sure to find a good woman to be his mate. But you need to hold up your end of the bargain and be a good husband. Besides my general disinterest in matrimony, the self-knowledge that I would make some poor woman's life a living hell was enough for me to forsake the institution. To thine own self be true."

"My father used to say that all the time."

"As well he should have. I always felt that Shakespeare was a little hard on old Polonius. But then again, I have a bias for people who talk too much. Reminds me of myself."

He gives a self-deprecating chuckle, and I join him. A bored Scott checks his phone and uses it as a pretext to go outside. Raymond's manner turns more serious. He huddles closer to me and lowers his voice.

"Have you found who killed my brother yet?"

"Afraid not."

"Too bad. You left quite the trail of tears at my house this afternoon. Katherine might as well be in a coma. She has locked herself away in her bedroom all day. Sammy has disappeared. No one has seen him for hours. Lucy is hot and cold. Crying one minute, spitting fire the next. She actually came tonight and is around here somewhere. She's tough like that. And that leaves Maxwell. For him I had to pull some strings with a friend on the judiciary to secure bail. Sexual assault, huh? I guess I shouldn't be surprised. I considered not taking his call. But duty to family runs deep in my veins, even if I can't stand that family much anymore. And you are running roughshod over all of them while telling me you still don't know who murdered my brother. To what end? Is there a purpose to your madness? Or do you just wreck lives because you can? Like a weapon of mass destruction."

Raymond uses his keen eyes to peer into my own, a seeming attempt to dive deep into my soul. I should get Lois Pressley to vouch for me and tell him that I'm one of the good ones. But his questions are fair. I often wrestle with moral doubt at the things my job sometimes forces me to do. Effective law enforcement requires a willingness to unleash daggers of cruelty to people who might not merit being on the other end of such treatment. Unless the guilty freely confess, hard questions have to be asked. I put people on the defensive—make them feel uncomfortable, inflict anguish—to see what might shake out of the tree. The unfortunate costs from my methods are the price of doing a good job. But I don't have to feel good about it.

I explain none of this internal turmoil to Raymond. Instead, I ask him a question.

"Have you ever destroyed a person on cross-examination who didn't really deserve it, but you had to do it anyway for your client's best interests?"

"All the time."

"Same thing. That is the life we have chosen. That is who we are—men who combine their mastery of the power of words with their understanding of human nature to trap people into telling on themselves. To what end? You tell me."

A wry smile overtakes his face. The effort does him some good. Raymond does not look nearly as old when he smiles. Some hidden light works to iron out a critical mass of his wrinkles. He clasps my shoulder with a firm grip. A little sparkle animates him just as he starts to speak.

"Justice is never pretty, is it?"

"Not in my lifetime."

* * *

Scott is outside still staring as his phone when I find him. Immediately upon seeing me, he jerks his head toward the hotel parking lot. I follow his sight path as directed and spy Lucy Kessler standing under a street light. We haven't talked to her since learning about the semen stains in Donovan Kessler's office. The moment seems opportune. Fresh off my conversation with Raymond, I make a command decision to delegate the unpleasant task to Scott.

"Why don't you go tell her about the seminal fluid in her father-in-law's office and ask if she has anything to confess?"

"Me? You're the one who usually talks to lawyers."

"I'm lawyered-out."

He scoffs but heads her way. I watch the scene from afar. When Lucy notices his approach, she acts startled and takes a step back from him. Scott doesn't waste any time starting his spiel. Moments later, Lucy's hands rise to cover her face—the kind of gesture a person instinctively uses when on the wrong end of bad news, as if shutting ourselves off from the world can make the terrible thing go away. But that never works.

The conversation is short. Lucy hurries off on heavy legs, like a groundhog scared of its shadow—almost stumbling a couple of times but managing to stay upright. Scott doesn't go after her and instead makes his way back over to me.

"No confession. She didn't say much of anything. But I'll give you any odds that you want that she participated in the acts that led to the bodily discharge of fluids picked up by that blacklight."

Supposition confirmed.

Working as a prosecutor in Atlanta for so many years, I grew over time to believe that the city was dirty. The idea is true as far as it goes. But the dirt doesn't stop at the city limits. The grime is baked into all of humanity—part of our evolutionary DNA, the inheritance of original sin. And those of us charged with cleaning up the mess cannot escape the stains that adhere to our skin in the blowback.

The brochure for justice might feature pristine marble halls, but the road to get there is littered with filth.

47

The Saturday night crowd at the Shore of Shadows likes to drink. The out-of-town lawyers who have descended on the area like a plague of locusts have their own hospitality lounge at the hotel, and none of them in their penguin suits appear to be present. Instead, the patrons now in our midst are a more blue-collar crowd. They look and act the part. Having always felt more comfortable with the common folk, I'm thankful for the reprieve. After I finished law school, my well-connected father could've arranged—despite my indifferent grades—a job for me with just about any white shoe law firm in Atlanta. But billing my labor in six-minute increments for multi-national corporations never appealed to me. I instead became a prosecutor for half the money.

Scott, J.D., and I snag a corner booth located in the back of the pub. I order the fish and chips in keeping with the English pretenses of the establishment. For the same reason, I decide to drown my sorrows with a glass of sweet tea—the Southern spin on a British classic. All of us raise a toast to the Queen. Her stately presence peers down on us from a portrait on the wall. Long may she reign.

Cecilia Franklin is our waitress. We tell her about Maxwell Matheny's arrest, and her big smile in response is the best thing I've seen since I arrived on Jekyll. When she leaves us, J.D. says, "I talked to that guy who Savage said he sold the drugs to. After I promised not to arrest him if he told the truth, he admitted to the transaction, the time, and the place—eleven-twenty that night on the pier. Bought some oxy for a back injury that still hurts him all the time. What does that mean for pinning Savage for the murder?"

I answer, "It means we don't. Rickie Savage is not the person we're looking for."

Scott explains the timeline to him. J.D. looks disappointed, which is fair. I can still see the bitemark on his neck. Plus, when he tells his grandchildren about the football spear he delivered to Savage on the dock, the story would sound better if he had tackled a murderer instead of a pill pusher. I turn to Scott and ask, "What do you think about the case?"

"Shaping up to be the first murder we don't solve. Some murder squad. Should do wonders for our reputation in the rest of the state outside Atlanta."

He raises his beer and gives another salute to the Queen. His joy at seeing me dress down Burt Pressley must have worn off. I try to steer him back on track.

"Surely you have some theories. Let me hear them."

"My best suspect is Rickie Savage, who apparently has an airtight alibi based on the say-so of someone whose whole life revolves around watching reruns of classic television. Have you considered that Otis Harper could be wrong about either the time Rickie made it home or got his nights mixed up somehow? We're talking about an old man here. The simplest solution is usually the right one. Otis made a mistake, and Rickie arrived home later than midnight because he was too busy killing Kessler—the man who murdered his daughter."

"What about the knife? You're the one who told me you didn't like Savage for the crime because he would've used his knife and not the brick."

"I was just talking."

The response lacks enthusiasm. He still doesn't like it. Me, neither. If Savage went over to the Kessler house to commit murder, he damn sure would've taken a murder weapon with him and not stumbled upon the idea of the brick on the way. I ask, "What about Sadie as a suspect?"

"You could get a conviction. No problem. Woman moves in with the man suspected of killing her girlfriend. Man turns up murdered shortly thereafter. Not a lot of imagination necessary to connect those dots. You know juries better than I do, but they would eat that up. Throw in the fact that she gets the multi-million-dollar house. Throw in all her lies. Throw in the admission that she actually tried to kill him through sex. A guilty verdict would be a cinch. Like shooting fish in a barrel, even for a bad shot like you. But did she actually do it? No idea. I don't like the brick for her, either. Say that Sadie goes to all this trouble to play the long game of killing this guy—is she really going to rely on a brick she picks up on the way to the beach? Doubtful. The brick as a weapon suggests an impulse killing."

"Someone who's angry and impulsive like Lucy Kessler."

Scott smiles and motions to Cecilia for another beer. He points to his temple and makes the case against Lucy.

"She has been on my mind more and more. The storming down the stairs that you described points to a volatile personality. The flat-out lie about not leaving the bedroom is pretty damning. She even admitted seeing Donovan Kessler in the backyard walking to the beach. I mean, she confessed to going downstairs, opening the door, and calling out to him. Lucy was there—exactly where we theorized the killer would be at exactly the right time. Sometimes the answer is just staring you in the face, right?"

"Except we have no other proof."

"Correct. We have no real evidence pointing to anybody. Maybe we should expand the suspect pool. What about the old man? He was right there in the house next door."

"Raymond?"

"Why not?"

While I mull over the suggestion, Scott adds, "Didn't you say that Donovan managed all the business of their law firm? Suppose he caught Raymond with his hand in the company till. Some kind of embezzlement or hanky-panky with Judy's massive settlement. She can't spend it all, that's for sure."

"Do you know how much money Raymond has won as a trial lawyer over the years? He has to have at least a hundred million in the bank. Probably more. I heard one time that he even owns his own airplane."

"Who knows? Maybe he squandered it all. Those billboards aren't cheap. Airplanes, either. And Madoff was once worth over $50 billion. All I'm saying—"

J.D. interrupts, "What the hell?"

I turn around from my place in the booth to see what catches his attention and wish I hadn't. After the past two days, the needle that measures my tolerance for drama is all the way past empty, but some people are hellbent on dishing out turmoil in spades. With a little bit of luck, I might've gone the rest of my life without ever seeing this person again. Instead, I didn't even make it eight hours.

Maxwell Matheny walks into the pub through the front door.

48

Maxwell—wearing the haggard appearance of a recent jail stint—hardly wastes a second before becoming disagreeable. He strides straight to the bar and finds the only stool not occupied, nudging a mean-looking woman to create the necessary room, all without so much as a sorry. The woman aggressively stares at him for a few seconds, and I wonder if she might have a go at kicking his ass before she lets the matter drop.

But Maxwell barely notices. His eyes scan around the crowded bar like a junkie looking for a fix. When he sees Cecilia waiting on a nearby table, he slides down off the stool and is hot on her trail. J.D. stands up and announces, "I'll handle this." If J.D. requires reinforcements, Scott can serve as his backup and perhaps land a death punch to Maxwell's other kidney. I sit back and watch. If a situation arises where I have to leave my seat to become involved, all hell will have broken loose.

Cecilia's back is to Maxwell as he approaches. He reaches out and puts a hand on her shoulder. When Cecilia turns around to see him, her body flinches. I'm too far away to hear anything being said in the noise of the bar, but my eyes capture everything. The round tray that she is carrying—full of glasses filled with beer—drops to the floor. The resulting clamor brings a sudden hush to the pub. J.D. reaches Maxwell and blocks him off from Cecilia. Maxwell doesn't take the intervention well.

"Who the hell are you?"

J.D. answers the question and sticks his badge in front of Maxwell's face in case a problem exists with the angry man's hearing. The gun at his side isn't exactly invisible, either. None of that matters to Maxwell.

"Get out of my way, kid. I just want to talk to the lady. There's a misunderstanding that we need to clear up."

Raymond shouldn't have arranged bail for this idiot. Maxwell needed at least one night in a cell. The humbling might've improved his manners. Now he's just angry without the benefit of being broken. From the legal side of things, coming here seemingly straight from jail sinks for good any defense he might've concocted to the sexual assault and will probably add at least another year to his jail sentence. His eventual lawyer figures to read of this incident and weep, assuming that Maxwell survives the night.

Scott gets out of the booth to provide backup. J.D.—who continues to shield a cowering Cecilia behind him—stands his ground.

"Look, Matheny. If you don't leave, you're heading right back to jail. Go home and get to bed."

A loud snort is the only response. J.D. places a firm hand on Maxwell's chest to keep him at bay. Maxwell holds his hands up in a gesture of surrender, but the malice lurking below the surface would be plain even to a blind man. The crooked grin on his face signals the formation of a very bad idea in a mind on tilt. But the smile vanishes in world record time when Maxwell sees Scott walking up. The pain of the devastating kidney punch must be still a fresh memory. Good. Maxwell starts to whine.

"What are you doing here? Why do you keep harassing me?"

The large room is deathly still. That this many people out drinking on a Saturday night could get this quiet so quickly suggests that the confrontation is as explosive as I fear. People have an innate nose for such things—the wisdom of crowds or some similar concept. A few patrons have their phones out recording everything. That development is unwelcome. Video is highly manipulable, and the wrong angle can tell a false story to the rest of the world not in the room. The good news is that Scott knows a lot of subtle methods not readily visible to hurt a man. For the time being, he plays it cool.

"Hi, Max. How are you feeling? I didn't expect that you'd would be upright this soon after your injury. You've had a long day. If any part of your brain is still functioning, you need to realize that no scenario exists where staying in this bar right now ends well for you. This young lady doesn't want to speak with you. Leave and go home. The only other choice is a one-way ticket back to a jail cell—or maybe a hospital if you try to act tougher than you are."

I can't see Scott's face, but I would bet my last dollar that his expression conveys the impression that he would enjoy inflicting more injury upon Maxwell's body if afforded the chance. Maxwell's own face, which I can see, appears to confirm my certainty on this point. He no longer looks like a man entertaining a bad idea but rather someone scrambling to come up with a face-saving retreat. Scott takes one step closer and growls, "Leave."

Maxwell hightails it out the door, spouting militant nonsense along the way. The crowd erupts in thunderous applause, but Scott barely acknowledges the attention. He returns to the booth like a never-nervous gunslinger. J.D. helps Cecilia pick up the broken glass off the floor. Charley the bartender assists with a broom. With the mess cleared, J.D. exits the pub for a minute before coming back in.

Scott complains, "I was really looking forward to hitting him again."

"Best not with all the cameras around."

All I get out of him is a dissatisfied grunt. J.D. returns to the booth and says, "He got in his car and drove away. Think this time he got the message?"

No one has an answer. Maxwell's behavior the last few days is a testament to his not getting the message. Cecilia refused his advances. His family excluded him from its meeting. Scott rearranged his kidney. Any one of these happenings should've prompted him to have a long, penetrating inspection of himself in the mirror.

But some people like to wallow in their own lack of self-awareness, which makes it hard for the rest of us.

49

The food arrives. After setting down our orders, Cecilia gives J.D. a side hug and proclaims, "My hero." He blushes while she scurries away. I'm too hungry to pay it much attention. Skipping dinner earlier in the evening seemed like a good idea at the time, but now the bill is due. I attack the fish on my plate as if it personally offended me somehow. The rest of the table pays similar attention to their plates. Between bites of his steak, Scott poses a question to me.

"Why did we move Maxwell down on the suspect list again?"

"Because he was too busy attacking Cecilia."

"Yeah, that. Always the timing. We just saw how that one handles adversity. Maxwell went home the night of the murder after being rejected by Cecilia and knocked down by Charley. He already resents Donovan Kessler because of Sadie. Hates the whole damn family, including his wife. He has a predisposition to violence already and fancies himself a tough guy. Hell, he tried to attack you with three police officers in the same room. If Maxwell sees Kessler on that beach, then he's picking up that brick."

"Except Kessler went for his walk nearly an hour and a half before Maxwell arrived home."

"Do I have to do everything? You figure that part out."

I'll get to work on it. We return the bulk of our attention to the food. As the hour gets later, the crowd in the bar gets more boisterous. The mere normalcy of the moment is a treasured oasis in the non-stop running around of these past two days. Just yesterday morning, I stood on the fourth fairway playing golf with George the Alligator. That moment feels like a week ago. But most investigations take on a similar life of their own—a time warp where the rest of the world barely continues to exist. The hope is to plow through the rough patch and come out alive on the other side.

J.D. asks me, "Who does that leave? Any other suspects?"

"The children. Katherine Matheny and Sammy Kessler."

Scott makes a disagreeable face and says, "The sleepwalker and the mouse. Katherine admits having dreams about a child killing his father with a heavy object. A little bit on the nose, don't you think? She also made sure that we knew about her sleepwalking habit. Convenient. If we somehow found enough evidence for an indictment, she has already set the stage for high-priced doctors to get her off the hook. As for the mouse, Sammy's under the radar as far as evidence goes, but that makes me suspect him all the more. He did yell at his wife the day his father bought it. For the mouse to scream at the lion is something. He had plenty of motive and enough opportunity when Lucy was in shower. That's all I got."

He finishes off the rest of his beer, and we digest his analysis in a contemplative silence. Cecilia comes over to tell us that the meal is on the house because of our help in expelling Maxwell from the premises. She does accept a fifty-dollar bill as a tip after I explain that the money is courtesy of the Governor. When the three of us again have the booth to ourselves, I give my parting monologue of the evening.

"Well, you've convinced me. They all did it. Rickie Savage—because he is a violent man with an avowed desire to kill Kessler and happened to be right down the street at the time. Sadie Foxx—to avenge the murder of her lover and collect $5 million in the process. Extra credit since she even admitted to plotting to kill him. Lucy Kessler—a liar, consumed with both love and jealousy, who confessed to seeing him walk toward the beach. The best opportunity of anybody. Maxwell—a person who was already in a frenzied state looking for anyone to hurt. Katherine—a woman trying to sell us a bunch of sleepwalking and dream nonsense that is clearly a put on. Sammy—because he yelled at his wife. And lastly, Raymond, as it would be unsporting not to include him, too. Plus, maybe he's an embezzler. You two have your work cut out for you. I look forward to hearing your final answer when I get back from Italy."

The suggestion about my trip I receive from Scott in response would probably land me in an Italian jail. He stands up. The idea is an excellent one, and I join him. But J.D. remains planted in the booth, saying, "I'm gonna stay to ensure that Cecilia makes it to her car safely. Maxwell may come back and try something." Scott peers down at the younger man and pats him on the shoulder.

"Good idea. Please remember, though, that she's a witness in our murder investigation. You can look but don't touch."

J.D. blushes for the second time that night but nods in understanding. He's a good kid.

Walking out of the bar, I realize that we forgot to include Meredith Bixby in our rundown of suspects.

50

In contrast to the heat that we endured most of the day, the night air packs a spring chill. I stare at the hotel with hungry eyes, eager to rest and spend at least a little time with Cate. Scott has other ideas.

"Let's drive past the Kessler place."

"What on earth for?"

"Call it professional curiosity. Shouldn't take long. About a minute with the way you drive."

I should make him walk. Two minutes later, the Expedition sits idling in the street in front of the neighboring homes of the Kessler brothers. The door to Donovan's place is draped with yellow crime scene tape and still legally off-limits to intruders. Little investigative reason exists to keep the previous inhabitants from returning, but I remain wary of putting Sadie and the Kesslers back together while ownership of the property remains murky. If I can stall long enough to Monday, the courts can sort out who gets the house for the time being.

Cars are a passion of mine, and I process them with the same instinctual understanding as a chess grandmaster does when analyzing the position of the pieces on a chessboard. All the cars that were here yesterday, except for Sadie's Ford Mustang, are present and accounted for. Even Sammy's BMW has returned. The prodigal son's threat never to come back didn't last long.

Tolstoy wrote in *Anna Karenina*: "Happy families are all alike; every unhappy family is unhappy in its own way." The Kesslers prove the last half of that wisdom. Consider that Sammy, his wife apparently in love with his father, cannot make himself sever—even for one night—the bonds that torment him. The story is an old one. Home is always a hard habit to break.

Scott studies both residences. I ask, "Can I go to sleep now?"

"Look upstairs in Donovan's house."

The tenor in his voice barely reveals his excitement, but the undercurrent is there if you know what to listen for. I do as instructed and don't even have to squint to see the item of interest. A movement of faint light darts in fits and spurts through the cracks of some blinds. Someone is up there with a flashlight. I turn back to Scott in sheer amazement.

"How did you know?"

"Didn't. But half of police work is simply showing up to see what happens. And a lot tends to happen after dark."

We exit the vehicle and make our way to the front door. I ask, "Guns drawn?"

"A midnight trespasser is rooting around in the dark with a flashlight in an off-limits area and you actually think I'm not going to have a gun in my hand?"

"Good point. Should we call J.D. for back up?"

"Nah. Let him keep watch over his girlfriend. We've got this."

The difficulty we encountered in corralling Rickie Savage is still fresh on my mind. The memory makes me terminally unsure about a two-man operation. Scott's injured knee should give him similar caution, but the die is cast. I follow his lead and take my gun out—switching the safety off so it's ready to use on a split-second's notice.

As we remove the police tape and enter through the front door, the blue light on the Ring camera activates to record our movements. At least Cate can see how I looked shortly before death if this reconnaissance mission blows up in my face.

Scott's flashlight illuminates the stairs, and we take them one at a time—quiet and slow. When I performed the noise test on the steps yesterday, I never figured to be so thankful that the carpet deadens amplification of sound. But in the silence of the night with a gun in my hand—when the beating in my chest feels like my own telltale heart—every slight creak clangs in my ears like a gunshot.

We stop and listen hard after both of us reach the second floor. Scott switches his flashlight to off. From the street, the movement in the house appeared to originate from Sammy and Lucy's bedroom suite. That hypothesis is now confirmed. A faint glow from the intruder's flashlight appears under their door and reaches us in the hall. Scott uses that bit of illumination to sneak his way to the door.

He makes some type of hand signal as an instruction, but the meaning is lost on me. I put my palms up in a shrug-like gesture. He just waves it off and hands me his flashlight. After a further round of charades, I figure out that he wants me to shine the light into the room when he opens the door, preferably right into the mystery person's eyes.

Everything happens fast. Scott bursts through the door, and I'm right on his heels trying to find a body to shine the flashlight on. A high-pitched scream—full of blood-curdling terror—slashes through the quiet like a mass murderer wielding an ax. The shriek allows me to focus the beam on the source of the noise.

Sammy Kessler, the mouse, looks as scared as any man I've ever seen in my life. The focus of the flashlight on his face dilates his pupils, and he blinks a number of times to ward off the attack. No one fires a gun, and I count that as a win. I feel for the switch on the wall and flip on the room's overhead lights. One more unpleasant surprise awaits us.

Sammy stands next to the bed buck naked.

51

Being naked with two guns pointed at him makes Sammy appear less like a mouse and more like a frightened turtle. The only thing missing is the protective shell to cover him. He stands there shivering all over, nearly on the verge of tears. I re-holster my weapon and take a deep breath—unsure of whether to laugh, cry, or leave town immediately to escape this case forever. Scott keeps his aim on the target. I demand of the turtle, "Explain yourself and make it good."

"I ... I couldn't go back there and be in the same room with Lucy. Not anymore. I decided to spend the night over here."

"But why are you naked?"

"That's how I sleep."

He scans his eyes down at himself as if to make sure. I ask Scott, "Should we allow him to put some clothes on?"

With his gun and laser-like focus still trained on Sammy, Scott says, "We let you go change, you're not going to come back out with a gun or knife or anything else like that are you? Because that would be bad for your health."

Sammy has a hard time processing the words. He remains shaking for a spell and finally stammers, "A gun? No way. I've never fired one of those in my whole life. Too loud."

We let him go to the bathroom to make himself presentable for company. Scott notes, "I was worried that whoever was in the house might have a gun, but Sammy's not packing much of anything, if you know what I mean. Not surprising that Lucy would want to plant her flag on firmer ground."

Harsh but fair. I remember Maxwell's words to me yesterday about Sammy and Lucy that he "*never got the feeling that there was much loving regard between man and wife.*" Maybe their problems started in bed. On cue, Sammy emerges from the bathroom wearing a teal green silk bath robe. The wardrobe choice makes him appear even less manly than he did trembling in the nude.

When I mentioned his putting on clothes, I had an outfit more substantial in mind. Not a lot of fabric separates him from us. The thought makes me uncomfortable. He asks, "Can I stay here tonight? Please. I have no other place to go. Once the memorial luncheon for Father is over tomorrow, I'm going back to Savannah and may never come back."

I answer, "What did you do with yourself tonight? You told us you were going drinking, but you seem stone cold sober to me."

"Went to Florida to go see some dog racing. Watching greyhounds run has always had a calming effect on my mood. They're beautiful animals. I had one daiquiri. That's it. I'm not a big drinker and don't really know how to get drunk."

The scene is absurd. I should take the opportunity to ask him more questions but don't even know what to ask. He already admitted to yelling at Lucy on the day of the murder, and I have no evidence to prove that he ever left this room while Lucy was in the shower that night—his one chance to kill his father. Out of better options, I decide just to agitate him and see what happens. Instead of a question, I provide an update on the investigation.

"You deserve to know what the GBI discovered during their tests today in this house. Using black light technology, technicians found the presence of seminal fluid on the couch in your father's office. Sadie swears she never goes into the office. Detective Moore asked your wife about it and, based on her reaction, concluded that she engaged in romantic activity with your father that led to the discharge of the semen."

Scott offers a solemn nod to reinforce the validity of his conclusion. Sammy starts the shivering again. We watch him—doing the part of police work that involves just showing up to see what happens. He makes a sudden move but nothing that is a threat to us. Balling up his fists, he starts to smack himself on the head. The force is hard enough that I feel compelled to say something.

"That's not going to do anything but you give yourself a headache, Sammy."

The blows continue. I'm not exactly sure what a demon-possessed man looks like, but Sammy would seem to be in the ballpark. A stream of incoherent mutterings adds to the case. I step toward him, wary that a lot of those punches might land on me if I get too close. Except letting him continue to hurt himself is not an option, either. A kidney punch from Scott would put a stop to the display and allow Scott to smack his second lawyer of the day. But Sammy's so thin that Scott's fist might come out the other side. I bite the bullet, rush in, and encircle Sammy's entire chest from the back with the strongest bear hug of my life.

He squirms and squirms. I hold on for dear life. Scott moves closer, ready to intervene if necessary. For his own sake, Sammy had better hope that he doesn't slip away from me because my partner figures to use enough force to knock him down for at least a ten count. The writhing continues, but I'm the stronger man. The fight seeps out of him, and the tension in his body releases. I relax my grip.

Sammy uses the opportunity to turn the front of his body toward me and move in for a tight hug—burying his now-crying face into my shoulder.

***

The torrent of tears is violent. I give him an awkward pat on the back and look out over his head to Scott, whose struggling attempt to hold back his laughter might create enough pent-up pressure to burst his appendix. I flash him a look of murder that does little to abate his bemusement. Sammy whimpers out some words.

"My father never hugged me."

The man in my arms is at least a decade older than me yet somehow I am now serving as a surrogate father figure to him. How did I end up in this mess? I start to rethink my life choices but decide that the moment might be right to illicit some raw honesty from the witness.

"Sammy, sorry that your wife and father hurt you like that. I really am. But I have to ask. Did you kill him? I'd understand it if you did."

He stiffens for a second before crying harder on my shoulder. After this goes on for long enough to make me even more uncomfortable, Sammy begins gasping for breath while he pants out a response.

"Lucy. It was Lucy."

That's an attention-grabber. The bemusement drains right out of Scott's face, replaced by a deadly seriousness. My emotions aren't far behind. I've been around enough murder investigations to recognize that you never know. Solving our case by stumbling upon a man buck naked in his own bedroom wasn't on my bingo card, but life rarely goes according to script. I pat the back of the man in my arms to provide him more encouragement.

"Why do you say that, Sammy?"

"She was so mad. It had to be her. You don't know her like I do—how she reacts to betrayal. That's why I wanted to spend the night over here. She scares me."

The answer is disappointing, but I keep prodding and ask, "Anything more than that? Did she confess to you?"

"Her eyes. They were crazy—accusatory. She kept staring at me as if I killed Father, but I didn't. Lucy murdered him. I know her."

"Think carefully—do you have any proof? Besides her eyes."

"She left the bedroom when I was in the shower."

"We know about that. Anything else?"

He lifts his head off my shoulder and shakes it back and forth. And that concludes the hugging portion of the evening. I break away from him, and a wounded look of rejection saddens the whole landscape of his face. I turn to Scott, "Any questions?"

Scott says, "You sure you didn't kill your father? Tell us the truth now, and we can help you get a good deal. Mitigating circumstances. All that jazz. But if you're not straight with us, you're staring squarely at the death penalty. Lethal injection—where the State of Georgia kills you by pumping poison into your body. They tell me it's quite unpleasant. One more time. Did you murder your father?"

Sammy's crying jag has made his eyes the color of raw hamburger meat. He dabs his face with the teal bathrobe but the red pallor remains pretty much everywhere. He cranes his neck from Scott to me and back to Scott again before offering a response to the question.

"I would never."

52

I let Sammy spend the night in Sadie's house. The decision was the path of least resistance. For one thing, even if we kicked him out, he could just sneak back over once Scott and I left again. What's the point? After securing assurances from Sammy that he wouldn't harm himself or otherwise do anything stupid—the worth of such a promise being questionable—we leave the house through the backdoor. The yellow crime scene tape is already out of our way through Sammy's earlier burglary.

Once outside, Scott shakes his hurt knee a little to loosen the stiffness. He asks, "Can I go to Italy with you?"

"That would make for an awkward honeymoon."

We begin our way back to the street when my partner pauses in midstep. He points to the wooden bridge leading to the beach between the homes of the Kessler brothers, the same walkway that Donovan traveled on his way to getting murdered. Under the moonlight, I see the silhouette of a woman—quite thin, wraith-like—standing on the beach end of the bridge, just over the dune. Scott says, "Katherine Matheny."

"Think she's sleepwalking?"

"Let's ask her."

The air is calm, and our steps on the bridge are loud enough to alert her of our presence. But Katherine is oblivious to our arrival. Her whole body remains pointed toward the ocean. At the end of the bridge, I have enough of an angle to see that the tide is near high, close to the bottom of the stairs where Donovan Kessler ceased living. The thought that Katherine might be interested in drowning crosses my mind. That feat shouldn't be too difficult to pull off if her stomach is full of drugs, despite the calm waters around Jekyll.

Only when we are standing right next to her does she become aware that she has company. Even in the moonlight, I can tell enough about her appearance to discern that she is in a bad state. Her heavy eyelids droop to make her face near catatonic. Having never crossed paths with a sleepwalker before, I wonder whether this is the normal demeanor.

I ask, "Are you awake?"

Her nod in response takes more energy than she can spare. In a dead monotone, she says, "Yes, that's the problem. I can't sleep. Nothing works. Not pills, not reading, not a hot shower. Nothing. I'm so tired. Haven't stayed up this long in years. I want to go to sleep and never wake up."

My drowning idea might not be that far off from the truth. I touch her elbow and guide her back toward the house. She follows as led but with a painfully slow gait, each step labored and heavy. Once we make it to Donovan Kessler's backyard, I lead her to a bench adjacent to a flower bed, near the spot with the missing brick used to smash her father's head. The both of us sit down. Scott stands in front of us. I talk to her in a soothing voice.

"Why can't you fall asleep?"

"The fear of what I might do. Can I ask you a question?"

"Please do."

"Did I kill my father?"

* * *

That's a first—a suspect asking me if she is the killer. I turn to Scott to get his read on things, but he keeps staring at Katherine intently, trying like me to figure her out. Her question is a stumper, and I avoid answering it.

"Why would you ask me such a thing?"

"'Judge not, lest ye be judged.' The words of Jesus Himself. Yet I harshly judged Father for his fornication with that woman. Even grew to hate him. I refused to offer mercy, and now he is dead. Perhaps my hard-heartedness killed him."

"Anything else? Your father didn't die because you had mean thoughts about him."

She tries to focus her attention on me, but her weary eyes refuse to cooperate. Her breathing is rhythmic now, almost like a steady snore. She might fall asleep just sitting here. Hoping for a better answer to my question, I prod her again.

"Is there any other reason why you think you killed your father?"

"Visions. I have these visions of murdering him. Ever since you asked me about the night of the murder when I dreamed about *The Brothers Karamazov*, about Fyodor's being slayed by his son. I keep thinking maybe that wasn't a dream. That instead of Fyodor and his son, it was Father and me. The vision feels so real, and I don't know what happens when I sleepwalk. Everything is so confused. So please tell me the truth. Did I kill him?"

Psychological suggestion is a real thing. And while I'd give a lot of nickels to crack this case and put it far behind me, tricking a woman with obvious mental issues into believing she's the murderer is not the way. But her fragile bond with reality does not clear her as a suspect, either. The problem with Katherine is separating fact, fabrication, and hallucination. The best way I can figure to chisel for the truth is to unearth whether she knows things that only the murderer would know.

"How did you kill your father in your vision?"

"With a gun, of course."

"Do you remember firing the gun?"

"I'm not sure. But how else would I kill him?"

"You mentioned before dreaming about Fyodor being beaten with a heavy object, like in the book. Could that have been you hitting your father?"

"You mean I beat him with a gun?"

Scott curses under his breath. I know the feeling. If Katherine is perpetuating a giant fraud, that is one thing. I have ways of handling a dishonest witness—tricks of the trade learned long ago. But if she is more lunatic than liar, the waters become more choppy. Is she a lunatic that kills or merely a lunatic who thinks that she kills? And how do I ever go about proving which one?

"What was your father wearing during these visions when you killed him?"

"I … don't know. The vision is unclear."

"What did you do with your clothes after the murder?"

Katherine acts like she doesn't understand the question. She sits there stupefied, teetering on falling asleep again.

"I … don't remember what I was wearing. Should I?"

That's a wrap on my end. No point exists in prolonging a pointless exercise. Katherine and I should both be in bed. I ask Scott, "Do you have anything?"

"Yeah."

He picks up a twin of the brick that killed Donovan Kessler and brings it back over to us. Staring down over Katherine, he issues a command.

"Stand up."

Her reaction time is slow, but she eventually rises on unsteady legs to face him. I notice for the first time that she's barefoot. Scott extends the brick out in front of him and tells her, "Hold this."

Katherine turns to me to make sure, and I nod my head. She puts her hands out, and Scott lays the brick onto them. The red block careens to the ground, missing her big toe by a few inches and sparing her a broken bone. Scott reaches down to pick the brick back up. The look on his face indicates a determination to take another trial run. He gives further instructions.

"Be strong with it this time. Get a good grip. The brick's not that heavy."

It looks heavy from where I sit, especially in her weak hands. But that's the point of the experiment—to see what shakes out. The two of them repeat the same ritual as before. This time a struggling Katherine holds on.

Scott says, "Now hit me with it."

Her eyes show more life. She turns again to me. Her thin face is wide with surprise. I say, "Go ahead. He has a thick skull." My words are ridiculous, but she doesn't stop to question them in her sleep-deprived state. Instead, Katherine does as told and tries to hit him.

The attempt fails to launch. She maneuvers the brick in front of her and almost pushes it on him in an awkward movement. Halfway through the motion, she loses her hold and the brick again falls to the ground—this time almost smashing Scott's toes. He returns it to the border of the flower bed. Katherine asks, "Why did you want me to do that?"

I answer, "You tell me."

She shows no emotional disturbance from re-enacting a scene straight from her father's murder. Nor does she answer me, instead saying, "I'm ready to go to bed now."

We lead her back to the backdoor of Raymond's house and watch her enter. Alone with Scott once again on the way back to the Expedition, I ask, "Still think she's faking?"

"If she is, she deserves an Oscar."

Probably. But I once knew a disturbed woman that delivered an Academy Award-winning performance right before my eyes. You never know.

53

The time is after one in the morning when I use the keycard to open the door to my hotel room, trying to be as quiet as possible so as not to wake Cate. But that stealth is unnecessary. The lights are on, and my wife sits upright in bed reading the latest from John Grisham. She smiles and says, "I was wondering when you might turn up."

I kiss her on the cheek and hand over the red rose courtesy of Raymond Kessler. The petals still retain enough of their character after riding around with me in the SUV all day. Cate tells me to thank Raymond on her behalf before changing the topic.

"Last time I saw you a couple of hours ago you were on the warpath."

Ah, yes. Burt from Bainbridge. The encounters with Maxwell, Sammy, and Katherine since then had all but erased him from my mind. I explain, "Burt Pressley talked out of school and came close to jeopardizing the whole case. I got pretty harsh with him. You probably shouldn't expect a campaign donation. Why are you still awake?"

"Not sleepy. I enjoyed a long nap this afternoon all by myself. Solved the murder yet?"

"Nope. Probably won't, either."

"That bad?"

"Lots of suspects. Mostly terrible people. But not a lot in the way of evidence."

"Anybody try to kill you today?"

I actually have to pause and think.

"Maxwell Matheny swung a beer bottle at my head, but Scott reached him before the beer bottle reached me. Punched him in the kidney—where it hurts."

Cate appears dismayed. The peaceful weekend jaunt we had planned before flying off to Italy has morphed into a horror show. So much for golf and sitting out on the beach staring at the blue water. But unless someone actually succeeds in killing me, we're leaving town later today. My wife says, "Poor baby. Go and take a quick shower and I'll make you feel better."

Her seductive look confirms the suggestive meaning. But my fatigue is rising to Katherine Matheny levels at this point.

"I'm too tired."

"Not a problem. You can lay back, I'll do all the work."

She's good to her word.

* * *

Nothing in the world can quite capture the magic of a Sunday morning. I wake up early but with bright eyes, thankful for at least some sleep. Cate is next to me, dead to the world. I pull the sheets down to appreciate her nude body and conclude that she's a heck of a lot more attractive buck naked than Sammy Kessler. She gives a slight shiver at the covers being off her. I kiss the small of her back and give her rump a love pat before tucking her back in.

I grab coffee and a newspaper from downstairs and return to sit on our hotel balcony. Far off in the distance, the sunrise sits on top of the ocean. I take a series of deep breaths. The solitude—my one moment of unhurried peace since the Governor's phone call—tastes sweet.

For all my mocking of Meredith Bixby's meditations and mantras, my own practice is not so different. Every morning I try to find a quiet place and get alone with God in prayer. One of the things my rocky road of faith has taught me is that spiritual cleansing is a never-ending process of renewal. Kinda like how I have to shower every day to wash the dirt off of my body. I skipped this time alone with God yesterday and already feel waste deep in ugliness. Bowing my head and closing my eyes, I recite the Lord's Prayer:

> Our Father who art in heaven, hallowed be thy name. Thy kingdom come, thy will be done—in earth, as it is in heaven. Give us this day our daily bread. And forgive us our debts, as we for-

give our debtors. And lead us not into temptation, but deliver us from evil: For thine is the kingdom, and the power, and the glory, forever. Amen.

The words aren't magic—nor a money-back guarantee of spiritual protection. But they work for me. And that's where Meredith and I diverge.

"*My positive thoughts guide me to new heights*" is not the worst message in the world. Negativity can be a self-reinforcing quicksand that's hard to escape. Meredith's way to get out of the quicksand involves willing herself forward to climb out of the muck. Mine asks God to throw me a vine.

I take a sip of the coffee—one of the Lord's gifts from above for making it through each day, much like the manna from Heaven for the Israelites in the desert. After savoring the sip and letting the caffeine do its work, I pick up my copy of the *Brunswick Times*.

* * *

Newspapers are dying. That reality saddens me. Reading the paper next to my father on our front porch—me with the sports section, him poring over the news—was a constant part of a happy childhood. The ritual is still strong with me. Something about holding the paper in my hand, the ink giving my fingers a little stain, just feels right.

Kessler's murder makes the front page. The article mentions the murder squad's involvement and states that I was unavailable for comment, which is news to me but true enough given all my running around of the past two days. The main thing I look for in stories of this sort is information that I don't know. But the reporting is light on facts. The meat of the story is dedicated to the biography of the deceased.

In the back of the paper, Kessler's obituary has top billing among all the other death notices of the day. I read it in full.

> Donovan Charles Kessler—husband, father, lawyer, pillar of the community—passed away on Thursday. He was 72. Born and

bred in Brunswick, Donovan was a local football star who went on to gridiron glory at the University of Georgia. Playing under legendary coach Vince Dooley forever remained one of Donovan's most cherished achievements, and he proudly wore his UGA letterman's jacket around town up until the day he died.

But Donovan found something even more valuable than football in Athens: love. While in law school at UGA, Donovan married his childhood friend, Judy Wright. The couple moved to Jekyll Island where they lived for nearly fifty years, raising two children who were the joy of their lives.

As a lawyer, Donovan's work on the Port of Brunswick helped transform the city into a major economic player. He also represented the area with great diligence in the Georgia House of Representatives for over two decades. Last year the lawyers in the state selected Donovan to serve as their State Bar President—a worthy capstone to an outstanding legal career.

Donovan is survived by his wife Judy, son Sammy (Lucy), daughter Katherine Matheny (Maxwell), and brother Raymond. A private graveside service will be held on Monday.

I stare at the last paragraph of the obituary for a good minute. Sammy. Lucy. Katherine. Maxwell. Even Raymond. No mention of Sadie, but I toss her in for good measure. I go back to my Tolstoy.

Every unhappy family is unhappy in its own way. I know the answer to the case lies there but cannot make heads or tails as to why.

54

I meet Scott downstairs with no ideas for how to spend the morning. I'm plum out of them. Like most of the state bar members attending the conference, Cate plans to attend the luncheon honoring Donovan Kessler. After that, the schedule for both of us is wide open, and I hope to be driving home by the afternoon. Scott says to me, "Let's go."

"Where?"

"To pay Leslie Hamrick another visit. I want to kick the tires again on Sadie. Leslie told us yesterday about Becky Savage's girlfriend but never mentioned her by name. She obviously didn't know that Sadie had moved into Donovan Kessler's house. I want to get her reaction to that bit of news. She's a tough, smart cop, and I always like to pick the brain of such people."

When we arrive, Leslie is back on her front porch just as we left her. Instead of lemonade, the drink of choice this morning is coffee. She gets out of her rocking chair to dole out the cups. From the smell, I get an inkling of its quality. The fact is immediately confirmed by my taste buds. I compliment her.

"Good coffee."

"Mr. Hamrick was a connoisseur and taught me how to make the perfect blend. But you guys didn't stop by to talk coffee. Have to admit I didn't expect to see you again. Now you got me curious. How can I help you?"

Scott takes the lead.

"You mentioned yesterday that Becky Savage had a girlfriend. Would that girlfriend's name happen to be Sadie Foxx?"

"It would."

"What if I told you that Sadie Foxx moved into Donovan Kessler's house as his girlfriend and eventual fiancé?"

"Damn."

Leslie takes a drink of her excellent coffee—her active mind processing the new information. She puts her cup down on a side table and says, "And you want to know whether I think Sadie could've killed Kessler?"

"That's right."

"What does Sadie say?"

"She admits that at the start of their relationship she tried to give him a heart attack through vigorous sexual intercourse, but as time went on she decided to sell out for the money."

That earns a deep chuckle and a lot of nodding from Leslie.

"Sounds like Sadie all right. On both fronts. That girl was broken up about Becky's murder and wanted revenge. We checked her out for the killing, of course, being that close to the victim. Sadie had nothing in the way of an alibi. Home alone. But no evidence pointed to her at all. That doesn't mean I trusted her. You could tell that she was the sneaky type—a master manipulator. And Rickie Savage had Sadie's ear. Over time, she started to drink his Kool-Aid about Kessler being Becky's killer. Except what you said about her change of priorities jives with her character, too. I can totally see that once she got comfortable in the big house, maintaining that position would supersede her earlier desire to exact some payback. A girl's got to be practical."

She chuckles again, a nice authentic laugh. Scott asks, "Any bit of evidence that would make Sadie for the Kessler murder?"

"Not a single solitary thing."

* * *

Back in the Expedition, Scott says, "Just got a text from Tripp. He says we have to come by and pick up our evidence."

"Tripp? Who's that?"

"Ridgeway. The medical examiner's kid. Mr. Metallica."

I remember now—the potential future serial killer with an inordinate interest in dad's work of cutting open the dead.

"He doesn't mean we have to take the body, does he?"

"Text didn't say. If so, he's going to be disappointed."

For the second time in two days, we arrive at the county elections office, which doubles as the home of the medical examiner. Because government buildings are just as empty on Sunday as they are on Saturday, we again have to wait for Tripp to unlock the front door for us. By my reckoning, he is wearing the same heavy metal shirt as before. The guess is that he didn't shower last night. Without saying a word, he whirls around to lead us back through the building's maze to his father's examination room.

Dr. Abe Ridgeway is elbow deep in another cadaver when we enter. While still focused on the nude female corpse on his table, he says in a brisk manner, "As you can tell, I run a small shop here, which means there's no room to store your victim's clothes. You have to take them. Over in the corner in clear evidence pouches."

His head jerks to the spot while his eyes remain affixed to his work. I wander over to inspect each individual bag of evidence—Kessler's letterman's jacket, a white button-down shirt, olive gray chinos, and denim blue slip-on shoes. Blood is apparent on the shirt and pants. The jacket is harder to tell since it is red anyway. The thought of finding a place to stash the stuff is an annoying one. Most likely, all of it has to ride home with Cate and me. Scott says to Ridgeway, "Can I ask you something?"

The doctor winces a little. Although unhappy with our presence in his sanctuary, he relents and grants Scott permission to ask his question.

"The nature of Kessler's wounds—could a person significantly shorter than the deceased have struck those blows?"

"Were the wounds indicative of an upward trajectory, you mean?"

"Exactly."

Ridgeway mulls it over. The diminutive Meredith Bixby argued last night that she was too short to smash Kessler's head with a brick. Scott's taking that theory on a test run. Of course, Sadie, Katherine, and Lucy—while not as tiny as Meredith—could all have a go at making the same claim.

The doctor's interest in us is a tad higher since we asked him about his work. He answers, "Nothing conclusive was indicated. My thinking is that the victim went down after one or two blows, but the killer didn't stop there. Hammered the victim's head some more after he was on the ground. Like I said yesterday, the killer was thorough. Those later blows made it impossible to get a good handle on the original angle of attack."

The mental picture of the murderer repeatedly hammering Kessler's head with a brick while he lay helpless on the sand is an ugly one. But I knew that much since the second I first saw Kessler's body on the beach. And Ridgeway's information, while informative, isn't terribly helpful because it doesn't allow us to eliminate any of the possible suspects. That's the case in a nutshell. A line of suspects a mile long but nothing concrete to take any of them off the board.

We take our evidence and go.

55

The Kessler family, Sadie, and Meredith Bixby are all together at the state bar conference honoring the late Donovan. Part of me wants to head over there, lock all of us together in the same room, and wrestle it out until someone confesses. We could transport Rickie Savage there to make the party complete, but that feels unnecessary. My faith in the reliability of Otis Harper's obsession with *Perry Mason* is stronger than Scott's. Rickie didn't have enough time.

But putting everyone together in the same room wouldn't solve the case, and the celebration of Donovan Kessler will have to go on without me. I tuck away the evidence bag with the dead man's clothes into the back of the Expedition and return to the driver's side. Scott says, "Want to check on J.D. and Dave Ketchum?"

J.D. and Captain Dave are supervising Operation Garbage at our second trash collection site in Brunswick. No one has unearthed a stitch of bloody clothes yet. If that evidence existed, we should've found it already. Now we're just floundering. I reflect on the Governor's money going up in smoke and debate whether I should go ahead and pull the plug on the search. The whole investigation has me down, and the ride over to the landfill is another quiet one between Scott and me.

He hops out of the vehicle when we arrive, but I stay in my seat. A thought starts to nibble at the grey matter in my brain. Before long, I feel a pressing need to pace around to help me gather my thoughts. But when I jump out of the car for that purpose, the rancid smell immediately catapults me back into the driver's seat with the door firmly closed.

I get down to thinking. The steering wheel is tight in my hands as I squeeze it, reflecting my body's need to release its excess energy as the adrenaline surges within me. Scott walks back over and opens his side with a question on his lips.

"What's going on?"

"Get in and close the door."

Excitedly, I talk him through the series of deductions circling within my head that point to the identity of the murderer. He is not impressed.

"That won't even get you a search warrant on probable cause. Much less an indictment. And a conviction? You'd get laughed out of the state."

"But it all fits. Everything."

"And how do you go about proving it?"

"No idea."

We exit the vehicle, and I hold my breath while trying not to smell anything. I tell J.D., "Send everyone home."

"Why?"

"Change of plans."

He goes off to give the troops the news. Captain Dave comes over. I ask, "Do you have anybody on Jekyll now?"

"Sure, Morelli."

Everyone should still be at the luncheon, but that won't last long. I give Captain Dave instructions for Chad Morelli. When finished, I emphasize the most important part.

"Tell Morelli to keep it simple. All he has to do is keep an eye on things from a distance. No need for him to be a hero or even get close to the suspect. Just watch. If our person of interest leaves, that's fine. We'll be on the island soon enough."

Captain Dave takes out his cell and walks away to relay the information to Morelli. Dave struck me as a little stiff at first, but he's a fine soldier to have at your side. Good at taking orders, too. J.D. rejoins us, and I fill him in. Once Dave is off the phone, the four of us head to our respective vehicles for one more trip to Jekyll Island.

Back on the road, Scott asks, "What are you going to do when we get there?"

"Tell the murderer how I think things went down and see what happens."

The element of surprise is only a one-time chance. I feel like a stumbling Barney Fife with my single bullet. The likelihood of success is nil. But that one bullet is all I've got.

***

Scott asks me to connect the dots again on the way back over to Jekyll, and a second time through doesn't alleviate his skepticism.

"Shaky."

He'll get no disagreement from me. But a lot of little points that accumulate eventually lead to one big point. We cross the bridge back onto the island. I don't bother to scan for dolphins this time. J.D. tails me in the Corolla. Dave is behind him in his state patrol car. At the conference center, we all find parking spots and join together to walk inside. Based on the time according to my watch, the luncheon should be breaking up around now, and a steady drip of lawyers heading to their cars confirms the hypothesis. Right as we near the outer doors, Dave asks me, "What exactly are you going to do here?"

"Well, I've been thinking—"

A gunshot rings out. To hell with my plan.

We race to the sound of the boom, around a corner to the main hallway of the conference center. Fleeing lawyers block the way. I run over Sammy Kessler but don't bother to help him up. A symphony of screams gives me a sick feeling in my stomach. Once we make the turn, the first sight to grab my attention stops me cold.

Chad Morelli writhes in pain on the ground. A circle of blood expands on the blue shirt of his uniform.

Dave Ketchum drops to his knees to be at Morelli's side. The Captain's face is a mix of fatherly rage and heartbreak. Scott's pistol is in his hand, and he scans the scene looking for someone to shoot. I frantically look around, too, but fail to see the person I figure to be the shooter. My legs feel like jelly, and a small voice inside my chest taunts, "All your fault. All your fault. All your fault."

A female bystander breaks me out of my self-pity. She shrieks, "They went in there." The woman points to the doors of the big banquet hall. Dave stands up with a dangerous tint to his eyes. The four of us—Scott, Dave, J.D., and me—rush into the ballroom with guns drawn.

Raymond Kessler stands with his back against a wall. He holds a gun to Cate's head.

56

Raymond tightens his grip on Cate with his left hand when we burst into the room. The right hand points the gun at her temple. My wife's face is wide with fear, and she struggles to breathe against the power of Raymond's near chokehold. But I have more immediate problems at the moment.

A shaken Captain Dave raises his gun and approaches the murderer—the same murderer now using Cate as a human shield. Raymond barks at all of us to back off, but Dave keeps moving forward with single-minded focus. Realizing Cate might very well get killed before I have an opportunity to figure out a way to save her, I yell at the top of my lungs, "Dave! That's my wife! Back off now!"

He at least acknowledges the words and turns to face me with utter confusion written all over him. He coughs out, "What?" The voice is soft and distant, too detached to think straight in a high-pressure situation.

"My wife! Stand down!"

"He has to answer for shooting Chad."

"And he will. Let us handle it."

"No. That's my man out in the hall bleeding."

"And you should go check on him!"

"No."

J.D. stands five feet behind Dave. I turn to him and order, "Get him out of here! And keep everybody else out, too!"

God bless that kid. He doesn't hesitate at all and moves with lightning speed to karate chop Dave's hand. The state trooper's gun falls safely to the floor. J.D. picks it up and pushes a shocked Dave right out of the door. The Captain shoots me a searing look of deep betrayal on his way to the exit. He'll get over it.

With just four of us in the big room now, a tense calmness settles in the air. I try to will my heart rate to a more reasonable speed with middling results. Scott is off to my right, and Raymond jerks his head toward him and says, "Him, too. Out."

"Not happening. I want a witness."

Raymond grins at my tough talk. Wearing his usual seersucker suit, he could pass for a friendly church greeter. Except for the gun. He scoots away from Scott and drags Cate along with him. I calculate the distance between Raymond and Scott at thirty yards—three first downs in football, a soft pitch shot in golf, the gap from home plate to first base in baseball. I shift laterally to match Raymond's movements. He and Cate stand roughly ten yards in front of me. The Smith & Wesson pointed at them is heavy in my hands, almost like an anvil. Raymond turns toward Scott.

"Fine, you can stay. But don't move. You understand? Try to get closer to outflank me and she dies. I fought in Nam and know about sneak attacks from the enemy. You going to behave?"

"As you wish. I'm good where I am. Won't move a muscle."

"Keep it that way."

His orders to Scott complete, the murderer switches his attention back to me. I'm calmer on the outside than what's happening internally. I hold the gun steady, but pulling the trigger with Cate in the way strikes me as unfathomable, which means I have to talk my way out of the crisis.

"What do you want, Raymond? No one else needs to get hurt. It's over. You have to know that."

"First things first. Will you do the courtesy of explaining how you figured out it was me?"

"Courtesy? How very Southern of you."

"No substitute exists for good manners."

"Says the man with a gun to my wife's head."

"Many apologies. That was not in the plan. But please, tell me. How did you know?"

Seeing Cate held hostage leaves me feeling impotent all over. She's right there, and I can't do anything about it. I already have one dead wife and child as part of my life story. To have to watch a sequel play out before me would be too cruel. I would probably spend the rest of my life in a monastery, the kind where the monks don't talk, where I could sit in quiet and pepper God with hard questions until I die.

But Cate is still alive, and taking a vow of silence would be premature. If Raymond wants to talk, I'll talk. That I can do. Maybe he'll get tired and drop the gun.

"Your brother's letterman's jacket—that was the start. The medical examiner returned it to us this morning. I stuffed it into the back of my vehicle with barely a thought. But something stirred. I remembered the obituary of your brother that I read this morning—the one you composed because no one else in the family could be bothered with the task. You wrote about the jacket in the obituary, said that Donovan *'proudly wore his UGA letterman's jacket around town up until the day he died.'* Except only a few people on Jekyll knew that he was wearing that jacket when he was killed. You're not one of them—unless you're the murderer. But the obituary doesn't quite say Donovan was wearing his jacket at the moment of death. The wording is ambiguous enough. Easy to write off as just one of those things."

Raymond stares at me full of curiosity, as if I am delivering an academic lecture that particularly interests him. I steal a glance at Cate but don't dare hold it for too long before picking up with the monologue.

"But once my mind focused in that direction, I realized that another part of the obituary was not so ambiguous. *'Donovan Charles Kessler—husband, father, lawyer, pillar of the community—passed away on Thursday.'* Did he die on Thursday? The answer to that question depends on whether he died before midnight or after midnight. Only the killer would know that. The medical examiner couldn't even pinpoint the time of death with that kind of accuracy. Still, not enough proof. Maybe you just assumed Thursday. Maybe in your mind Thursday night included the time right after midnight. Maybe you simply inferred Thursday from my asking if you saw anything suspicious that night."

I pause—still holding to the strategy that the longer the stand-off goes on, the better are Cate's chances of living through it. But Raymond doesn't let the quiet linger.

"Is that all? Surely there is more than that."

"There's more. The obituary just steered me to really analyze for the first time the evidence through the lens that you might be the killer. I started to do that last night but got interrupted and never circled back. This morning, I tried again, beginning from the first moment I met you."

"And?"

"Everything suddenly made sense."

57

"The first time we met, you led me into your house through the covered patio at the back. A bourbon glass sat on an outside table. The water ring from the melted ice suggested that the glass had been there for a good while. Most certainly from the night before since you left for work the first thing that morning. You picked up the glass, washed it, and put it away. All normal. But once inside I watched you drink two different glasses of Johnny Walker while we talked. Both times you immediately washed the glasses and dried them off. I didn't think anything of it. So what? You are a neat freak. No part of your house is out of place. But once my mind finally focused on you, I started to wonder why that other glass was left outside overnight. Seemed out of character."

When I drank lemonade on Leslie Hamrick's front porch and held the perspiring glass up to my eye for further inspection, I concluded that the empty crystal had no answers for me. Little did I know that such a small detail would be the key to the whole case. Raymond stands there confused, no longer appearing curious but rather startled. He says, "A dirty glass? You must be joking."

"Not joking. After thinking more about that glass, one theory clicked into place. You were sitting outside that night drinking on your patio and saw your brother walk to the beach. That's how we figured it from the start. Someone witnessed Donovan going for a midnight stroll and decided to take that opportunity to kill him. The bourbon glass puts you in your backyard the night before—a perfect spot for you to see your brother head to the ocean. The story writes itself from there. You followed, grabbed a brick on the way, and murdered him on the beach. Coming back to your house, you forgot about the glass on the patio. You had other things on your mind. Neat and tidy."

The man with the gun to my wife's head laughs. Not the demented chortle of a madman, but the relaxed laugh of a guy in a bar who just heard a good joke. He readjusts his grasp on Cate's chest to make it tighter and calls out in a strong voice, "And why under your theory did I kill my brother?"

"Because of Judy. It's always been about Judy."

He stops laughing. The old man's eyes withdraw a little and lose some of their light. He solemnly nods at the accuracy of my conclusion. Scott's speculation last night about possible embezzlement didn't really move me. But love is an even more powerful force than money.

Raymond didn't exactly hide his feelings toward Judy during our conversations together. I just wasn't paying attention and fell too easily for his repeated proclamations that he wasn't the marrying kind.

Judy is one of the finest women I've ever known. She went all the way through grade school with Donovan and me over in Brunswick. Thought I might even marry her myself at one point… He told me yesterday that he intended to divorce Judy to marry Sadie. We had words over it… Judy's still alive—seemed cruel to me for him to abandon her in that condition… Judy deserved better.

I keep talking.

"You freely admitted to me that you and your brother had words on the day of the murder because he intended to divorce Judy—the same Judy who you expected to marry once you returned from Vietnam. The woman you loved. Except she chose Donovan instead while you were gone. But that didn't stop your love. You moved next door to her. You became her gardener and worked with her to create a beautiful garden landscape in both your backyards. After her terrible accident, you were the only one that would even visit Judy. Not her husband. Not her children. You. The brother-in-law. In isolation, a strange fact perhaps. But viewed as a continuation of your five-decade devotion to her—not strange at all."

The discussion about Judy makes him smaller and almost non-threatening. The change in demeanor portends that Raymond may simply give up, which could cut two different ways. Giving up could mean surrendering. It could also mean killing himself and Cate. Deciding that continued engagement is the best diplomacy, I ask, "You want the rest of it?"

"Please."

"The murder weapon—a brick that is part of a border surrounding a flower bed. Such an odd choice for the killer to make. Most people in enough of a frenzy to murder would never even notice the flower bed. But you know who might very well notice? The gardener. I bet you placed the brick there in the first place. Part of me believes that you also picked the brick because of its connection to Judy. Some form of poetic justice."

Raymond stays silent about the brick. I use the break in the discussion to take Cate's temperature. The fear in her eyes is too much. I release the gaze to stop from breaking down. The adrenaline running through me could fill the ocean, but I feign calmness to try and trick my nerves. Raymond asks, "Anything more?"

"Yes—the killer's bloody clothes. The GBI assured me that the murderer had to be on the other end of significant blood splatter. If true, where are the bloody clothes? We searched your brother's house and found no sign of blood. We've ransacked all the trash on Jekyll. Nothing. The only suspect who could've disposed of the clothes off the island was Rickie Savage. You made a point to put me on his scent during our first conversation. Nice touch, by the way. But Rickie has an alibi. What then happened to the clothes? Once the trail pointed in your direction, I realized that you actually left the island early the morning after the murder for a court hearing in Jesup. You had plenty of time and about fifty miles to get rid of the only evidence that could convict you."

The murderer just stands there, holding Cate in place. Scott, too, remains frozen in the same ready-to-fire position. But he's too far away for much comfort. For such an incredibly tense moment with lives on the line, the stillness of all of us reflects the clarity of the situation. Raymond shows no signs of letting go of my wife, so I keep talking to keep his mind on me.

"That leads to the final clue that points in your direction. But first—since we're exchanging courtesies—I have something to ask you. Why did you kill that innocent girl?"

* * *

Cate reacts to the question with a gasp. I force myself not to look at her. Raymond settles into a smirk. The change concerns me. I asked him about Becky Savage hoping to rekindle a part of his lost humanity—to spark some flame of morality that would stop this madness. For no matter how he mentally justifies the murder of his brother, killing Becky for the sins of her father stretches rationalization past the breaking point, even for a world-class advocate like Raymond.

The smirk, though, suggests a mind too far gone for moral persuasion. Raymond wears it still and doesn't answer the question, so I start filling in the gaps.

"No murder investigator alive believes in coincidences. Rickie Savage causes Judy Kessler to lose all of her cognitive functions. A tragedy. But the misfortune doesn't stop there. Someone murders Rickie's daughter. Someone murders Judy's husband. Now we're up to three tragedies. They have to be linked. But how? The obvious answer is a back-and-forth cycle of revenge. Rickie hurts Judy. Donovan kills Becky in retaliation. Rickie kills Donovan to settle things once and for all. A double quid pro quo, easy to understand."

The sound of sirens in the distance—police and ambulance—reaches my ears. With a bleeding officer just outside this room, cops arriving on the scene figure to be full of bloodlust. One itchy trigger finger could get Cate killed. Hopefully J.D. can keep them at bay. I try again to make Raymond feel bad about Becky Savage.

"You fed me this scenario by saying that you thought your brother murdered that girl. Strangely, only you and Rickie believed that Donovan had anything to do with Becky's death. Everyone else scoffed at the idea. But not you. That should've been a tell, if I had been thinking about you at all. When I began looking at things with fresh eyes, another angle emerged for how the murders of Becky and your brother might be linked. Both killings delivered vengeance for Judy—first for the accident, then for the divorce. Except who's the avenger? The same person who fought for her in court against Rickie Savage and the trucking company. As part of that case, you told me that you *'hired a private investigator to unearth as many facts about Savage as possible—from when he stopped believing in Santa Claus to his favorite brand of underwear. Family, friends, everything.'* No doubt that dossier included where Becky worked and her normal hours. All in your hands. Rickie had it correct from the start. Becky was killed to punish him for the accident with Judy. Right idea, wrong brother. But you never answered my question. Why kill the daughter? Why not kill Rickie himself?"

"Because death would've been too good for a man like that. Real pain in life is living with loss. And that's why you're going to help me get out of here."

58

"Apologies again for taking your sweet wife captive. If I had known the basis for your suspicion of me, there would've been no need. What you just described may not contain a single piece of admissible evidence in court. Speculation upon speculation. Random dot connected to random dot. What exactly was your plan?"

"Tell you what I just told you and hope that you broke. Absent that, searching every trash can in the fifty miles between here and the route you took to Jesup for the hearing that morning. Tilting at windmills basically. Strong odds in your favor that you would've walked. Except all of that is now moot."

"Yes, I panicked. A rare mistake for me. That state trooper kept staring at me with suspicion-laced eyes. Made me uncomfortable. When I tried to leave, he blocked the door and ordered me to stay put. I thought you had the goods, but all you had was a bunch of weak conjecture. Shot the poor kid for no good reason."

Morelli. Damn, I wish he had listened. *Tell Morelli to keep it simple. All he has to do is keep an eye on things from a distance. No need for him to be a hero or even get close to the suspect. Just watch. If our person of interest leaves, that's fine.* Hard to be mad at him when he might be dead at this moment. I should've kept my instructions to watch Raymond to myself and waited until all of us were here before tipping off a double murderer that we were on to him. But having finally identified the killer, the instinct to keep eyes on him carried the day. Lesson learned. Raymond continues.

"One of my strengths as a lawyer was always the ability to adjust on the fly. To reassess a situation immediately and chart a new course. Hell, even in Vietnam, that talent saved my life on more than one occasion. Before I shot that state trooper, my thought was to get in my car and leave the island with all deliberate speed. But he got in the way, and I needed an alternative strategy. Your lovely wife stood there in the hall shocked along with everyone else, and I saw her value at once. She was my ticket to getting out of here—a bargaining chip to negotiate with the one man with the power to get me off Jekyll in something other than handcuffs or a body bag. Now, it's time to deal."

Cate screams, "Chance, don't you dare let this baboon take me anywhere! Shoot him! Shoot him now!"

Raymond tightens his hold, and Cate winces. He even slumps down more behind her in case we decide to act upon her orders. But that's a non-starter. I'd love nothing better than to empty my six bullets into Raymond Kessler's body. Except the person I love most in the world stands in the way. I look at her and say in a soft voice, "Keep out of it, please."

"I think I'm in it, Chance."

Her eyes flame with terror, and her body shakes with small shivers. The murder of Amber and Cale gutted me for years, but I didn't have to watch it happen, at least. My stomach churns at this possible horror. I offer the murderer a deal.

"Take me instead, Raymond. Walk me out right now with your gun to my head. We'll head straight to my SUV, and I'll turn on the siren to drive you wherever you want to go. If things go sidewise, you can kill me in good conscience. But let the woman go. You're a Southern gentleman. Act like it."

"Can't do it, Chance. I'm sorry. You're too big and strong for an old man like me. Besides, I want that quick brain of yours figuring out the best way to keep your wife alive. That's my best hope of getting what I want."

He actually does appear chagrined, which is worth absolutely not a damn thing under the circumstances. His endgame remains unclear. Once he gets off the island, then what? Raymond cannot truly believe any opportunity exists for him to escape.

"And what do you want? You're not going to be able to simply disappear. You cannot be so far gone as to believe that."

"No—you're quite right. I'll never live to see another morning. But in death, I want the one thing denied to me in life. To be with Judy. Once I reach her, my need for using your wife as a hostage will end. She will return to you to live happily ever after. I will say my goodbyes to Judy and take my own life."

* * *

The words are full of sincerity. He means to kill himself. The firmness of his voice—the same baritone he used to seduce hundreds of juries—carries with it an implicit guarantee of truth. But something's still off in the story. That he's willing to kill Cate just so he can die a few miles from here strikes the wrong chord with me. The guess is that he has only shared half the truth, and I put the issue to him.

"You're going to kill Judy, too, aren't you?"

Raymond peeks around a little further from behind Cate's head and beams an impressed smile. He says, "Your powers of intuition and deduction are top notch, Chance. Facing you in the courtroom would've been something. It's a damn shame that we never got the opportunity to square off."

"There's still time. Surrender and you can be your own lawyer at the trial. I'll come back down and prosecute you myself."

"Nice try. But you're quite right. Even though Judy and I couldn't be together in life, we can be as one in death. We both deserve it. She realized early in her marriage that Donovan was a narcissist and that she should've waited for me to get back from the war. But the obligation of duty and honor ran deep in both of us. The most we would do was hold hands on my back patio late into the night while Donovan was out of town whoring himself to different women. And that was enough for both of us. But then Rickie Savage took her from me. I paid him back in full."

A sheen of vileness radiates from him. The absence of any conscience about murdering Becky Savage makes me question whether he'd keep his end of the bargain that he proposes. Could be that Raymond kills Cate for spite just to pay me back in full for revealing that he is a murderer.

"As for my brother, he moved on with his life as if Judy were already dead. Fine. That gave me more space to care for her all by myself. But then he decided to divorce his wife of fifty years so he could whore around some more with another new tramp. The man was sick. Just as you surmised, I sat on my back patio drinking my whiskey when I saw Donovan head to the beach. I raised a mock toast to his bad health. A minute later, Lucy stood behind his house calling out to him with the whimper of a wounded dog—his own daughter-in-law. Enough is enough, I thought. My brother was hellbent on hurting everyone around him, and it needed to stop. When Lucy went back inside, I followed him to the beach. I passed the flower bed on the way, thought of Judy, and picked up the brick. You know the rest."

The story is an old one. Cain and Abel. Cain—the first murderer who killed his brother out of jealousy. But while God punished Cain with a lifetime of wandering, Raymond tortured himself by anchoring his entire life to the source of his envy—flowering the seeds of an unquenchable bitterness for over fifty years until that final last straw. The lesson, like the story, is timeless. We ignore the Ten Commandments at our peril. Especially the last one.

Thou shall not covet your neighbor's wife.

59

Slow tears run down Cate's cheek, and part of me dies inside. I weigh the merits of shooting her in the leg to drop her to the ground. With Raymond exposed as a sitting duck, both Scott and I could empty our guns into him. But all it would take to kill Cate is one little flinch of the murderer's finger. I dare not take the chance.

Raymond says, "We're talked out—you and I. Time for you to come up with a way to get your wife and me away from this place."

"That would've been a lot easier before you shot that state trooper out there. Likely a thousand cops are waiting just outside those doors to shoot you dead on sight. I'm not a magician."

"I concede the dilemma but also know how powerfully motivating the feeling of love can be. You're resourceful. Figure it out."

He gives me too much credit. Once we leave this room, I'm no longer in charge. For all I know, the police have already blocked the one road off the island, likely with a sore Captain Dave barking out instructions to shoot to kill. Or maybe Raymond thinks we can just slip out the back toward the beach and flag a passing boat. But the long odds that we can waltz out of here through waves of trigger-happy police is too weak a bet to place on Cate's life. One angry cop decides to play hero, and she is dead.

And that's setting aside the ethical qualms of aiding and abetting his stated desire to murder Judy. In law school, a professor challenged us with the famous Trolley Problem. Suppose a runaway train will soon kill five people standing on the track. But you—an onlooker—have the ability to hit a switch and divert the train to another track where it will only kill one person. What should you do? Most philosophers opine that you are under a duty to hit the switch. The moral math is simple. The lives of five people outweigh the life of one. But I could never get comfortable with that solution—the idea that I could play God and decide that some stranger should die because his life didn't measure up in the split-second calculus of the moment.

The same discomfort gives me pause now. Who am I to say that Judy's life is so worthless that I can simply discard it so that my wife can go on living? Even in her deteriorated state, Judy is a person with dignity entitled to some consideration that she still has value. Raymond himself chided the rest of his family for denying Judy's ongoing worth. But expecting moral consistency from a double murderer is bound to leave one disappointed. I stall for more time.

"How do I know you'll keep your word and release Cate once you reach Judy?"

"You're going to have to trust me."

"That's a big ask under the circumstances."

A shrug is the only response Raymond deigns to give. I analyze my options. The sight of my revolver points straight at Raymond's left ear. My hand is remarkably steady. But the memory of my time in the shooting range just before the trip down to Jekyll makes me skittish. That day I jerked everything to the left of the target. A repeat of that performance would place my shots in the dead center of Cate's temple. I take a peek at Scott so far away. His total focus is on the murderer, and I consider the words he said to Raymond. *As you wish. I'm good where I am. Won't move a muscle.* The noise from outside the room is louder now—sirens blaring, cop voices yelling, maybe even the sound of J.D. arguing with someone. After inhaling a calming breath, I return all my concentration to Raymond and notice a change in him. His body starts to gets antsy, and a growing agitation is rubbing him raw.

Him and me both. With each passing second, the fear I feel becomes more paralyzing. Like I'm playing *Let's Make a Deal* with Monty Hall but no matter what door I pick, a goat is guaranteed to be behind it. And picking the goat means that Cate dies.

Raymond snaps, "Stop stalling and get me out of here. I'm tired of waiting. Unless you intend to do something with that gun."

I keep the revolver still and try to draw on the resolve I used to kill a Navy SEAL. A terrified Cate mouths, "I love you." My heart collapses into my stomach. I take a mental photograph of her to make the image last—just in case I never see her alive again. The world around me moves in slow motion. Everything becomes silent—a black hole of quietness until the murderer flares up again in an angry tone.

"Well? What's it going to be? Are you that good with a gun? I highly doubt it, but you keep surprising me. Can you make the shot or not?"

My arm drops. I make a big production out of holstering the weapon. Cate's eyes cloud—in relief or fear, hard to tell.

"You're right, Raymond. I cannot make that shot."

He displays a wry smile, exhales a little, slackens his trigger finger, maybe even loosens his grip on Cate. I point to Scott.

"But he can."

Confused, Raymond turns to look at the almost forgotten man damn near on the other side of the room. The movement exposes the entirety of the murderer's forehead, which is hopefully enough.

Sight and sound converge in an instant. The pink mist of Raymond's brain explodes in a wide radius at the same moment I hear the thunderous crack of Scott's pistol. Cate's screams pierce the air in the wake of the gun blast. She stands there immobile—hands to her head, the murderer's arm no longer pinning her against him. I rush to close the distance between us and encircle her body tight in my arms. Her screams turn to jagged sobs. I try to soothe away her terror.

"You're all right. It's over. I have you. It's over."

She still shakes with hands covering her eyes against my shoulder. I feel all around her head and back checking for potential wounds but come up empty. The gunshot apparently brings a rush of more people into the room, but I close my eyes to tune the rest of the world out, content to be intertwined forever with the woman that I love.

When I do open my eyes—seconds, minutes, hours later, I'm not really sure—the body of the murderer lies there on the banquet floor a few yards away. Half his head is now missing. Bits of it are splattered around on Cate and everything else in the near vicinity of the point of impact.

Shakespeare wrote in Henry VIII, "Men's evil manners live in brass; their virtues we write in water." Until today, most people would've pegged Raymond Kessler as a great man, a living legend who labored tirelessly to make injured people whole. I even admired him myself—a bias that made me slow to give him his proper due as a suspect.

But a bad ending can wash away all the deeds of a good life. No one is likely to write a fine-sounding obituary for a disgraced killer. Raymond knew the score. He made his choices and received his due. Glancing down at what's left of him for one final look, I reflect on what he told me just last night.

Justice is never pretty, is it?

***

I stare at my haggard face in a mirror hanging in a hallway outside the conference center's main ballroom. Blood smears mark my cheek and forehead from holding Cate close. She's now in the restroom trying to wipe clean the remnants of the murderer's head off her. Wanting to be here when she comes back out, I leave my stains as they are—a visual reminder of how close I came to losing another wife.

Scott approaches and asks if I am okay. Not knowing the answer, I simply shrug. He says, "You didn't need to get him to turn his head toward me. I had him all the way. Why did you wait so long?"

"The distance seemed a little far. And I wasn't sure I interpreted your words right—that '*I'm good where I am*' meant that you had a clear line."

"What else would it mean?"

"Probably being a little extra cautious since a gun was pointed at my wife's head. Plus, to be honest, your knee worried me. Might have affected your aim."

"Man, I could make that shot blindfolded on one leg."

He probably could. I wondered on the gun range a few days ago whether his aim would still be that true during live action. Raymond Kessler learned the hard way that the answer is yes. Good thing for Cate, too. No other way she would've come out of the situation alive. A question I should've asked earlier pops into my mind.

"Morelli?"

"Don't know yet. He was alive when the ambulance carried him away."

The news is better than the alternative, and I lift up a silent prayer to God to save that kid's life. Scott and I loiter in the hall while other law enforcement personnel from more agencies than I can count crawl about the place like busy ants. The GBI has already taken Scott's gun—a rote piece of investigative procedure whenever a cop kills somebody in the state. He'll get it back soon enough. I study my best friend and try to put myself in his shoes.

"How are *you* doing? You did just kill a man."

"The hell I did. That man killed himself. I saved a life. Probably two."

No mystery exists as to the second life he saved today. Mine. Scott walked by my side in the aftermath of Amber and Cale's murders—the only person I really let get close to me at all. Back then I tried to run away from my pain but learned from the experience not to suffocate hurt. The pent-up emotion will rebound against you with even greater force. Better to meet your agony head-on. But an acknowledged torment is only slightly less painful than a buried one. And a life without Cate—now that she has made herself an indispensable part of my existence—would not hold much purpose for me.

She comes out of the restroom. Alive. The view is as beautiful as any I've ever seen. The full weight of relief hits me in the moment. Fighting to hold back my tears, I clasp Scott on the shoulder and manage to whisper, "Thank you." He pushes me toward Cate with a parting salutation.

"Have fun in Italy."

EPILOGUE

Cate rests in my lap on a sunny verandah overlooking Lake Como. Her head lies on my shoulder. The closeness mirrors the dominant theme of our time together in Italy. Touching. Lots of touching. Cuddled together in the back of a gondola in Venice. Walking hand in hand while ascending the Spanish Steps in Rome. Nights becoming mornings with our bodies entwined in perfect, unhurried rest. And now Lake Como. Holding one another again to make sure that the other person is still there—real, tangible proof that the both of us remain bound together as one.

She says, "I could stay here forever."

The thought is appealing. I've seen lots of awe-inspiring sights in the world—the Grand Canyon, the Cliffs of Moher, the Great Barrier Reef among them—but none compare to the vista of turquoise-infused water set against green treetop mountains now before me. The overwhelming sensation is a feeling of peace—the kind of deep contentment so fleeting that you better savor it whenever you get the chance.

The happy news from America helped put my mind at ease. After a couple of precarious days, Morelli survived. His recovery spared me a double-barreled shotgun's worth of guilt. The instructions to keep eyes on the suspect stung bad enough. But my resolve to get Cate out of the country after her own personal hostage crisis would've meant missing Morelli's funeral if the killer's aim had proven deadly. That choice felt gutless while sitting in first class on the plane ride over, still unsure of the young trooper's condition.

Except I'd do it again—no matter the residual remorse. Life belongs to the living, and Cate comes first. For that I will never apologize.

Neither of us has spoken once about the murderer during the trip, but his presence lingers as a warning never to take a single day for granted. Death lurks everywhere. Driving a car. A heart attack. The final act of a madman with a gun. All are random lightning bolts of terror that threaten to snatch loved ones away from us with furious speed. But sometimes the lightning bolt misses—coming close enough for a good scare, maybe even a deep wound, yet veering off course before that fatal, irreversible loss. I press my lips to Cate's forehead to feel her presence once more.

Thank God for second chances.

The End

ACKNOWLEDGEMENTS

For *A Hard Way to Die*, my Dream Team of Nancy Boren, Browning Jeffries, Joanna Apolinsky, and Tom Lacy once again graciously donated their time to give me feedback through the reading of various rough drafts. Their collective insights proved invaluable as I completed the book. I appreciate every one of them from the bottom of my heart.

The dedication of this book reads: "To My Daughter Emily—For Always Making Me Smile." Emily and I take a Daddy-Daughter trip together every year, and the dominant memory from all those journeys is one of laughter. We always have the best time together. Her presence brings me joy every day, and I am so proud of the young woman that she is becoming. I love you, Emily!

As always, the biggest thank you goes to my wife, Carla. Without her love and support, my writing career wouldn't be possible.

Finally, many thanks to my team at Bond Publishing for their encouragement and support—especially James.

All mistakes are mine alone.

ABOUT THE AUTHOR

Lance McMillian is a recovering lawyer who gave up the courtroom for the classroom. For over a decade, he has taught Constitutional Law and Torts to future lawyers at Atlanta's John Marshall Law School. Lance is married to Justice Carla Wong McMillian of the Georgia Supreme Court. *A Hard Way to Die* is the fourth book in the best-selling Atlanta Murder Squad series.

Lance loves to hear from his readers. You can connect with him via email (lancemcmillian@icloud.com), Twitter (@LanceMcMillian), or Facebook (fb.me/LanceBooks). You can also follow him at BookBub (bookbub.com/authors/lance-mcmillian).

If you enjoyed this novel, help other readers discover it by leaving a rating or review on your favorite retailer or Goodreads. Even a very brief review can make a huge difference.

To receive updates on Lance's next book, sign up at
https://bit.ly/2ZIfY6L

CPSIA information can be obtained
at www.ICGtesting.com
Printed in the USA
LVHW110158301122
734318LV00004B/399